MOMENTS OF DOUBT

A Novel
by

Walter B. Levis

PublishAmerica

Baltimore

First printing

ISBN: 1-59129-627-7
PUBLISHED BY PUBLISHAMERICA BOOK PUBLISHERS
www.publishamerica.com
Baltimore

Printed in the United States of America

Acknowledgements

I would like to thank the faculty and students at Northwestern University's Medill School of Journalism, and Columbia University's Creative Writing Program. Both schools helped me appreciate the extent to which writing is a craft that requires practice. And more practice.

The importance of teachers in a writer's life can be a complicated subject. In my experience, the spell of influence concerns not so much literary style or aesthetics, but values. It's about conferring upon the enterprise of writing a kind of depth and integrity. In this spirit, I'm particularly grateful to Janet Shaw, Jon Ziomek, Romulus Linney, Stephen Koch, Richard Locke, and Ted Solotaroff.

Many friends helped me with this book. Special thanks to John Murphy, Adam Sexton, and Patrick O'Sullivan. Also, Mitchell Redman and Jayne Connell were extraordinarily insightful. Adam Kraar, whose own work is a steady inspiration to me, helped in ways too numerous to count. Also, Rick Coffey's support over the years has helped me "keep up the practice." A special thanks to Barry Williams, as our time together remains a source of creativity, and to Jake Thiessen, for helping to hold the space where possibilities emerge.

I would also like to acknowledge the importance of an abstract group: readers. The writer E.M. Forester once said, "Literary history distinguishes between major and minor writers but makes no such distinction between major and minor readers." I have benefitted greatly from knowing "major readers," some of whom are listed above. But major or minor, it's readers who, finally, complete the circle for writers. And to any reader who wants to spin the circle back the other way, please try me at Wlevis3507@aol.com

Lastly, this book is dedicated with love and gratitude to Mara.

"We work in the dark—we do what we can—we give what we have. Our doubt is our passion and our passion is our task..."

Henry James, *The Middle Years*

"Most serious matters are closed to the hard-boiled."

Saul Bellow, *Dangling Man*

Prologue

I'm sorry if my candor is offensive. My father (and my mother, too, if she were alive), Uncle Max, Gloria, and, of course, Malaika and Heidi——none of them deserves this. And I wouldn't do it at all if I didn't think it would help. Jung once wrote: "We are fated to suffer that which we fail to make conscious." So, you see, I want to tell you this story as candidly as possible in an effort to make conscious whatever it is that might help me avoid making a terrible mistake, thereby hurting more people than I already have. I mean, it's possible to simply marry the wrong person, isn't it?

But my guilt is far enough behind me now, I hope, that I can see it clearly. "Please God, just a little clarity," as James Agee said. I need all I can get right now, although I know that in the name of clarity many of us take flight into abstraction, trying to think our way out of our feelings. Even in therapy I often rushed into interpretation and insight, avoiding affect. For example, working honestly to understand my situation right now, I find myself considering the survival of the Jews through five thousand years of civilization in conflict with the emerging multicultural identity in postmodern urban America at the dawn of the twenty-first century. Absurd, I know. A pompous inflation of a puny love triangle. But I've even gone so far in my search for perspective to think that what's at stake in my little problem is the future of the human species, how we work out our identities as individuals and members of a group, learn to respect each other's differences, live in peace, etc.

Ridiculous, of course. Yet I'm unable to entirely dismiss this sort of bold, grand view. The universe, after all, is bold and grand. I want to take that into account. At the same time, I'm on guard against my own defensiveness. I mean, I don't want to inflate my problems into some grand abstraction as a way to avoid the sharp pinch of ordinary emotional pain.

Chicago, my neighborhood, the people I've loved and hurt——it's a question of contacting this basic reality, and trusting it. Like the gentle support of a comfortable chair, a soothing swallow of warm tea, or the just-right temperature of a breeze through a bedroom window on an autumn night. It could be stated, I suppose, in the form of an epigram: Out of the experience of our senses, we try to make sense of our experience. And then do whatever's right.

In this way, Malaika and I were, in fact, trying to be honest with each other right from the beginning.

1

We met at a yoga class, which was a complicated setting, with such a heavy mix of sexual and spiritual energy that it seemed to hang in the air like a scent. I first spotted Malaika just after she'd stepped out of the women's dressing area, a section of the loft separated by a mauve-colored curtain that didn't quite reach to the ground. This meant you could watch the women's naked feet shuffle along the bare wooden floor as they slipped off their street clothes and wriggled into their leotards. At least I imagined them wriggling, imagined with all the powers I could summon. I admit—and in the interest of objectivity, I want to admit it—I was a lusty voyeur of this little dressing room scene. That mauve-colored curtain appeared in more than a few fine fantasies, which Malaika and I, later, shared quite openly.

She stepped out wearing a forest green leotard and pink running shorts and our teacher said hello to her right away. He called himself Shahms, although his real name was Stephen. He'd taken this other name based on the spiritual master of Jalalludin Rumi, the Sufi poet. He claimed to have read everything Rumi had ever written. He also sold his own silk-screened T-shirts with quotes from Rumi. "Only Love. Only the holder the flag fits into, and wind. No flag." These little turns of phrase dating back to the thirteenth century were sources of genuine inspiration for Shahms, and for me, too. In those days, I found in Rumi an enormously appealing vision of spiritual surrender. Although, unfortunately, much of what I called "spiritual" back then was a form of escapism, and what I thought of as "surrender" was mostly an excuse for my predilection toward passivity. I didn't read Rumi's poetry so much as I read *into* it.

Anyway, Malaika walked over to Shahms and flashed him an impish smile that I could tell conveyed a shared joke between them. I was watching her so closely because, to put it bluntly, she was gorgeous.

…How can I describe her? It seems almost better to leave her undescribed and let your imagination fill in whatever is your image of a sensually and sexually alive person. For me, it's a presence, a way of imbuing the smallest of gestures with an effortless intentionality so that, for example, grabbing the phone or folding the newspaper or any other tiny and usually meaningless physical act is performed fluidly and with a relaxed but complete attention. The quality is rare. You can sometimes find it in great athletes, truly great athletes, of which I've only known a few, all of whom were playing the pro tennis circuit. But they had it, this confidence grounded so deeply in their bodies that it seemed to radiate—on and off the court—through every gesture. Call it timing, touch, the gift.

I can't imagine anyone, man or woman, *not* picking up on this quality in Malaika and, if she's your type, experiencing the whole thing as incredibly erotic. Of course, she was a certain type, and partly, I'm sure, it's that Malaika's physical type is so different from Heidi's.

First of all, Malaika is part Chinese. Her grandmother, who was born in Taiwan, married an American missionary, and her mother, born in this country, married a light-skinned Black. Malaika grew up in a small town in California called Isle of Vista, just outside of Santa Barbara. Not to get too bogged down in her whole life story, the point is that Malaika's got enough Chinese blood in her for my initial attraction to spring, at least partly, from that stereotypical fascination with the "inscrutable mystery of the exotic Orient." I'm not proud of it, but there it is. The China Doll syndrome. Although, in fact, Malaika's appearance is even more "exotic" because of the faint trace of African influence on all of her features. Her skin is just a shade darker than usual, a richer and deeper shade of golden yellow; and a little wave runs through her basically long straight black hair while her perfectly chiselled nose flattens out just the tiniest bit around the nostrils. Add to this that her small mouth is given a distinctive flair by the fullness of her lips and that her dark, deep-set eyes radiate calmness…

It was utterly unfair, but by comparison Heidi's quite remarkable presence struck me at the time as nothing more than a thin angular face filled with the most oppressive sort of Russian-Jewish intensity, as if she'd just trudged through the *shtetl* after standing in line for bread.

The truth is much different. Heidi's dark eyes can fasten on you from their deep-set sockets with a kind of singular intensity that is every bit as powerful as the "inscrutable Oriental gaze." I often feel like she isn't just looking at me; she's taking in and considering everything about me, including the smaller details of the particular shared moment, and its relation to some larger moral and historical moment. Her gaze is transfixing, transporting. And it's extremely sexy.

So why then did I break up with Heidi in the first place and start a relationship with Malaika? Well, the moment I saw Malaika flash that smile at Shahms I was, as the old Romance writers used to put it, *smitten.* But perhaps that's too grand. To keep it simple, call it lust. And, yes, putting my sexuality on display may not earn your sympathy, but it's not sympathy I'm after. It's advice. A cogent plan for how to do the right thing. I've done a lot of thinking in the last four years and coming up fast on forty gives me a certain desperation about the whole question of "settling down." Now, with the mess I'm in, if there's any hope at all it's a question of not just good, sound legal advice but ruthless, brutal honesty. I mean, really, for me (and most men?), "know thy self" means, basically, "know thy pig."

Anyway, I remember how Malaika glided across the room, her neck and ribcage aligned and lifted just enough to be elegant without being stately or forced.

"Whoa-baby-whoa-baby-whoa!" she said quietly to Shahms. Then she patted him playfully on the butt.

"Wild place last night, huh?" Shahms said, smiling.

"I'll say. Especially with wild men like you on the dance floor."

"You didn't look too domesticated yourself."

Malaika laughed. "It was the outfit."

I burned to blurt out, What outfit? What dance floor? Where?

Shahms smiled and did something flirty with his eyebrows. He had big, bushy eyebrows that went along with his generally wild look. He suffered from an overidentification with the 1960s. Long hair pulled in a ponytail, tie-dyed shirts, beads, the whole package. He once told me that before yoga he'd been "heavy into drugs."

Malaika leaned into him. "I think I did something to my shoulder," she said, slipping her hand under the strap of her leotard. "Woke up this morning with a kink."

"Let's see." Shahms rubbed her shoulder, then turned her around and placed one hand on the center of her back and the other on the back of her head, working on some sort of alignment. I watched closely. She was facing me directly now, though her gaze was focused beyond me. Her large, dark eyes glowed like a pair of polished stones, set off by her petite nose and golden complexion. While Shahms massaged her neck, she twisted her small mouth and groaned.

A moment later, class began. I rolled out my green rubber mat next to hers.

"We're going to do some partner work today," Shahms said.

Malaika turned quickly to me and, smiling easily, said, "Hi partner."

I smiled back. "Hi," I said. Then told myself to relax. My palms were sweaty. I remember that detail precisely because "sweaty palms around pretty girls" is an expression I'd once heard my father use, when I was just a boy.

We warmed up with side stretches, lunge stretches, forward bends—I don't recall the Hindu names of the poses anymore, although I once tried to learn them with flashcards. Malaika moved from pose to pose without looking up, and I was impressed as much by her quality of attention as by her physical ability, although, believe me, I wasn't simply admiring the alignment of her spine. I remember there was a slightly more pale shade of yellow visible beneath her tiny pink running shorts whenever she bent over.

Shahms finally called out, "Okay, everyone find a partner." Then he added, "Malaika, you and I can work together."

But I immediately blurted, "She's going to work with me."

And the room fell silent. Shahms's startled expression cooled quickly into an icy glare, aimed first at me, then at Malaika. She looked at me blankly, although I thought a faint smile hovered over her beautiful, small mouth.

"Now boys, boys, boys," she said, turning away from us as the other dozen or so people in the class laughed. "I think you both probably have cooties." The laughter erupted into a roar.

I waited for it to die down, then said quietly, "I've been vaccinated."

She looked at me, her head cocked to the side, birdlike. "What?" A frown creased her brow.

"Sorry," I said. "Just joking. But I would like to be your partner."

The room was quiet again. Our gazes locked. I noticed her golden skin had a small blemish, a tiny white spot on her cheek below her eye, where it looked like maybe she'd had a beauty mark removed. "I'm Eli," I said, and extended my hand.

There was another pause. She crinkled her nose slightly, as if she was trying to determine an unfamiliar odor, and she squinted, still looking directly at me. Then Shahms spoke.

"It doesn't matter, Malaika," he said. "One of the things yoga teaches us, of course, is to practice detachment."

More laughter, subdued now. "Right," she said. "In fact, I think I'd prefer to be completely detached." And she walked to the wall and performed a supported headstand.

Shahms smiled at me and shrugged, a gesture that struck me at the time as unusually expressive, as if with the rise and fall of his shoulders he was saying hey, the universe is a mystery, deal with it.

Malaika spent the rest of the time at the wall working by herself. Although her not rejoining the class was clearly a signal that she was less than irresistibly drawn to me, it had the opposite effect on my raging infatuation with her. The independence, the boldness of her simply removing herself from the group—how might such a woman, who feels free to say the hell with a whole room full of people she'd just paid money to be with (the classes cost, I think, about $12 each)—how might such a woman make love?

I was determined to put the question out of my mind. After class, I threw on my jeans and left as quickly as I could without so much as glancing at Malaika or speaking to anyone else.

Outside, the warm spring air soothed me. It was late April. Chicago had been having a rainy spell, and it was the first sunny day in about a week. I paid a lot of attention to the weather back then. As a tennis pro working at an outdoor club, bad weather meant bad business. So I stood out there in the sun, taking in the edgy city feel of Halsted Street, something I always appreciated on my days off, grateful to be away from the country club with its insufferable politeness and outrageously well-groomed landscapes. The owner of the Korean fish market on the corner came out waving a stack of yellow fliers and calling, in a high-pitched nasal voice, "Fish'n'chips, fish'n'chips, four ninety-five!" The smell of fried fish was mixed faintly—pleasantly, I thought—with the odor of auto emissions.

Just then, Malaika came out. She wore faded, snug-fitting blue jeans and a pale blue tank-top shirt. She also carried a plastic blue gym bag with a wide zipper. A cheap bag, I noted, although I found it charming in a campy sort of way.

She glanced at me, and our eyes happened to meet squarely.

"I'm sorry," I said, flatly. "I was temporarily insane."

She laughed, a tiny laugh that I'll never forget. The way she threw her head back and slipped her tongue over the top of her front teeth. It was completely spontaneous. And that kind of spontaneity, that moment of irrepressible expression—that was it, the cornerstone of what we had.

"Who are you?" she said, a small smile lingering as she spoke in a low voice.

I didn't know how to answer. Partly because of this spiritualized context of the yoga class, the question seemed layered with possibilities, comic and otherwise. Just to tell her my name again seemed inadequate.

I pointed to my chest and looked around, struggling to find a decent answer. Then out of the corner of my eye I spotted the brand-name logo on my tennis shirt. Above the small breast pocket, in bold script, it read: ***Prince.*** I pointed to it.

She smiled and shook her head. "You're unbelievable."

"No," I said, quickly. "You are unbelievable." There was a pause. I didn't really know what I was saying. I was on some kind of automatic pilot, just going with the first thing that came to my mind. She seemed to take the compliment without flinching. "You cast a spell on me in there, didn't you? You made me act like a fool, and now I'm destined to continue to act like a fool—maybe forever—unless you come have coffee with me, and lift the spell." I paused just long enough to catch my breath, then added, "Why dost thou wrong one that ne'er did wrong thee?"

She laughed.

"I mean, it's a terrible thing to do to a man," I went on. "Casting a spell like that—a fool forever. You don't really want that on your conscience, do you?"

She looked away, and I realized I'd gone too far. I could feel it, like losing your timing in the middle of a rally. My breathing felt choppy.

"Look," I said, stepping toward her. "I'm sorry, really I am. I don't know what I'm saying. It's been a rough week. I don't know what came over me up there. It was just when you said 'hi partner' I sort of figured…well, forget it. I'm sorry, really. You want me to leave you alone, just say so."

Before she answered she looked away and bit her lower lip just enough for the corner of one tooth to show. And she froze like that for a moment, hesitating. And it was as if everything stopped, like a still photo of a tennis ball frozen at the peak of its trajectory, not falling, not rising, just there, suspended, waiting to be struck.

"A cup of coffee," she said, slowly. "Sure, Prince. Why not?"

And as we walked away together I think I knew, at some level anyway, that I'd just taken my swing and hit my shot—a tremendous, seam-splitting smash—directed only more or less at Malaika, but definitely aimed at Heidi.

2

Because of that coffee with Malaika, I was late to meet Heidi. A big problem with me in those days. I was always squeezing into my mundane little schedule more than I could handle. Tardiness, I suppose, made me feel important. And since every appointment, meeting, or casual date began with a small fifteen-minute insult, I cultivated a weird gift for transforming a puny apology into poetic reverie. I'm not kidding—this shows a lot of what I was like back then. Once, when I worked at the East Bank Club, I arrived about twenty minutes late to a staff meeting of all the tennis pros because the employee parking slots were full and I couldn't find a place on the street. So I opened the door to the meeting room and—before the manager could start chewing me out—I began improvising:

> To park or not to park—that is the
> question.
> Whether 'tis nobler in the car to
> suffer
> the lurch and honk of outrageous
> traffic,
> Or to take the "El" into the heart
> of the Loop,
> And by so choosing,
> arrive late.
> …Or on time, perchance on time.
> But in that choice between the
> CTA and the plight of the car
> lay the mortal coil of Loop
> vitality and the pith and moment
> of downtown parking…

Silence, a few groans, some nervous laughter—and I was off the hook.

But that night with Heidi, no such luck. She greeted me at the door with an expectant arch in her dark brow. We'd planned to see a movie.

"Is there a 10 o'clock show?" I said, and shoved my hands into the pockets of my tennis shorts.

"I have to be up at six tomorrow morning."

"Right."

She held open the door, a huge door, solid oak with a brass knocker in the shape of a lion's head. This was her parents' house, in North Evanston. The house faced Lake Michigan, and that night one of those summer electrical storms lit the sky far out over the water. But it wasn't raining. Just jagged soundless streaks of light over the black water.

"Your folks home?"

She nodded, then exhaled loudly, rolling her eyes. Six weeks earlier, she'd returned from Rome, where she was doing research for her dissertation on Renaissance painting, and she was still waiting for the subtenant to move out of her place in Hyde Park. She was back earlier than she'd planned. Not that she didn't get along with her parents. She did. And they were crazy about me too. In fact, at this point in our relationship her parents, like almost everyone else we knew, expected us to announce our engagement any day.

But at that moment the thought of marrying Heidi gave me the chills. I looked out at the lake, its blackness deepened by the bolts of soundless lightening.

"How about a walk?" I said. "I don't think it's going to rain."

She looked at me. The light from the doorway cast a yellow shadow on her deep-set eyes, which flitted from my face to the ground and back again to my face.

I kissed her forehead. Hard, impulsively. Her head sprang back a little from the force of my lips. Then I quickly framed her face in my hands and kissed her again, just as hard, this time on the mouth. And I looked at her, at her mouth. Her full lips trembled. I knew that my affection seemed forced. Simulated spontaneity.

"Eli," she said, softly. "I thought you were going to be here at—"

"I'm sorry."

She paused, waiting for me to continue.

"I…I don't really know how to explain it right now."

"How complicated can it be? I'll concentrate real hard, OK?" She smiled.

I laughed, but a sense of panic came over me because I realized how deeply Heidi trusted me. The idea that I might have been late because I was spending time with another woman—this was the furthest thing from her mind.

Still smiling, she leaned forward, goose-necked, the way she sometimes does, her head hanging forward like an old peasant woman's. It jarred me. There was something quaint about the posture, its familiarity. It reminded me of pictures of my grandparents—immigrant Ellis Island-type of pictures of the bewildered Jews, the lost Jews, the head-hung-carrying-everything-they-owned-running-for-their-lives-determined-to-make-it-in-this-country-immigrant Jews. Our common ancestry, mine and Heidi's. No doubt coming straight from yoga sensitized me to this posture, which seemed to me to say so much. But this is also typical of the effect Heidi still has on me. With her I'm always reminded that there is no history which isn't the present. And Heidi and I have so much of it—history. For example, losing our virginity to each other.

At that moment, the weight of our history pressed on me like a thick heavy blanket, like one of those pads they place over you before taking an X-ray. My shoulders and neck suddenly ached, and I had an urge to walk.

"Come on," I said, taking her hand. "Let's go to the beach."

She resisted just long enough to pull shut the big oak door. Then she followed behind me, squeezing my hand tightly.

"If I get struck by lightning," she said, "you're going to be in big trouble."

"Don't worry. I'll finish your dissertation for you. I promise."

She laughed, and I placed my hand on the small of her back, and together we silently crossed the huge lawn in front of the house and headed toward the lightning-filled horizon.

What happened next is particularly embarrassing, but I'll try to relate it as straightforwardly as possible. It no doubt cuts to the heart of this whole crazy situation.

First, when we got to the beach, I wanted to jump the fence. Heidi wanted to walk the block and a half to the proper entrance. We fought.

"I can't climb it," she said.

"Why not?"

"For one thing, I'm wearing one of my favorite dresses."

This caught me off guard. So preoccupied was I with the business about being late that I hadn't even noticed that she was wearing the dress we had bought together before she left for Rome. It was the only time we'd ever bought something like that together. And it was one of my favorite dresses, too. A simple cotton pattern with small buttons down the front, the dress reminded me of an artist's smock. But it was low-cut, flattering to her full breasts, and it fit her snug around the waist without being too tight in the butt, which she's always self-conscious about since she has a full, fleshy, round butt, and large thighs.

She stood with her arms folded, determined not to climb the fence.

"Come on, I'll help. I'll lift you. I'll carry you over."

"You'll hurt your back. Besides, what's the big deal? It's less than two blocks."

I bent over and started to scoop her up.

"Get away." She laughed, slapping my shoulders with floppy wrists.

Then I said, "For chrissake, just be a little bit of an athlete, will you?"

Her wrists on my shoulders tensed. "Let go of me," she said.

I stepped back. We looked at each other. A breeze came off the lake and blew the thick curls of her wavy hair.

"Climb over the fucking fence if you want," she said. "I'm walking around."

And she turned her back on me and headed down the block. I watched her. Her familiar heavy gait—it struck me at the time as slightly masculine. The way her shoulders swayed, the width and length of the stride. And that's when it occurred to me that I'd made the crack about her being an athlete because I was comparing her to Malaika. You see, athletic ability is one of mine and Heidi's ancient sore points, dating back to our days in high school when I tried to teach her to play tennis, only to realize that she had no eye-hand coordination. But Malaika? With those long, sleek, flexible legs, she would have jumped this fence in a flash.

I tried to put this out of my mind as I caught up with Heidi and we walked together in silence. But a thin layer of sand covered the walkway near the beach's entrance, and the noise of Heidi's sandaled feet scuffing against the pavement made me think again of Malaika, who I was sure possessed such lightness and grace that she would have barely touched the ground as she walked.

Again I tried to dismiss these ridiculous comparisons. "Please, Heidela," I said, pulling her closer to me. "I'm sorry. That was a cheap shot."

"'Be a little bit of an athlete,'" she mumbled, with her teeth clenched. "You know I used to actually like you for your mind."

"And now—just my body?"

"That's all that's left."

"Touché!" I said.

"I'm serious," she answered. But then she laughed and wriggled out of my embrace and ran into the sand, kicking off her sandals. The beach was empty. I watched her run the whole way to the lifeguard's chair. I ran part of the way too, the cool night sand filling my sneakers.

When I caught up to her, she was breathing heavily, one arm slung over the bottom of the lifeguard chair's ladder.

"See?" she panted, pointing up. "They ground these things with a lightning rod."

"Good thinking," I said. And I raised my index finger and tapped the side of my head. "Heady chick."

She shook her head and smiled. "Fuck you."

I stepped closer to her, tapped first my chest, then hers. Then said, in my best broken accent, "Yaah, me fuck you."

She turned her head just enough to hide one eye, then lowered her chin and gave me that look of hers which, I must say, even after all these years, after all we've been through, remains genuinely seductive.

I looked around, figured that a passing car's headlights wouldn't reach us this far down, then pulled off my shirt. Heidi registered this with a small smile. Then I slipped off my shoes and shorts. She looked at me, still smiling coyly. I stood there in just my underwear and took a deep breath of the dark, fresh lakefront breeze.

"Nice," she said, quietly.

She stepped closer, slowly unbuttoning her dress. A gust of wind came off the lake, blowing back her hair. She squinted. Tiny grains of sand swirled at my ankles. The backs of my bare legs stung. I dropped to my knees, and Heidi followed, her eyes closed. Then we kissed, and as her tongue lightly circled mine, she moaned softly, slipping the tips of her fingers under the waistband of my underwear. And as she took the shaft of my penis in the palm of her hand——that's when everything fell apart.

Not that I lost my erection. That would have been much simpler, much more truthful, relatively speaking. Instead what happened is that Malaika, again, leapt into my mind, and I couldn't shake her out. In fact, I didn't even try. It was Heidi's full lips I was kissing but Malaika's small mouth I was imagining; Heidi's large breasts pressing against my chest but Malaika's much smaller ones I was envisioning; Heidi's soft, fleshy butt I was squeezing but Malaika's firm, toned one I was picturing.

And the truth is that while I told myself all this imagining and envisioning and picturing of Malaika was nothing more than those passing forbidden fantasies we all have——it was not mere fantasy. I'd have to say now that it was deception. The reality of deception.

Why? Because I was using the experience of making love on the beach with Heidi as a way of clarifying my feelings about Malaika. I don't know any other way to put it. Except maybe to transpose it into passive voice: My feelings for Malaika were clarified by making love on the beach with Heidi. "I" wasn't trying to do anything. The experience was, in a sense, doing it to me.

We finished and were lying quietly, wrapped tightly in each other's arms, when Heidi asked, "Where were you?"

At first I thought she had detected my distraction while making love. "Hmm?"

"You know. You were like an hour late. What happened?"

"Oh, it's sort of complicated."

"What do you mean complicated?"

"Just…complicated."

She pushed herself out of my embrace and sat up on one elbow.

"Let me assure you," she said, slowly. "Complicated things don't intimidate me. I'm a graduate student, remember?"

That cool edge of irony. She reminded me at that moment of a trial lawyer. One thing about Heidi——I know I can't outmaneuver her. She isn't just smart; she glows with a certain intellectual brilliance. It's difficult to describe, but it's as if she hears what you say and what you don't say. What is conscious and what is unconscious. This can be wonderful, allowing her to home in on a vague feeling and bring it out into the open. But it also allows almost no room for ordinary social politics. I mean, she can be amazingly blunt, articulating exactly what is better left implied. And especially during intimate moments, this quality can be damn unnerving. That night on the beach, the look in her eyes was all business.

"I ran into someone after yoga class and we went out for coffee——and I lost track of time."

She looked away, pushing out her lips like someone counting money, or measuring a very small amount of some precious substance with a fine instrument. Then she looked back at me.

"That doesn't sound so complicated," she said. "You ran into someone after yoga class, went out for a cup of coffee, and lost track of time. I think I've got it on the first take."

And she smiled, then stood up. I sat there for a minute in the sand, watching her. She quickly fit her breasts into the cups of her bra, then brushed the sand off her legs and butt and pulled on her underwear. I started to reach for her dress to hand it to her, but she bent down and snapped it up, throwing it on over her head and buttoning it almost simultaneously.

Just then a line of my Uncle Max's came to mind: "Find the rhythm of a moment and you've got that moment's truth." So be it. Anger moves at a clip.

I got dressed without a word. Then we walked back to her parents' house in silence. At the door, she asked me if I wanted to come in. And I said, "Sure, why not?"

And almost as soon as I said this a little jolt passed through me, like hitting your funny bone. It occurred to me that *Sure, why not?* were the exact words Malaika had said to me a few hours earlier. It's not an expression I use.

But Heidi just nodded and put her key in the lock, swinging a hip into the heavy oak door. Inside, a blast of cold, dark air hit me with a chill. Heidi's mother has asthma, so in the summer they run the house's central air conditioning almost twenty-four hours a day. A moment passed while Heidi stood there in the dark fumbling for the hall light, then she flicked the switch, and the hanging chandelier lit up.

"How about a drink?" she said. "Brandy?"

We sat on the couch in the book-lined study, which smelled faintly of Mr. Kirschbaum's pipe tobacco. He has a passion for tobacco and cognac that I've always thought perfectly suits his position as one of Chicago's best-known commercial litigation lawyers. A cultivated and influential man. Truly powerful. He's been known to have lunch with the mayor. Although with Mr. K. his influence is strictly behind the scenes; to see his own name in the paper doesn't interest him. He'd rather be at the opera. Which is another thing: his authentic high-brow taste. When you first meet him—with his pipe and tailored suits and unnaturally grammatical way of speaking— it might seem, in a way, like he's just a big, rich snob. But, in fact, he carries his elite baggage pretty lightly. He has a genuinely open mind. The trick, I think, is that he's just damn smart.

And that's partly what Heidi inherited from him: smarts, plus some. I mean, while Mr. K. has that lawyerly analytic gift for logic, which he can brilliantly apply to any abstract problem, he can be somewhat obtuse when it comes to the subtleties of emotional life. Heidi, on the other hand, possesses all of her father's analytic powers plus her own ability to sniff out the unspoken feeling in a situation, the basic emotion.

And this basic emotion is precisely what I was trying to avoid. I can say that now, although at the time I didn't know what was happening. I was just sitting there on that leather couch in that room full of books, sipping my brandy, looking at one woman and trying not to think of another.

"What would your yoga teacher say?" Heidi held up her snifter.

"Alcohol?"

She nodded.

"At least it's vegetarian." I laughed weakly. Heidi was silent. "I don't know. It's probably bad."

"You said some pretty interesting stuff about yoga in those letters."

"Yeah? Like what?"

"I don't know. Lots of things. Like…um… how yoga is your spiritual discipline? Remember that…?"

I remembered. I had written that because, when she first left for Rome, it was terribly important to me to make it clear to Heidi how seriously I was taking yoga. Standing poses, balancing poses, twists, backbends, inversions, pranayama (breathing exercises)…I did them all every day right by the book, following the sequences and timing outlined by guru B.K.S. Iyengar in *Light on Yoga*. And I ate vegetarian, and read Mircea Eliade and the Upanishads and studied the Maharabata—and all the time I feared that I was doing something that Heidi wouldn't understand. Although, in fact, I was quite deluded in thinking I understood it myself, this "spiritual discipline." I'm aware now how problematic such a label really is—that one man's spiritual discipline can be another man's profound waste of time.

But that night with Heidi, I just said, "Yeah, nobody writes letters anymore."

"Not like yours, no." She took a long swallow of her brandy. Then we looked at each other for a moment, each of us holding our snifter in front of our mouths. She went to get the bottle.

"So," she said, a little too loudly, as she stood over me filling her glass. "How much longer do you figure you'll be teaching tennis?"

"Oh, you know, same as usual. The outdoor season goes through Labor Day, but the club will be open for another——"

"No, I don't mean this season. I mean, how much longer?"

She sat back down, holding her gaze to mine in an eerie sort of way, like in the movies when someone is pointing a gun and is afraid to look away.

"You sound like my father," I said. " You know his rap: Tennis is something you learn so that you can rally politely with the partners at Lehman Brothers. You take tennis lessons—but you don't become a tennis pro."

I laughed, repeating this old family joke. Heidi didn't blink.

"I'm really curious," she said. "How much longer do you think you'll do this?"

"What do you mean? You make it sound like it's something I'm supposed to give up. Like smoking." I paused and finished my brandy. "I mean, tennis pros can make a perfectly decent living, you know."

She reached for the bottle and filled my glass. "So you see it right now as a career?"

The coolness in her voice—call it her father's lawyerly detachment— made me want to strangle her. She'd clicked into interviewing mode, and I was now supposed to comment on my career. A word, back then, I hated.

"What's the matter with tennis as a career?"

"Nothing of course," she said, taking another sip of her brandy with a gesture that I thought reeked of false nonchalance. "Nothing at all. It's just that I guess I've been—well, I think we've all been wondering if it was a career for you."

"Is that the royal we?"

"You know what I mean."

"No, Heidi, I don't."

She didn't say anything. She drank more brandy. Long gulps, obviously not tasting the stuff. She was drinking, I knew, to get drunk.

"Okay," she said, slowly, "forget I said anything. We were talking about something else anyway, weren't we? Oh yeah—yoga."

"What about it?"

She took another swallow. "I'm trying to remember something that you wrote…It was one of those grand pronouncements about Western civilization and how yoga fills some gap or other."

"Sounds like you don't quite agree, but in your letters you never——"

"I don't really know what to make of it, Eli. I'd just like to hear right now what exactly it is you think 'Western civilization' is lacking that yoga provides."

I sensed that I was about to step into a trap. Heidi cranking up her intellectual machinery. She still sometimes does this when she's upset with me—tear apart piece by piece some large theoretical construction of mine until all that's left are the small, simple emotions on which the whole thing is built.

I should have kept my mouth shut but instead, in my infinite arrogance, I said, "OK—fine. Western civilization has developed an enormous capacity to conquer and control external reality but has failed to develop a sufficient understanding of and appreciation for inner states."

She frowned and squinted her eyes, and I knew she was going to speak, so I quickly went on, "I know—psychology, you say. But psychology is geared primarily toward adjustment. I'm not talking about adjustment, or pathology. I'm talking about the exploration of inner states at a much more subtle and profound level."

"You don't need yoga to meditate."

"I don't expect you to understand—not ever having done yoga yourself. It can't really be appreciated intellectually."

She looked at me glassy-eyed, her mouth slightly parted, as if she had a cigarette hanging from her lip. Then, in a low controlled voice, she said, "Eli, with whom did you have coffee?"

I looked away. I think I even closed my eyes, I'm not sure. But I know I just sat there, waiting for I don't know what. Then I heard the upstairs bathroom flush, and the familiar shuffle of Mr. Kirschbaum in his suede slippers scuffing softly through the thick carpet. And a moment later, the stairs creaked, and then Mr. K. appeared in the doorway of the study.

I looked up at him. He wore his plaid wool bathrobe. A few tufts of his thin brown hair stuck out. He smiled.

"We're having a brandy," I said. "Care to join us?"

"No thank you. I don't want to disturb you." He looked over at Heidi. "I'm just looking for your mother's inhaler. The blue one. The yellow one is upstairs, but the blue one, she said, has the night-time medicine."

I got down on my knees to search under the coffee table. Heidi pulled back the couch cushions. Mr. K. wandered over to his desk, a large, well-polished mahogany desk, one corner of which was reserved for his famous circular pipe-rack. It held about a dozen pipes and had carved into the handle a lion's head that almost perfectly matched the front door-knocker.

"Your mother was reading in here earlier," Mr. K. said. "Which I tried to warn her against, since breathing in the smell of my pipe tobacco, I told her, would give her trouble later. But she didn't listen. She said she loves the smell of my pipes and that, in fact, it's part of the reason she married me!"

He laughed, a low chuckle. " 'But when you married me you didn't have asthma,' I said. 'Asthma-shmasthma,' she says, and marches off into this smokey room to plop herself down on the couch with Saul Bellow. She's reading his latest book."

He paused. From my position still crouched on the floor, I heard him shuffling some papers on his desk. "*More Die of Heartbreak,*" he said, after a pause. "Have either of you read it?"

I knew Heidi had, but she didn't say anything. Her silence made it clear to me that she was annoyed with this interruption. But Mr. K. didn't pick up on it.

"Heidi, didn't you say something to me once about——"

"Yes, Dad. I read the book."

"Alfred Kazin called it the most misogynistic novel he's ever read," Mr. K. went on. "But I didn't feel that way. And neither does your mother, so far. What did you think?"

"I don't know," Heidi said.

"Were you offended by the characterization of the women?"

"Yes, it's misogynistic, in a way. But Bellow is basically representative of men of that generation who were infatuated with the kind of women who——"

Heidi stopped herself. I stood up. I was interested in how she was going to finish that sentence, but behind a couch cushion she'd found her mother's blue inhaler. She reached over and picked it up. "Here it is."

"Thank you." He smiled. "Perhaps we can continue this in the morning. What you're saying, about the generations——" He turned suddenly to me. "Have you read it, Eli?"

I shook my head. "Not yet. Sure you don't want to come back down and join us for a brandy?"

I could feel Heidi glaring at me as her father said, "Well, why not? I'll give this to Mrs. K., and be right back. Pour me two ounces of Remy Martin, will you, Eli? And be so kind as to measure it out with the tumbler, please."

"Exactly two ounces of Remy coming right up," I said, grateful for the task.

Heidi sat silently on the couch for the few minutes it took her father to return from upstairs. He was holding a copy of the Saul Bellow novel, which he presented to Heidi as if she'd asked for it.

"Here you go," I said, handing him his drink.

Heidi crossed her legs and opened the book. I'm sure she wasn't conscious of it, but her legs were crossed in a rather sexy sort of way, with her loose-fitting dress pulled way up the side of her leg.

While she flipped through the first few pages, Mr. K. lit his pipe. I just stood there, sipping my brandy and enjoying the sweet-leaf burning smell of Mr. K.'s tobacco.

"Before you came down, we were discussing yoga," Heidi said abruptly. "Eli thinks Western civilization lacks an appreciation for the inner life."

"Western civilization?" Mr. K. said, exhaling a small, smokey laugh. "That's us, right?"

"He's serious, aren't you, Eli?"

I didn't say anything .

"Of course it's true in a certain sense," Mr. K. said, settling into the large leather chair behind his desk. He leaned back and set his slippered feet on the desktop. "But you don't mean East versus West in terms of contemporary politics—but rather philosophically, right?"

"Philosophically," I said. "Yes, I suppose you could call it that. I'm talking about a way of looking at the world. How we determine what's meaningful."

"Well, the big difference, in my opinion, and you know me, ready with an opinion on anything." He laughed. He was in good form that night. "Particularly from a Jewish standpoint," he went on, "the big difference is that we in the West view—of course this is an oversimplification, but Jews, in my opinion, view history as a sort of moral connective tissue that...well, it's not a question of being at one with Nature but of understanding the moral imperative that History, with a capital 'H'—"

"Moral imperative?" I said, with a squeak in my voice.

"Yes, that's right," Heidi chimed in. "The moral imperative to contribute. To try to make a difference."

"Of course," I said. "But there are an infinite number of ways to, as you put it, make a difference."

"I wouldn't say infinite," she said, flatly. "A lot—but it's not infinite."

"What activities don't count, Heidi? I'd really like to know."

She looked surprised by my directness. Then her father spoke. "But it all depends how you measure it," he said. "And there's an enormous social reality to take into account. Class, education, historical background—there's no escaping these things. Your contribution is measured against your potential."

"Exactly," Heidi said. "It's different for everyone. But I'm willing to say that—as an essentially privileged person—I'm willing to say that I have a responsibility to use my privileges the right way. That's my obligation, my moral obligation."

She looked at her father, who nodded, puffing calmly on his pipe. Then he said, "It could be argued that this feeling of obligation, in its various permutations, is part of what links one generation to the other. I mean, sociologists call it—well, I don't recall right now what they call it. But, put simply, my parents came to this country to give me opportunities they didn't have. And I've worked hard to give you opportunities that I didn't have."

This time it was Mr. K. who looked at Heidi, and she who nodded.

"So as the wealthy and privileged," I said, suddenly adopting an exaggerated British accent, "we have a moral obligation to help those less fortunate than us, is that what you mean?"

Mr. K. laughed. "When you put it that way," Mr. K. said, "it does sound rather patronizing, doesn't it?"

"I'll say it does."

"But why do you say it that way?" Heidi asked.

"Why?"

"Yeah—why make fun of trying to help people?"

"I'm not making fun of it. I try to help people all the time. That's what I do every day."

"You mean teaching tennis?"

"Yes."

"You mean that you help people with their tennis game."

Now it was out in the open, and my anger boiled over. "What's the matter with that?" I said, a little too loudly. "Isn't that on your list of 'contributions'?"

"Of course it's a contribution," Mr. K. said.

"But," I turned to face him directly, "we measure the contribution against the potential, right?"

"What measure would you suggest?" he asked, calmly.

But I wasn't really listening, not anymore. My buttons had been pushed, and I was out of control. I was standing as I said, "You don't even know me. How could anyone know anyone else's 'true potential'?"

"It's not all so mysterious, Eli," Heidi said.

"That's right, it's not all so mysterious—because you know what this is really all about?" I pointed at her, my hand shaking. "It's about guilt," I said. "You feel guilty. Both of you." I stepped back, moving away from them. "And that's why you're so critical of me—"

"Eli," Mr. K. tried to interrupt me. "Eli, I'm not trying to criticize you—"

"Yes, you are," I shouted, cutting him off. "You and her both. You're criticizing me because I'm my own person and who I am doesn't have a goddamn thing to do with you and your guilty feelings about being rich Jews!"

I turned around and headed toward the door. I felt my legs shaking. Anger frightens me. It always has.

"Eli," Mr. K. called after me. "Eli, wait…"

Out in the hall, I stopped when I saw Heidi's mother standing in her robe at the top of the stairs. She must have heard the shouting. "Hello, Mrs. Kirschbaum," I said, in a whisper. "Excuse me. I'm sorry. I'm leaving."

Behind me I heard Mr. K. scuffing along after me in his slippers and Heidi calling, "Let him go, Daddy. Just let him go."

3

After I walked out of the house, I sat in my car for about fifteen minutes. Then Heidi came out.

"OK," she said firmly, settling herself in the seat as if we were about to drive away together. Then she took a deep, chesty breath. "I just want to know. I can't believe I'm even asking. I can't believe it. You wouldn't. I know you wouldn't…"

And then she lost it. Her voice trailed off into a mucous-filled mess of sniffling and sobs. I leaned forward and tried to put my arms around her, but she pushed me away. Then she suddenly grabbed my wrist.

"Were with you someone else?"

I drew a blank, which I know sounds ridiculous. But I flashed on how Heidi and I had talked at such great length about being faithful to one another during her four months in Italy and how it had always been me who was so worried about *her* fidelity. Italian men and the charm of Europe. Heidi, on the other hand, was always perfectly undaunted by the notion of country club wives enchanted by the Local Pro, a scenario we'd been through a million times, always as a subject of mockery. Tennis pros as sex objects was a stereotype beneath us. We wouldn't fall for something so predictable. The Local Pro:

Follow through, bend your knees.

Sleep with me, if you please.

We made up that stupid verse right after I got my first tennis job, the summer of my sophomore year in college. And we had been scoffing at it ever since.

But a tennis court affair was the first thing I thought of when Heidi asked if I had been with someone else. I shook my head and was about to say no. Then I woke up to the obvious—my coffee with Malaika.

I put my hand over hers, resting my palm lightly on the back of her hand.

And that was all it took. This simple gesture, completed in silence. That, she thought, answered her question.

It was nasty as hell of me not to say anything right away, but I let her pull her hand out from under mine ever so slowly. I remember it precisely because at just that moment a bolt of soundless lightening lit up the sky. The storm had moved onshore. In the bright-white flash, I saw Heidi's flushed face, her nose dripping as she stared straight out over the dashboard, breathing heavily, forcing her tears to cease with a clenched mouth and hard swallows. Then, as quickly as the light came, it disappeared. And there was only her dark silhouette and the stuffed-nose sound of her tear-clogged breathing.

"It was just coffee," I said. "I don't even know her. We met in yoga class. Today. Today was the first time I ever saw her. Her name is Malaika."

"That's why you were late?"

I nodded.

"And...?"

"And what?"

She leaned forward and turned on the inside car light. Then she cocked her head to the side.

"Eli," she whispered. "What's happening?"

She deserved an explanation. But what was I to explain? Where was I to begin? With my desire to be anything but a "nice Jewish boy"? Or with my outrageous fantasies about Malaika? Or my inflated notions about tennis as a "spiritual path"? Or with my fear, which had just recently been substantiated, that my father had lied to me about the seriousness of his troubles? I didn't know where to begin because, of course, I could have begun anywhere, and Heidi would have listened. Patiently, and with compassion, she would have taken it all in and, gently, reflected it back to me. But to look at myself in the reflection of her kindness and compassion was more than I could handle.

I bounced the palm of my hand on the steering wheel a few times, then said, "What do you want—an essay on my general emotional state? First you give me a hard time about being a tennis pro—"

"I'm not talking about that—"

"—the significance of which you obviously fail to grasp."

"You want to argue now about being a tennis pro?" she said. "Fine. What significance do I fail to grasp?"

"Exactly. That's exactly what I mean. With your elitism."

"Eli...please."

"Please what?"

"Don't do this."

"Do what?"

Just then a clap of thunder struck, and a gust of wind whistled through the drafty car, and then the rain fell. And it was as if I interpreted the sudden break of that summer storm as some kind of divine sign permitting me to let flow a torrent of cruel words.

"Don't you think," I began, slowly, "that you're suffering just a tiny bit of status anxiety?"

She didn't say anything. She sat as still as a statue. So I closed my eyes and spoke, in my mind, to this statue.

"In fact," I began, "your concern for your place in the world, your constant worrying about your little niche in the social hierarchy, that's just the tip of the iceberg. What's at the center of your psyche, Heidi, around which your entire life is built—what's at the center is an abnormal, crippling fear of solitude."

This all seemed to rise up out of its own volition. The whole little lecture came the way a wild swing of the racket will sometimes produce a perfect shot. Not that the words perfectly described Heidi—far from it. What they did is perfectly achieve their undisclosed aim: to alienate Heidi from me entirely.

"The thing is," I continued, my eyes still closed, my voice rising above the low drumming sound of the rain pummeling the car's roof, "the thing is, you think you've got to be everyone's friend all of the time. You've got to listen to their problems, their loves, their losses, their physical ailments— and not just friends. People you don't even know, too. Total strangers. The way you read the paper from cover to cover and shout with moral outrage, cry, shed actual tears for the headlines, the political oppression, the senseless suffering, the absurd violence—you think you've got to show everyone that you feel everything, that, literally, you care about the entire world, and, then, because of your heroic extroverted emotionalism you think you count more than anything or anyone else... but it's bullshit, Heidi. Because I count too. Just as much. Even if all I ever do—something you can't see any value in— is teach tennis."

I opened my eyes, and in the weak, yellowish light of the car, I looked long and hard at Heidi. Her head hung down, chin to chest, with her arms crossed tightly, squeezing her breasts. Her legs, too, were tightly crossed, the cotton of her loose-fitting dress bunched-up between her thighs. She sat like that, motionless, for a long time. I found myself counting my breaths, something I'd begun to do since practicing yoga. I didn't want to speak. I think at some level I knew I'd already said too much. The speech, in fact, left me drained and a little queasy. Words as physical discharge, like vomiting. I felt better and worse at the same time.

Finally, without looking up, Heidi said, "Are you finished?"

"Yes," I whispered, then watched Heidi's arms uncross, and her hands slowly rise, and her fingers blindly massage her temples, and then she said, so simply, "Goodbye, Eli."

And she opened the car door and got out. It was still pouring, but she ignored the rain and took small, slow steps, hanging her head like a tired athlete. She stopped once, halfway up the driveway to the house. But she didn't look back. She stood there, oblivious to it all, the soaked dress clinging to her skin, wet hair matted to her scalp.

And me? I just sat there in the car—confused and frightened, but smug with my sense of shelter.

4

For the next couple of hours, I drove around in the rain thinking about when Heidi and I first started going out, back in high school.

In those days, she used to give me lots of little gifts. Small items, like a keychain, or a pressed leaf mounted on typing paper, or a polished stone to use as a paperweight, and with it a three-by-five notecard with some inspirational quote. Precocious as we were, the quotes ranged widely, anyone from Joni Mitchell to Kierkegaard. One of my favorites was a line from Ruskin taped to a handmade wooden letter-opener with an eagle's head carved on the top.

"The highest reward for man's toil is not what he gets for it, but what he becomes by it..." Soar, my love, soar...H—

She gave this one to me right before my big tryout for the high school varsity tennis team. She was a terrific inspiration for me back then. Of course, I was young. Blind-mouthed, barefoot-ranked. A typical swollen adolescent. In short, a teenager. But still, Heidi was a genuine Muse.

And she was, just as she wanted to be, a ubiquitous presence in my life. Not just throughout high school but in college, too. Even during the big test, the separation. Me at the University of Wisconsin, her at the University of Michigan. We had made the painfully "mature" decision not to attend the same college. And it followed naturally, then, that we formally break up. So we went months without speaking or writing to each other. And during this time we dated, slept around a little, and generally tried to forget about one another. To no avail.

Every holiday home was a trauma, until, finally, the summer after our college graduation we were back together, sharing more secrets than ever. It was as if our relationship had its own time zone. Four years had passed; but all we had to do was reset our watches.

The first night we were together after college graduation I'll never forget. It was at my house. My father was in the Orient on business; her folks were vacationing in Europe; she came over, ostensibly, to discuss Wittgenstein. Her final semester she'd taken a course on Wittgenstein, and so had I. A most interesting philosopher, we agreed. And made our plan to get together for a "discussion."

When she came to the door that night, she carried a large, leather shoulder bag, which she called her "suitcase of essentials." She'd had it custom-made out of an old postal sack, its leather worn and well-oiled, the color of dark chocolate.

"I didn't know what we might end up talking about," she said, pulling out three newspapers, several magazines, and about half a dozen books with titles like *The Industrial Society, Reading in the Philosophy of Religion,* and *Social Thought from Lore to Science.*

We talked for hours. Crazy for ideas, our excitement was absurd. We stood on the living room couch and shouted to make important points. It was ridiculous. It's embarrassing to remember it. But I was, in fact, incredibly in love with Heidi's urgency. She made it feel so important—everything. Every ten-cent idea, every sophomoric generalization, every ridiculous headline seemed absolutely alive. It was magical. She moistened the whole dry world of thought. And placed me in the center of it all.

Around three in the morning, we started in on Tillich's conception of God as the "ultimate ground of our being." We'd ordered a pizza and were still sitting in the kitchen, the oily cardboard box and open bottles of beer crowding the table.

Then she read this quote of Tillich's: *"Whether one has known God is tested by one question only: 'How deeply have you loved?'—for he who does not love does not know God; for God is love."*

There was a silence. Then I said, "Reminds me of Bonhoffer's idea of a non-religious understanding of the divine, in which a right relationship to God doesn't depend on any sort of creed or doctrine."

"Exactly," she said. And she leaned forward, her eyes fixed on me. "There are no barriers. God can simply be this wonderful energy between two people."

That clinched it. The end of the evening's intellectual courtship. Still sitting in our stiff-backed chairs at the crowded table, we kissed and fondled each other until a pale pink light shone through the kitchen windows, then we made love on the floor. Cool, bare linoleum under my naked ass. Heidi, being more forward than I'd ever remembered her, said she wanted to be on top.

I have to admit our sexual life that summer was terrific. I'm not sure we had half the deep love we thought we did, but in bed everything was wonderful. No hang-ups or emotional confusion. And no philosophical distractions there. A rare harmony of quiet minds and mutual doubt-free lust. We enjoyed each other. True, it wasn't the sort of sexual risk-taking I got into with Malaika, but we didn't seem to need any of that.

Yes, I thought a lot about Heidi while I was driving around that night in the rain, but by the time I arrived home, I was thinking again of Malaika. Through her, it seemed, I might get beyond everything that had to do with Heidi, including—and this is difficult for me to admit—being Jewish. That was definitely part of it. The way Malaika's beautiful, calm gaze seemed to offer escape from the whole twisted history of being a Jew. No doubt the obliteration of my personal identity enhanced the complicated, yogic spirituality of our great, physical connection: orgasm as transcendence.

I also think our ecstasy-seeking involved the influence of a terrific though little-known book, *The Universe is a Green Dragon*, by a cosmologist named Brian Swimme. I'd been reading the book just before that first yoga class, and in this slim volume, destined I believe to become a kind of New Age classic, Swimme argues that the Big Bang theory must be the fundamental context for all discussions of value, meaning, purpose, or ultimacy of any sort. Furthermore, he says that while scientists have just learned to see the fireball, what's most amazing about the discovery is "the realization that every thing that exists in the universe has come from a common origin." I was wild for this notion:

> The material of our bodies are intrinsically related because they emerged from and are caught up in a single energetic event. Our ancestry stretches back through the life forms and into the stars, back to the beginnings of the primeval fireball. This universe is a single multiform energetic unfolding of matter, mind, intelligence, and life. And all of this is new. None of the great figures of human history were aware of this. Not Plato, or Aristotle or the Hebrew Prophets, or Confucius, or Thomas Aquinas, or Leibniz, or Newton, or any other world-maker. We are the first generation, and our future as a species will be forged within this new story of the world.

Ah, yes, all is one. And my generation the first to realize it! Whatever blather there might be in this, it's still essentially true and when I sat across from Malaika—she wasn't just a beautiful woman I wanted to take to bed. She was the vessel through which the universe stretched back to its fireball origin.

Of course, I still didn't really know anything about her. But that was a mere detail. And I was too high on my own big ideas to give any attention to something as trivial as a personal biography. Until she forced me to.

5

A few days later, I knew that it was Heidi I should be calling, but it was Malaika's number I dialed.

She picked up on one ring. We exchanged greetings. then I suddenly blurted, "Look, have you been sleepless, unable to concentrate and bumping into things?"

"No." she said. flatly.

"No?"

"But I'm glad you called." She laughed, then there was a pause, and I heard the sound of opera music in the background.

"You like opera?" I asked.

"Uh, not really."

"But you're listening to——"

"I'm taking a course. Music appreciation. Does that sound stupid to you? Like if you've got to work so hard to appreciate something, it's probably not coming naturally."

"I don't know. With opera—well, my father is a subscriber to the Lyric, and whenever I've gone I always feel like——"

"I knew you were an opera-goer!" Her voice suddenly trembled with excitement. "I knew it!"

"I wouldn't say I'm an opera-goer, my father——"

"Wait," she said. "Do you know this…?"

She held the receiver for a moment right up to the stereo's speaker. "Well?" she said. "Do you know it?"

"Yes, Mozart's *Magic Flute*."

"I knew you would know it. I was sitting here listening to this, and I was thinking that you would know this opera—and I was right!"

"Well, it's kind of famous."

"It's based on the legend of Armor and Psyche—did you know that?"

"Yes," I said. "In fact, I did."

I couldn't quite tell what was going on. The conversation seemed to have a rhythm of its own.

"So, your father is an opera-goer? Wow." She sounded awfully impressed.

"Yes, a subscriber. But sometimes he doesn't use his tickets. Maybe you and I—"

"Oh, I'd love that," she said quickly. "This class I've been taking—well, it's one of those Learning Annex type of things…" Her voice trailed off. She had a way of letting her words fade out as she simultaneously sighed. An erotic little mannerism.

"I think it's a great thing to do," I said. "Most people, you know, just sit around watching TV."

"Yeah, well…"

"So how about a cup of coffee?" I said. "Or a drink?"

"Tonight?"

"Sure tonight—why not?"

"I'd love to, but…" She paused. "Well, why don't you tell me about her first?"

I was shocked. "What?"

"Your last girlfriend—or the woman you're still seeing. Whatever."

"What makes you think—"

"Nobody comes without strings attached," she said. "I like to know what I'm getting involved with."

"Are we getting involved?"

"You just asked me out for a drink, didn't you?"

"Yes, but a drink doesn't mean—"

"What—" she interrupted me. "You just want to be my friend?"

I felt like I could hear the coy smile on her face. I didn't say anything.

"Look," she said, finally. "I don't really know what this energy is between us—but it's there. I guess I just want to get it out in the open, OK?"

"OK," I said. "It's out in the open."

"Fine. So are you sneaking around behind anyone's back to call me?"

"No," I said, feeling extremely righteous. "I am not sneaking around behind anyone's back to call you." I took a deep breath. All of this candor was refreshing. "And you? Any lovers hiding under the bed?"

She laughed. "No. But I sleep on the floor."

"On the floor?"

"A futon mattress."

"I see."

"But let's not talk about my bed, OK? Not yet."

"Right," I said, then added: "You are a world-class flirt, aren't you?"

She sighed, and then there was another long pause. The opera music in the background stopped suddenly. For several moments I heard only the dead-space crackle of phone silence.

"Malaika?"

"Yes," she said, in a small voice. "I'm here."

"I was just kidding——"

"No, you've got it right," she said. "That's what I am…" Her voice trailed off into that little sigh, and then she added, in a drowsy voice, "but I'm going to change it…with your help, OK?"

"OK," I said, quietly. "OK."

So that night Malaika and I met for a drink. Determined not to be flirtatious, we put a safe gap between our uncomfortable bar stools and told each other about our lives as if we were distant cousins. Malaika insisted on paying for her own gin-and-tonic, and the evening ended with a polite kiss on the cheek. Still, the energy was there, perhaps strengthened by our self-conscious formality.

In any case, the next morning Heidi called. She was in the neighborhood and wanted to come over for breakfast. I told her that I'd prefer to meet at a coffee shop.

In a cool low tone, she said, "Fine. Just don't bring a date, OK?" And then she hung up before I could answer.

I got dressed and sat for a while on the stoop in front of my building. Back then I lived over on Sheffield, near Wrigley Field. I remember Chicago had been having one of its summer heat waves, which seemed even worse that day on account of the Cubs traffic. The street was already jammed with rock'n'roll and the smell of hotdogs and candied peanuts and the intermittent shouts of someone selling "Cubs' pennants, Cubs' pennants, Cubs' pennants…" Also contributing to the heat's oppressiveness was the complete absence of any lakefront breeze. As a rule, on a hot summer day without a breeze, once you get as far west as Sheffield, the whole city stinks. Exhaust hangs in the air. A faint fried-beef odor lingers everywhere. Dank, muggy.

I was about to head around the corner to Ann Sather's restaurant when the mailman approached. We nodded at each other. Half-moon sweat stains, large and dark, shone from the underarm of his pale blue shirt. His mouth was twisted. Sweat dripped from his forehead. What a horrible job, I thought. Having to walk around all day in this furnace. I felt sorry for him, even though if it hadn't been a Monday I would have been out on the tennis court sweating like a pig myself.

After nodding wearily at me, he said, "Your name Eli?" He mispronounced it *Eee-lee*, but I let it go. I didn't want to aggravate him, on account of the heat.

It didn't entirely surprise me to find a letter from my father. We had stopped speaking to each other about three months earlier, when I first suspected that he was lying to me. Since that time, he'd written twice. Long letters filled with rationalizations, justifications, apologies. I'd written back only once: a postcard from the country club, wishing him a happy birthday.

At the time of this particular letter, I knew only that his bank was one of several being investigated by the U.S. Attorney's office and that his name had appeared in an article with the headline: CITY DUPED BY PHONEY FIRMS.

The article had appeared on page one of the *Tribune*, and as soon as I saw it I phoned my father. It was his refusal to discuss it with me in any but the most vague and general terms that led me to my suspicion of him, and, shortly after that, to my refusal to speak to him at all.

So that morning I sat back down on the hot front steps and read his letter. It had the same familiar two-note refrain: 1) banks were frequently investigated by prosecutors searching for a paper trail; and 2) he was "deeply hurt" by my questioning his integrity. I took the letter, damp now around the edges from my sweaty hands, and stuffed it back into its envelope, which I carefully folded and placed in the pocket of my tennis shorts.

Then I sat there, waiting for my feelings to pass. The idea that my dad had really done something wrong gave me this strange sense of instability, a kind of light-headedness. Like a helium balloon that's gotten away from a small child. That was the image in my mind, a red helium balloon rising into a clear blue sky and growing smaller and smaller until it gradually disappears. I sat there pressing my hands down hard on my thighs—until it occurred to me that, once again, I was going to be late to meet Heidi.

I hurried through the Cub-game traffic. A group of shirtless Latino teenagers with crown-tatoos on their arms and chests were leaning against the doughnut shop under the El tracks. The smell of sugar and oil hung in the air around them like an odd cologne.

"Got a cigarette?" one guy asked.

I shook my head. Then, out of nowhere, a small, muscular black guy on roller skates whizzed past, nearly knocking me over. A red bandanna tied around his big bicep actually whipped the side of my face. The same guy who'd asked for the cigarette shouted, "Fuckin' nigger," and, in spite of myself, I shot him a quick look.

"What're you staring at?" he said, puffing out his bare chest, which had two small crowns tattooed above each nipple.

I shook my head, then the kid—— he couldn't have been more than about fifteen——turned bug-eyed and stuck out his jaw, baring his teeth, which were cracked and yellowed.

I hurried away, grateful that an El train directly above us rumbled to a wheel-screeching stop. The sound of metal on metal was strangely soothing. Seemed to match my inner state.

Heidi was standing in front of the restaurant with her head buried in a newspaper when I arrived. I had to walk right up to her and touch her elbow to get her attention.

"Sorry I'm late," I said.

She nodded so nonchalantly that it occurred to me maybe she was only pretending to read the paper. "This OK?" She flicked her head toward the restaurant.

"Sure."

We went inside, and I followed her to a booth. Before sitting down she swept some invisible crumbs off the table with her folded-up newspaper. We sat there in silence looking at the menu until the waitress came. Then, for no good reason except to buck Heidi's expectations, I decided to order a corned-beef sandwich. She pretended not to notice——and this time I was sure she was pretending. She ordered a bowl of tomato soup.

When the waitress left, Heidi sat there for a long while looking at the lunch counter as if there might be someone sitting there she knew.

"So…" I said, finally. "What's up?"

She squinted. "What's up?"

"You wanted to talk."

"Yes."

"Well…?"

She looked away from me again, then tore off a tiny corner of her paper napkin and twisted it between her thumb and forefinger. "Were you with her last night?"

"That's what you want to talk to me about?"

She dropped the torn-up corner of her napkin in the ashtray, then said quietly, "I just want to know—is that so unreasonable?"

I realize now I was being a real asshole, but I just shook my head. "That's not the point, Heidi. Whether I saw her or not doesn't matter."

"It matters to me," she said. Then she clenched her jaw. The first sign of her control cracking—her lip quivered, her eyes glistened with fought-back tears.

The waitress came with our food. Heidi quickly pulled the bowl close to her and began eating, not looking at me. I watched her lift spoonfuls of the steaming red tomato soup to her small red-lipped mouth. The soup steam fogged her glasses. And her not wiping them was meant, I figured, to insult me. I mean, I did feel a little like I was eating lunch with a woman wearing work goggles.

While Heidi slurped her soup, I took a bite of my corned beef sandwich. I hadn't eaten something like that in ages. After a few chews, I pulled a tiny string of corned-beef fat out of my mouth. Another small string was stuck between my teeth like a piece of thick, waxy dental floss.

Finally, Heidi took off her glasses and said, "What is it—you just think we need different things right now?"

She'd regained her composure.

"Yes," I said. "That's a good way to put it. We want different things out of our lives."

She dropped her spoon in her bowl, splashing a few drops of soup onto the table. "That's not what I said."

"But it's true, isn't it?" I said. "We don't want the same things."

"Oh? What do *you* want?"

"Me? I just want what I already have."

"To keep teaching tennis?"

"And practicing yoga—that's the main thing."

"Right—practicing yoga," she said. "But I'm not saying there's anything wrong with all that."

"What? You know that you wish I were—"

"I don't care what you do, Eli—as long it's what you really want."

"This is what I want."

I didn't say anything more, although obviously my glib little line concealed more than it revealed. Looking back, I'm amazed at the way my fear and insecurity masqueraded as courage and confidence. Perhaps it's social conditioning: scared and uncertain, men explain things, beating our chests as we clarify that we are in control and everything is fine.

While I composed my little exegesis, I reached for the jar of mustard and poured a big glob onto my plate, then dipped my sandwich and took a large, deliberate bite.

"Look," I said, as I chewed, "I'm sorry about what I said to you and your father last week. I was just…I don't know. I lost my head. But in terms of you and me, Heidi, you know this has been coming on for a long time." I paused just long enough to be sure I had her attention.

"I think it's obvious," I continued, "that we're moving in different directions. I mean, your university friends and everything. And someday you're going to be this famous art historian travelling all over the world and lecturing and——"

"And you?"

"Me?"

"Yeah."

"I don't know where I'll end up, but that's part of the point. Part of the basic difference. I'm not worrying about that right now. I'm on a certain path, and I'm trusting that——"

"Look, Eli," she said, cutting me off. "I don't care if you keep teaching tennis and practicing yoga. I just want to feel like…well, like we're in this together."

"Which means…?"

She looked down into her soup, and there was a long pause. Then she pushed the bowl toward the center of the table.

This, I have come to believe, is another scared man's move: accuse the woman of being unclear. "Which means what?" I said. "What exactly are you trying to say?"

"I guess if you've got to ask…"

"Look, Heidi, you obviously want some kind of commitment from me that I can't make."

"It's not about commitment. I'm not trying to pressure you into some sort of commitment——"

"It's understandable, we're getting older. You just turned thirty-four. I just turned thirty-five. Everybody we know is, you know…"

She leaned forward quickly. "Look," she said. "Here's my big fear, OK? That you will end up just like your Uncle Max."

"Max?"

"Especially now with this bank investigation and everything——"

I slapped my hand down on the table. "Jesus, that's a stretch. What's going on with my dad's bank doesn't have anything to do with us, Heidi. For chrissake…"

"OK, OK," she said. "Take it easy. I'm sure you're upset about your dad, all I'm saying——"

"Just leave my dad out of this."

"OK, fine. Just listen to me for a second. What I'm saying is that Max—— and I know you love him, I love him, too——but Max doesn't function in the world. You know that. He's just an utterly lonely old man refusing to recognize the pain of his loneliness, which is right there, in his deteriorating body. His failing health. Now you love him, I know. And so do I. But that's precisely why I'm so worried."

This whole riff about my Uncle Max caught me off guard. He's my father's notorious older brother who was almost fifty when he went off to help a group of Marxists fighting in Somalia and lost one leg. Blown off in battle. Tragic, yes. But it's family mythology. A story told and retold a thousand times in the last twenty-odd years. This is what worried her now? I didn't know what to make of it.

"Remember the last time we visited Max," she said, growing more animated. "In that stuffy, little attic?"

"It's not an attic."

"There's no window."

"It's a small window, and he had a fan in it."

"What was in that room?"

"What do you mean?"

"Books. Books, books, books. Notes taped to every inch of the walls, and stacks and stacks of books piled everywhere. Piled on the floor, stuffed under the bed, if you call that little cot a bed, and even books stacked on the table with the hot-plate. No room even to put down a cup of coffee! And what's the purpose?"

"You of all people to knock a guy with books? He reads."

"But who is Max?"

"What do you mean 'who is'——"

"How does he live? On disability insurance, right, while proudly refusing your father's 'hand-outs.'"

"For Max there are principles involved in not taking that money."

"It's just normal familial generosity!" Heidi said, her voice rising. "But forget the money, that's not the point. The point is there's no flowers, no painting, no decoration anywhere. Only piles and piles of books and that single, paint-chipped, wobbly table, crammed with more books and the hot-plate and his arsenal of medicine—pills for asthma, migraines, stomach cramps, nausea and, of course, insomnia. The drugs. Those drugs are Uncle Max's only companions. Do you realize he doesn't have any friends?"

"That's not true."

"But he doesn't think he needs any friends because his task, he believes, is 'to overcome himself.' And I'm not exaggerating. Max is——"

"There's Charlene."

"Who?"

"Charlene."

"Right—she brings him bagels once a week. Look, Max believes he's living like his cherished Nietzsche, about whom he is completely mistaken, by the way. I mean, Nietzsche is not a man of great self-knowledge; he is simply history's most articulate adolescent. And that's something someone ought to say to Max face to face."

I laughed. "What are you talking about? So Max reads a lot of Nietzsche—so what? He's interested in German philosophy."

"Yes, he's interested——"

"I don't know why you even mention Nietzsche——"

"The point is that to be taken in by Max's glorified bohemianism is extremely dangerous—and I can see you're tempted."

She paused, looking at me intently. I did my best to conceal my emotions, which were, to put it mildly, extremely mixed up. You see, I hated her characterization of Max as nothing but a lonely eccentric, but at the same time I was, at some level, flattered that she thought me capable of ending up like him. I mean, in those days especially I thought of Uncle Max as an unquestionable heavyweight. A thinker, a man of conviction, a man who had faced fear in a way I'm still not sure I'll ever be able to comprehend. Going to Africa? Losing a leg in war? What can I ever pretend to know about something like that? A brave, principled man. That's how I thought of Max.

After a long glassy-eyed moment, Heidi went on in a low, intimate voice, "You know that I'm right, Eli. Max is not some kind of an inspired outcast. He's simply alienated. And what's frightening is that he ignores it. He ignores precisely what he must pay attention to, the deepest of human needs, which is…the need to defeat solitude."

This, I thought, was a not-so-thinly-disguised counterattack to my previous charges against Heidi. At least, that's how I interpreted it. And, after letting it sink in for a few moments, I responded accordingly.

First I laughed, a low chuckle. Then, with what must have been a little swagger in my voice, I said, "Let it rest, Heidi. That's your song—not Max's. And certainly not mine."

She frowned.

"I mean, if you think 'alienation' is life's big problem, then go out and solve it. I wish you well."

I pushed my uneaten sandwich toward the middle of the table and reached into my pocket for my wallet. Then, unable to contain myself, I said, "But you know what the other side of this is, don't you?"

She answered in a surprisingly clear, strong voice. "No, Eli. What is the other side of this?"

"That if you weren't so afraid—you would make art instead of just studying it."

She winced a little, which I have to admit on some level must have pleased me. This, too, was an old wound of ours: Heidi's desire to paint.

"Here," I said, counting the money out for my portion of the bill. "Here's for my sandwich." I dropped the money on the table and started to slide out of the booth.

"So I get it," she said, swallowing hard now to keep her tears in check. "I'm laying my fears on you. And you're not afraid of anything, right? Life's a blank canvas and you're just painting your own picture, is that it?"

I didn't say anything. Then suddenly she slid out of the booth and was standing in front of me.

"Well, good luck, Eli," she said in a choked-up whisper. "I wish you well."

And then she turned around and walked out of the restaurant, leaving me sitting there alone.

6

I went immediately to Malaika's. But on my way I got caught in the rain. In true Chicago fashion, a summer storm had come out of nowhere.

"You're soaked," she said, opening the door.

I nodded, smiling.

"You're also a day-and-a-half early." She was referring to the plan we'd made the previous night at the close of our officially un-flirtatious date.

"I needed to see you," I answered.

She laughed softly, then shook her head and lowered her gaze. "Is that a need or a want?"

The question made me fear that she'd seen the erection bulging in my shorts. It also made me think I was wrong to show up uninvited. But—and I know this will sound shallow—the sheer physical beauty of her face, her high cheekbones, big eyes, full lips, and the proportions, the relation of the parts to the whole…what can I call it? Her aesthetic power? The immediacy of her magnificence made me feel bold, as if there were a moral imperative to act on what I felt. It all seemed a simple question of courage.

"Passion is a need," I said, quietly.

She shook her head and pulled at the bottom of her shirt. She wore a snug-fitting T-shirt. "You know," she began, "you're the one who is a world-class flirt."

"Oh no!" I said, raising my hands, like in a stick-up. "I must protest. Me? Amuse myself in unserious amorousness? Play lightly or mockingly at courtship? Deal triflingly, or coyly? Toy? As in 'The bullfighter flirted with death?' Not I…"

I stood there with my hands in the air, then she spoke, finishing my sentence, " 'Not I, said the prince.'"

I looked down at my shirt. I had again worn a tennis shirt with the brand name *Prince* stitched above the corner pocket. Was it an accident? No, there were no accidents.

"Right. 'Not I, said the prince.'"

"Look, Eli, I really enjoyed our drink together last night, but I just want it out in the open."

"What's that?"

"That I've known a lot of guys like you."

My damp clothes suddenly felt slimy and cold, and a nasty draft seemed to whoosh through the big hallway of her building.

"What does that mean?"

"We don't know each other well enough to argue, so let's——"

"Just get to know each other."

She stared at me, without blinking, "What are you doing here?"

"I like you—does that need some justification?"

"Not if it's genuine."

"How can I convince you of that?"

"You mean how can you earn my trust?"

"OK, yes. How do I earn your trust?"

"Say something true. One thing, right now, without hesitating, that's completely true."

I hesitated, laughing nervously.

"I guess I just blew it, huh? Is this a game you play often?"

"Not too often. Here's another chance, OK? One true thing: Go."

"I...uh...I think my father might go to jail."

She smiled, the corner of her lips rising. "That's supposed to earn my trust?"

"It's true. I've got a letter here from him. I can explain." I quickly pulled the folded envelope out of my back pocket.

"Don't show it to me," she said. "You might regret it later."

She averted her gaze with a dramatic turn of her head, then paused. "I shouldn't do this," she said, finally.

"Do what?"

"Invite you in."

"Why not?"

"Because I've been in this situation before."

"Where a guy said his father was going to jail?"

"No, that's an original line."

"It's not a line! It's true. He's in real trouble. It was in the papers."

She turned sideways, propping herself diagonally in the door frame. Her running shorts were cut high enough for me to see the grooved indentation of her thigh, just below the buttocks.

"You're either the greatest bullshit artist ever to walk the earth," she said slowly, "Or just incredibly...I don't know what..."

I shrugged. "You asked for something true."

"Your dad's really in trouble with the police? The opera-goer?"

I laughed. "Yeah, the opera-goer. I don't really know for sure if he's in trouble, but, yeah, I think he is."

"What did he do?"

I hesitated, not sure where to begin.

"He didn't beat somebody up, did he?"

"My dad? No, he's not—well..."

"Not that sort, huh?"

"I guess it's a long story."

She nodded. "Your mother know all about it?"

I paused. I knew that telling her about my mother's death would change everything. It's just one of those things that people react to. And I'm not proud of it, but I have to admit there are times when I've used this to my advantage.

"My mother?" I began. "She...uh, my mother's dead."

She looked at me closely. The facial muscles around her jaw and under her eyes seemed to soften.

"I'm sorry," she said.

Just then the elevator doors behind me hissed open and a big fat lady with a grotesquely large red hat stepped out, breathing heavily. She stopped in the middle of the hall, looked one way, then the other, and started trundling toward us, her great rolls of fat jostling with each step. I started to back away from the doorway to let the big woman pass, but Malaika took my wrist and pulled me toward her, into the apartment.

"You must be freezing in those wet clothes," she said. "I'll get you a robe. You can change in the bathroom."

I did as I was told, enjoying her take-charge style. A moment later, wearing a terri-cloth robe that reached only to the middle of my forearms, I stepped out of the bathroom and looked around. There were just two square rooms, a small kitchen/living area and a bedroom around the corner. The place lacked character, but seemed to have all the comforts, including central air conditioning, wall-to-wall carpeting, and all new appliances.

I sat down opposite her on the corner of a small couch.

"Well," she said, "now that I've got your clothes off…"

I laughed. "That didn't take long, did it?"

"How about a drink?"

"A drink?"

"Too early for you?" She looked at her watch, the sort of big, plastic watch you might buy for a little kid. It couldn't have cost more than about ten dollars. "It's a quarter to one," she said. "Myself, I never have a drop before twelve-thirty. What about you?"

"Twelve-thirty in the afternoon sounds like a reasonable curfew."

She looked at me, a little puzzled. "Isn't a curfew just at night?"

"What?"

"Curfew—isn't that something that just refers to nighttime?"

I shook my head, not sure whether she was joking or not. The expression on her face suggested she wasn't. Eyes wide, mouth slightly parted.

"I guess what I'm saying," she said, as if she were thinking out loud, "is that maybe I don't understand that word."

I nodded. And I remember thinking: this is a weird moment.

Then, as the silence between us became awkward, she turned quickly away and said, in a sing-song voice, "But I shouldn't worry my pretty little head about it, should I?" She headed toward the refrigerator. "Last night you were drinking gin-and-tonic, no lime—right?"

"Good memory," I said.

"My best friend back home would kill me if she heard me say something like that—'worry my pretty little head.' She's a hard-core feminist. Just moved onto an all-women's commune near Mendocino, a couple of hours north of the city. Growing their own food and everything. Men aren't even allowed to visit without all kinds of special arrangements being made. They say it's an energy thing—that the feminine energy needs to be ritually prepared. I said to her, 'Star,'—that's her name, Star—I said, 'Star, you're going too far with this feminist thing.' You see she's not a lesbian or anything. She's crazy about men. And all she does is just look at a man and he wants to marry her. No kidding. She once stole a guy from me who——"

Malaika stopped suddenly as the bottle of tonic opened with a loud fizz and splashed on the floor. "Shit," she said. "Excuse my language. I'm rattling on, not watching what I'm doing. Be a sweetheart, will you, and grab me a paper towel."

I jumped up and hurried to the sink, glad that her little riff about the "hard-core feminist" had been interrupted. It was not so much what she was saying but the hurried quality of her saying it that made me nervous. She was screwing up my picture of her. My calm, serene, exotic beauty.

When she finished making the drinks, we sat down again on the couch. The patient calmness in her big, dark eyes returned.

After a long moment of silence, she said, "I'm glad you're here."

I nodded, and we both took a sip of our drinks. "Let me just get this out of the way, OK? About my mother. She died when I was eighteen, my senior year in high school. Throat cancer. It came out of nowhere. She was diagnosed, and then six months later…"

My voice trailed off. Malaika sat there patiently, then crossed one leg over the other, a pleasing little gesture, quietly dignified.

"I just wanted to tell you," I said, still feeling guilty about the way the sympathy card had helped me get into the apartment.

She nodded. "I feel…well…privileged."

"It's not like I want to lay it on you——"

"Do you have a picture of her?" she interrupted.

The question caught me off guard, but I liked it. "I'll bring you one, OK? I'd like to show you what my mother looked like."

She smiled. But she didn't say anything. And this silence, the space, seemed encouragement to say more.

"Now my father," I said. "I'm not quite sure where to begin about him…"

"Is he some sort of gangster?"

She said this with a straight face, but I laughed. The label——at this point, anyway——sounded ridiculous.

"What's so funny?" Malaika continued. "There are plenty of Jewish gangsters, aren't there?"

The previous night I'd told her I was Jewish, a fact she seemed to register with interest. "He's a banker," I said, then gave her a brief explanation of how the papers had reported that phony firms were charging the city for work they'd never done, and that one of the firms had opened an account at my father's bank.

"But maybe he doesn't know anything about it?" she said.

"Maybe."

"But you don't think so?"

I shrugged. "I don't know. It's just the way he won't talk to me about it. It doesn't make sense."

"You guys are close?"

"Sort of."

"No brothers or sisters?"

"No."

"Me neither." She smiled, then said suddenly, "Do you think being an only child can screw you up?"

"Nah. That's not why I'm screwed up."

She laughed. "But maybe an only child can understand another only child better than someone with brothers and sisters could understand. I mean, if one person has brothers and sisters and the other person—you know what I'm trying to say?"

"Yes, I think so. That children without siblings have a unique experience."

"Exactly. That's exactly what I mean. I get confused a lot with words," she said.

"Confused?"

"I mean I wish I were more, you know, good with words. I really like listening to the way you use them. Like last night. I've been thinking a lot about some of the things you said last night."

"Such as?"

She took a sip of her drink. "I don't know. Like about tennis. The way you talked about the 'inner game,' about how 'it's a question of the quality of consciousness you bring to it.' I liked that phrase. I wrote it down."

"Really? I get most of that stuff from the book I was telling you about, *The Inner Game of Tennis.*"

"But the way you put things—I don't know. It reminds me of this yoga teacher I had in California. He used to end each class with a little poem, or a Zen reading."

"Any favorites?" I asked.

"Poems?"

"Or Zen readings. Whatever."

"Yeah I've got a few that I live by—but I'd never tell anyone."

"Why not?"

She ran her fingers through her hair and closed her eyes.

"Oh I don't know, I can take my clothes off in front of a man in a minute but I guess I like to keep my soul covered up..."

This was a turn-on—yes. But I also sensed that, beneath the flirting, she was trying to tell me something serious about herself.

"What if you kept your clothes on and—"

"Instead showed you my soul, right?"

I didn't say anything. Her eyes were still closed, the expression on her face soft, dreamy. She continued to run her fingers through her hair.

"That's what my friend Star says—that I use my sexuality to avoid my 'deeper femininity.'"

"Do you?"

Now, she opened her eyes. The directness of my question seemed to startle her. Small lines creased her brow.

"No," she said, in a low tone. "I don't believe that. I believe my sexuality is a deep femininity."

I nodded.

Then she said, "Can I trust you?"

"I hope so."

"If you promise me that you won't laugh, I'll——"

"I promise."

"This is, truly, a little saying that I live by. So if you laugh——"

"I promise, Malaika, that I will never laugh at anything you live by."

She bit her lower lip just enough for the corner of one tooth to show, the same way she'd done that first time we spoke out in front of the yoga studio. Then she smiled. "I believe you when you say that."

"I'm glad."

She took a deep breath. " 'Consciousness is attention, and complete attention is prayer'…That's it. I don't even know whose saying it is, but I have it written on a piece of paper that I carry around in my wallet."

"Consciousness is attention, and complete attention is prayer," I repeated. "That's nice." I raised my glass, toasting her. She leaned forward, and we kissed.

"Thank you," she said, "for not laughing." She kissed me again, this time more passionately, one hand moving to the back of my neck, squeezing it tightly. Then she moved her hand from the back of my neck around to the front of my open robe, and down my chest to my stomach.

I moaned, then she whispered, "I want it to be different with you."

I leaned back, still holding her hand. "Different…in what way?"

"I don't know. I just——I know it doesn't sound right. But it's just that I've got a lot of experience as——what Star would call——being a 'sex object.'"

I let go of her hand and slid back to my corner of the couch. "Am I making you feel like that?"

She shook her head. "It's not you. It's just… I don't know how to explain it. I've known a lot of guys like you."

"How can you say you've known a lot of guys like me—you don't even know me yet."

"I didn't mean it like that."

"I mean if I'm making you uncomfortable, Malaika, just say so. And I'll leave."

"No, that's not what I'm saying. Please don't be angry with me." She climbed over to my side of the couch and again took my hand. "What I mean is good-looking guys who talk smooth and who are gentle and not into playing society's games and——it's just, well, the last relationship I had——"

"With the painter," I interrupted her. She'd told me the previous night that her last relationship had been with a painter in San Francisco.

"Yeah, the painter. Jake. His name was Jake. At one point, you know, things were pretty serious between Jake and me, and we were talking about the future, about getting married, and he says to me, 'Malaika, one thing I don't get is how come a beautiful woman like you isn't already married?' And I said to him, 'Jake, it's because I keep falling in love with gorgeous, irresistible fuck-ups like you.'" She paused, gazing down at my hand. "This is crazy to be telling you all this."

"No, it's not. I want you to tell me…whatever it is."

"It's just that——you know I'm thirty-nine years old now."

"I know. And I'm thirty-five. We went through this last night."

"It's just that I feel like——" She let go of my hand and quickly stood up, the firm muscles of her legs flexed as if she were about to spring across the room.

"So," I said, "you think I'm just…somehow another Jake?"

She turned and started to pace back and forth in front of the couch. "No," she said, finally.

"Then what? What is it?"

"I want to show you something. You'll either think it's great or you'll run the hell out of here."

She walked past me and went into the bedroom. For a second I thought maybe she was going to come out in some kind of outrageous lingerie.

But then she called from the bedroom, "Do you know how I'm supporting myself now?"

"How?"

"Remember what I told you about where I got my money."

I thought for a minute about what she told me the previous night, how she'd worked as a model in San Francisco and had come to Chicago to try her hand at being an actress. "Your work as a model," I yelled back.

She stepped into the room holding a small, ordinary brown paper bag, like a lunch bag. "Right," she said quietly. "My work as a model."

She threw me the bag.

"What's this?"

"Open it," she said. "It's my 'deeper femininity.'"

7

I opened the bag and took out a small stack of pictures. They were of Malaika nude. I started to put them back.

"No, don't," she said.

I froze, and there seemed to be a great silence in the apartment. The rain was falling outside and I heard the sound of my own shallow breathing. I also became aware of the smell of my own rain-soaked body. A faint, salty, masculine odor—it stunk.

She turned around and started to cry. I put the pictures back in the bag and went to her. Tentatively, we hugged. I remember suddenly feeling like a total idiot wearing her robe. I hadn't noticed before that there was a little lace pattern stitched along the bottom of the sleeves and around the neck.

"Take it easy," I said. "It's OK."

She took a quick, gasping breath, then said, "Star says I'm afraid to let anyone see these because—"

I squeezed her shoulder and gave her a little shake. "Hey, your friend Star is doing her thing, and you're doing yours. She isn't here in the room with us. You don't have to show me these pictures just to…just to prove something. You don't want to show them to me—fine. I'll give them back to you—or throw them in the garbage if you want—and we'll never talk about it again."

She shook her head. "No, I…" She broke out of my embrace and quickly stepped over to the coffee table, where she picked up her drink and took a long gulp. Then she forcefully, almost angrily, set the glass back down. "No," she said again, and she whirled around and faced me. Her pupils were dilated, the dark brown deepening into blackness. She picked up the paper bag and handed it to me. I sat back down on the couch.

"I'm gonna have another drink," she said. "Want one?"

"Sure." I put the bag next to me.

"Go on. Look at them. I want you to."

She went to fix the drinks. I reached into the bag and pulled out about a dozen three-by-five snapshots. They were tasteful, artistic even, in their own way. Malaika, of course, looked beautiful. In one picture, she was simply standing nude in the center of an Oriental rug. Behind her, in the background, a fireplace and an antique bookcase gave the setting an elegant ambience. She stood with one knee bent, accentuating the curve of her hips, and she held a glass of red wine in one hand. Her other hand rested at her side. She smiled, looking directly into the camera. It looked a little like an advertisement, except, of course, that she was nude.

When she came back with the drinks, I again started to put the pictures away, but she said, "No, don't." Then she sat down cross-legged on the floor at the foot of the couch and closed her eyes. She took a few deep breaths, as if she were meditating.

"This photographer," she began quietly, with her eyes still closed. "I met him about nine months ago at Stinson Beach. "He came up and told me this stupid joke. He was an older guy, you see. Sixties, maybe even seventies. He refused to ever tell me his exact age, and it was hard to tell because he looked real fit and had a thick, full beard that he kept well-trimmed and was only grey around the edges. Also he was real lean and tall, six-four, at least. A jogger. A total exercise freak. Used to run every day and had all kinds of equipment and weight sets all over his house. And he almost always wore running shoes and a sweatsuit. Anywhere he went—he wore a sweatsuit. But fancy ones. Made out of that thin, velvety cotton. All the most expensive brands. It was the only thing he ever wore."

She smiled suddenly and opened her eyes, then looked at me, as if this sweatsuit thing were some sort of joke I was supposed to join her in.

"He wasn't a bad man," she said.

I just nodded. She looked away.

"So the joke," she continued, and closed her eyes again. "A group of senior citizens had been holding some sort of exercise classes at the beach and nicknamed it Elder Park. So I'm lying there in the sand and he comes up to me and says, 'Don't you know the name of this strip of sand? This isn't a place for a pretty young lady like you.'

"Well, I'm out there especially to get away from this sort of thing because at that time, you see, I was working in the city as a bartender. The only reason I was there at all is because the owner of the bar, a real first-class asshole, had asked me to house-sit for him at his place in Inverness. You know where that it is?"

"No."

"No? It's gorgeous, not far from the Point Reyes National Seashore Park. Anyway, it was like his second house—or third house, for all I know—and it was a great big place with a view of Tamales Bay and a hot tub and everything. Even though I couldn't stand the guy, I jumped at the chance to house-sit for him because it meant five days of luxury—and five days without being behind the bar. So that's why I was so pissed off about this old guy coming up to me with a line. But right after he said it, as if he were reading my mind, he said, in his old-fashioned elegant sort of way, 'I apologize. I don't mean to disturb you or to offend you. I mean only to suggest a compliment—that your beauty is a gift.'

"I don't know why, but I looked up at him and, instead of shooting him a get-the-fuck-away-from-me look, I said: 'Well, thank you for the compliment.' And he smiled. I'll never forget it because it was this beautiful old man's sort of smile, with the wrinkles around his mouth and eyes coming alive. I felt like I'd really made him happy, you know? And he didn't say anything else. He just made this polite little bow and walked away."

Malaika paused and took another long, slow breath. Then she gulped down the rest of her drink and got up to fix herself another. I looked down at the picture on the top of the stack, then began glancing through the rest of the pile. The next one was of Malaika with her back to the camera. Her hair was much longer then and reached to the top of her bare buttocks. Then there was a picture of her sitting in front of the fireplace, legs crossed, carriage and neck nicely extended; and one shot with her knees pulled up to her chest, her hair this time piled on top of her head. All of the pictures, with the wine glass and the fireplace and the antique bookcase, conveyed pretty much the same mood, a kind of eroticized elegance. Nothing even remotely resembling smut.

Except for the last one. The last picture in the stack looked as if it had been handled a lot. Bent, corners torn, it was a picture of Malaika sitting on the Oriental rug. Her eyes were closed, head tilted up, her back arched so that her chest was open, lifting her breasts. She'd placed one hand behind her. It looked like it helped support her weight and arch her back. The other hand was hidden by her thighs.

It took me a minute to comprehend what I was looking at: a photograph of Malaika masturbating.

My first thought was: I shouldn't have done this. I shouldn't have looked at these pictures. Then I wondered if it was a mistake, if maybe Malaika hadn't intended for me to see this last one.

"A few days later," she said, while still mixing her drink, "I went back to the beach, and there he was, painting. He had an easel set up facing toward what I think was like a willow bush or some kind of tree hanging over a small, rocky part of the shore…"

As she spoke, I buried the picture in the middle of the stack and stood up. Suddenly, I felt hateful. I hated everything. My whole life. Heidi, my father, Uncle Max. And Malaika, too. Who was this woman telling me her life story? What was I doing there?

I was about to walk into the bathroom, get out of that ridiculous robe, put on my clothes and leave, when Malaika looked at me and, so nonchalantly, the way she must have a thousand times before, said, "Can I freshen up your drink?"

And I don't really know why—a moment of weakness, or my predilection for passivity kicking in, or a fascination with the bizarreness of the whole thing? Whatever. I looked down at the coffee table and picked up my drink, took a big gulp, and said,"Sure, why not?"

She took my glass. "So he said he wanted to paint me. You know, like be his model. And I was intrigued. His age, his manners, everything about him. Such a change from the guys who'd come into the bar. Also, I figured that he was taking me to be some rich Marin County type, since I had my boss's car and was showing up at the beach in the middle of the day and everything. I don't know, it was all just a big fantasy. I was living in somebody else's house and so it was easy to just pretend I was somebody else.

"The next day I went back to the beach, and when I got there, he saw me walking down these wooden steps out onto the sand, and he waved. He was back in that same spot, with his easel set up facing this tree hanging over the rocks. I walked right over to him."

She handed me my drink and raised her glass in a silent toast. I thought about how she was on her third drink but still seemed completely sober. We each took a small sip and sat back down.

"At first he didn't say anything. He just stood there looking at his drawing. I remember I was freezing because the wind was blowing like crazy. The easel wobbled. There were these huge waves. I was about to walk away. Then, finally, he turns to me and says, totally straightforward, 'I'll pay you five hundred dollars a day to be my model.'"

Malaika shook her head and made a soft clicking sort of sound with her tongue. "I'm sure the expression on my face must have given me away," she said. "The idea of that much money just…well, I was blown away. And the next thing I knew I was parking my car in this big, paved driveway in front of a huge, wood-frame house that had this great porch with an old-fashioned hammock in the corner. His studio was on the top floor, and I followed him up there without saying a word. I was nervous, but somehow I knew that whatever this was, it wasn't dangerous.

"When we got inside his studio, he offered me a glass of tea and then disappeared into a small dinette. I stood around looking at some of his paintings on the walls. Obviously, they were all his. Mostly of the ocean, the shoreline. Then he came out with this little tray, that I remember thinking was so charming and sort of European. There was a small clay pot, two cups and a little plate of crackers. But not regular crackers. You know, fancy ones. He set the tray down on a small table in front of a two-seater couch, a love-seat, I guess you'd call it. And he motioned for me to join him.

"'I must talk to you,' he said, pouring out the tea while holding the top of the pot real carefully with one finger. And then he said: 'No doubt I should have told you this before you got here, but I am going to ask you to take your clothes off. If you don't want to do that, I understand. But I'm afraid it's the only way that—'" He hesitated, and I felt like he was waiting for my reaction. But I just looked at him, and I was thinking, I have to admit, about that five hundred bucks.

"'You must understand that I'm interested in art,' he said quietly. 'You may, of course, conclude that I am just well… a 'dirty old man,' but, I assure you, I am motivated by a belief that there is only one temple in the world, and that is the human body. Nothing is more sacred than that noble form.'

"And he paused again, waiting for me to say something. And I remember thinking that my not saying anything was getting to him and that I didn't really want to put him off—I just didn't have any idea what to say.

"But after a moment he leaned back and went on, 'You are a very beautiful young woman,' he said. 'Your beauty is like a kind of genius, a gift. And it must be very difficult for you. You are the kind of woman that men want to own.' And he looked down into his cup of tea, then said in a real low and quiet voice, 'All I want is a picture.'

"And then he reached into his pocket and took out five one hundred dollar bills. He tucked them under the edge of the plate of crackers. I just sat there for a second looking at the money. I'd never seen anyone just pull out that kind of money before. When I looked back up at him, he was staring down into his teacup.

"So I picked up the money, and a moment after I did, he said, 'Good.

Thank you.' Then he stood up and said, 'I'll get my things ready. I'm going to start with some photographs. You can take your clothes off in the bathroom. On the white shelf, you'll find a clean robe.'"

Malaika stopped and, swirling the ice in her glass, looked at me. I was still holding the stack of pictures.

"I modelled for him for the next five months—six days a week. Twelve thousand dollars a month." She hesitated, then took a swallow of her drink. "You've never been poor, have you?"

I shook my head. "No, I haven't."

"You think I'm a slut because of what I did?"

"No."

"Damn right I'm not," she said. "That money got me out from behind the bar and——"

She broke off and started to laugh, and for the first time I thought I was seeing the effects of the alcohol. It was a bitter, sarcastic laugh.

"Star…" she said. "She doesn't know shit. She said that I should've…" Her voice trailed off into that little sigh of hers. "*Exploited*—that's her big fucking word."

She looked at me with a sneer, one lip curled upward. "I moved in with him," she went on. "Stayed in a little room in the coach house—and I know what you're thinking. But he never even tried to lay a hand on me. Never. We became friends, sort of. I mean he was always giving me books to read. Stuff on art and psychology and religion. And astronomy. He was crazy into astronomy. Loved to take me out to the beach at sunset and talk about how the sun isn't setting, you know, the earth is moving. And he'd tell me to close my eyes and see if I could feel it, the earth slowly rotating away from the sun. He was also into yoga, though not as good at it as me. I mean, not as flexible. So I helped him with the poses and a few times we went to classes together. But the strange thing was that we never were really getting close. Like, we never talked about our past or our families or anything. It was some sort of unspoken agreement. Once, we were looking at the color and lighting in one of the pictures and I said something about my father being a real light-skinned black. But he seemed to not even hear me. He really didn't care about that sort of thing. It seems almost spooky when I look back on it. Like there was just one whole level of reality, all the day-to-day stuff that, you know, makes up who we are—but he just wasn't interested in it. At the end of every session, every single session, he'd say to me, 'Your beauty is a gift. Thank you for sharing it.'

"And it got to the point where I started to want him just because he was so, I don't know, mysterious. In fact, that's why, right before I left…" She stopped suddenly. "This is all freaking you out, isn't it?"

"No." I reached my hand out to her. She pinched my wrist with her thumb and forefinger. A little kid's gesture, I thought. Endearing.

"You know," she said quietly. "I never… Jake thought I was just living up there in the old man's house and stretching the canvases and stuff. In fact, I never told anyone—except Star. She drove up from the city a few times to visit me."

I took her hand in mine and squeezed it tightly. "I'm glad you're telling me."

She shook her head. "I don't know, though. I mean why am I telling you?"

I shrugged. "I'm your prince."

"That's explains it." She smiled.

"No seriously," I said. "You're going through something right now—some sort of change. And I'm the right person to go through it with."

"And what is it?"

"The change?"

"Yeah, Prince. Tell me what the change is? When I kiss you do I turn into—"

"You want to show me your soul," I said, angered suddenly by her joking.

"Yes," she said, quietly. "My soul…" And she let go of my wrist as a gloomy feeling seemed to overtake her. Her head hung forward, and her shoulders rounded into an uncharacteristic slouch. "Did you look at all of them?"

I held up the stack of pictures in my hand. "Yes."

"Including the one that shows me…" She hesitated. "The one uh…that shows me…"

Our words overlapped as I said "yes" at the same moment she said "touching myself." Then she stood up and turned her back to me. Her head was lowered so that the soft nape of her neck shone beneath some loose strands of her dark hair. I got up and stood behind her, placing my hands firmly on her shoulders. "That last picture was my idea," she said, without turning around. "I set it up and everything. I smoked a bunch of dope first and told him that I wanted a picture of me that would be about pleasure. And while the camera was snapping, I kept thinking over and over that he's right, he's right, I'm beautiful, it's a gift, I'm beautiful, it's a gift and I thought about his whole astronomy thing about how the sun is the center of the universe and how he used to say that each second the sun transforms itself into light, and it's a kind of sacrifice with the sun giving itself over to vanish into this energy going off in all directions and making everything possible, all of life, and how the energy of the sun is inside of us because it's the source of us, the source of all life…"

Her voice trailed off and she started to cry. I was moved by her tears but also fascinated by the cosmology she was articulating: it was Brian Swimme's living universe, minus the detailed understanding of atomic and nuclear physics. But she had the essence right: we are composed of the very fabric of the universe, and through us the universe becomes aware of itself.

She kept talking through her tears, and her mood quickly darkened. "But afterwards…afterwards I was just angry," she said. "I hated myself. I hated him and all his big ideas. Hated how mysterious he was—how aloof. How he never made any attempt at all to get to know me, to touch me. And I didn't know what to do—but I felt like I couldn't stay there anymore. I couldn't face him. So I went back to the city and when I told Star what happened—"

She turned around and faced me. There was a long silence. Then she stepped forward, and we kissed—a long, slow, passionate kiss, until she let out a soft, little moan and said, "This feeling inside of me right now…I'm going to follow this feeling as far it takes me. Wherever it leads." And her mouth was clenched so tightly that I could see the outline of the muscles of her jaw, as she added, in a whisper, "So I hope you're ready." And then she didn't wait for an answer. She opened my robe and pulled my underwear down to the middle of my thighs and took me in her mouth.

I felt dazed and a little scared because she seemed so experienced and sure of herself that I immediately feared I would disappoint her—in more ways than one. But I pulled off the robe and slipped off my underwear. Then she took off all her clothes and lay down nude right there on the floor and looked up at me with her big, dark eyes wide open.

8

So that's how it started, and for the next couple months Malaika and I spent every free minute together, and the world was a happy place.

I succeeded in pushing Heidi completely out of my mind by telling myself that I couldn't have anything to do with her because she didn't respect me. She didn't respect my tennis, or my yoga, or my whole view of life. She was simply too Jewish. That's what it boiled down to. That her intellectual-historical-analytical-moral "Jewish way" of looking at the world failed to respect what I knew about life. And I knew plenty——or so I thought.

Until Malaika got pregnant.

She gave me the news at six in the morning while I was on the phone with my dad, who had just broken our three-month silence to tell me that one of his bank's senior vice presidents had mysteriously disappeared. If the police contacted me, I was to refuse to answer questions, he said. Meanwhile, Malaika, nauseated for the fifth straight day, was sitting on the side of the bed holding her stomach, one hand scrunching up the fabric of the grey, oversized T-shirt she slept in.

I covered the phone. "You're what?"

"I can just tell," she whispered. "Tell your dad I want to meet him, and that he's going to be a grandpa."

"Are you serious?"

"Yes. I've got to pee." She walked down the hall to the bathroom, her sleepy feet slapping the wood floor.

"…but I can't really explain it any further," my dad went on, in a low, tense voice. "Bill Greengoss's wife said that Bill didn't come home last night. He left the office as usual, but then—— "

"So you were the last one to see him?"

As soon as I said this I wished I hadn't. There was a long silence.

"OK, Eli, OK," my dad said, quietly. "Come out to the house and I'll tell you the whole story, all right?"

"Dad, I'm sorry. I didn't mean to suggest that you——"

"It's my fault, Eli, not yours. Nature abhors a vacuum, right? So you don't know what's going on, and your imagination fills it in with…whatever. Sunday night, OK?"

"Yeah, Sunday's fine."

"OK. I'll lay it all out for you then, the whole story. But listen, Eli…" He paused. "Anyone contacts you, you just give him Irv Kirschbaum's phone number."

"Heidi's dad?"

"Yes. Do you have Irv's office number?"

"Mr. K. is your lawyer?"

"No. I mean, yes. But not formally. I don't need a lawyer. Look, this is all going to be resolved soon. But Irv's handling it all for me—as a friend."

This shook me up. Did Heidi know more than me about what was going on with my own father?

"Do you have Irv's office number?" my dad asked again.

"Yes, I've got it."

"Good. OK." He paused. "So how are things teaching tennis? Your back holding up?"

"Pretty good."

"I'm sorry to call so early."

"That's OK."

"Well, I'll see you Sunday."

We hung up, and I heard the sound of the toilet flushing and Malaika jiggling the loose handle on the bathroom door. It was stuck, so I started down the narrow hallway, crammed with boxes of books, an exercise bicycle, tennis rackets, and a broken ball machine. I opened the bathroom door for her.

"What did he say?"

"I'll tell you about it later. What are you saying? Are you really pregnant?"

She paused. "How about lighting a candle, OK? I think we need that now—a candle burning. Unless, do you need to sleep some more?"

"No, I'm fine."

I grabbed two silver candleholders that had once been my mother's. They were absurdly fancy for that dumpy little apartment, with its cracked plaster, grey peeling walls, and the permanent mildewy smell that drifted in from the bathroom. I sometimes think that the only reason I lived in that apartment was to prove to myself that money wasn't everything.

Anyhow, I took the candlesticks back into the bedroom, where Malaika had spread a blanket for us on the floor at the foot of the bed.

We sat down cross-legged, facing each other, our knees touching.

"There's a meditation I would like to do with you," she said. "Will you let—"

"Yes, yes, I will, of course I will, but, Malaika, if you're really telling me—"

"Shh. Shh."

She closed her eyes and took a deep breath. I knew that I was supposed to close my eyes too.

"If one locks one's attention to the entrance door of breath," she began quietly, "and in that terrible darkness makes the spirit a lamp... then the indefinable supreme reality can be felt—and the inexpressible experience of unity can be attained."

She took my hand, her eyes still closed. What she had recited was word-for-word the lines Shahms used to accompany *savasana*, the "corpse pose," where you simply lie flat on your back. We did it at the end of every yoga class.

The truth is I liked what she was saying, and it upset me that I couldn't concentrate on a damn thing.

She took both of my hands rhythmically moving first one, then the other, back and forth, like pedaling. "The union of a man and a woman," she whispered, "is like the union of the sun and the moon..." She opened her eyes. I blinked, pretending my eyes had just opened too. Then she nodded at me.

"The union of a man and a woman," I repeated, our clasped hands continuing to move back and forth, "is like the union of the sun and the moon."

"And the core polarities of the human soul lose their finite quality..."

"And the core polarities of the human soul lose their finite quality..." I repeated.

"As love knows no limit but burns beyond every limit..."

There was a long pause, and her lips were parted as if to continue—but instead she leaned forward and kissed me.

"I have something to tell you."

"Yes?"

"I really am pregnant. And this isn't the first time."

I was silent. I wasn't sure I'd heard her correctly. We'd discussed our previous relationships—with utter candor, I thought.

"What?"

"I was pregnant once before."

"But you told me—"

"I lied," she said, looking directly into my eyes.

"You...lied?"

She nodded. "I'm sorry, Eli. I'm so sorry."

I pulled my hands away from hers, then I slowly stood up, and I remember suddenly feeling self-conscious about being in my underwear. In those days I wore this black, bikini-style underwear.

"It was with Jake," she said. "And there was never any doubt about my having an abortion. I didn't even tell him about it."

I wandered to the closet and stood there, holding the door. There was a ball of dust in the corner of the closet and I imagined it hanging in the air, entering my lungs. She lied to me, I kept thinking, she lied to me.

Then she stood up, and I thought maybe she was going to come over to me—but instead she blew out the candles, then walked right past me and went quickly down the hall and back into the bathroom.

What emotions she was experiencing at that moment I can only guess. I've often wished I hadn't been so narcissistically absorbed in my own feelings of betrayal. I mean, I'm sure that for her the sheer physicality of being pregnant made the moment between us much more intense than I can ever imagine. After all, the baby was inside *her*.

But I just stood there at the closet for a long time, saying nothing. Finally, I decided that maybe I ought to get out of the apartment, just go for a walk, get some air, but then I heard the toilet flush, and the pipes whistling, a familiar, strangely soothing sound. So I stepped into the hall, listening in the early morning stillness to the faint rattling of the door handle. Then there was a soft but distinct *kchunk*—and instantly I knew what had happened: Malaika had pulled off the loose handle on the bathroom door.

This somehow pierced my brooding and struck me as ridiculously funny: she was trapped inside the bathroom. Would she call to me? What would she say? *"I'm your prisoner, let me out, let me out...."*

She always hated that bathroom. The separate hot and cold water spigots, the rust spots in the ceramic bowl, the chipped mirror, cracked tile, cockroaches under the sink. I must have stood there for several minutes, then suddenly there was a loud *whaaak* on the door, several quick clanging *plunks* against the bathroom tile, and a low ripping sound, Malaika tearing down the shower curtain.

I rushed forward and threw the door open so quickly that it banged against the side of the tub. Malaika stood near the toilet, her hands clenched in front of her forehead as if she were protecting herself from blows. Her eyes darted up at me through the space between her trembling wrists. I watched her shoulders rise and fall with each strained breath.

We stood there, silent, frozen, looking at each other. Then I caught a glimpse of my reflection in the mirror. A blank, blood-shot gaze stared out of sunken grey sockets. A two-day stubble darkened my chin.

It frightened me, the weariness, the strain I saw in my reflection. I guess partly in reaction to it—and partly just on an impulse—I dropped to my knees as Malaika slowly lowered her hands and sat down on the toilet's seat cover.

She had swept her make-up bottles from the shelf and sent everything crashing to the floor. I brushed a bottle of clear nail polish out of the way and watched it roll under the sink where a bottle of red polish, cracked, lay in a small, red puddle. Then I leaned forward, resting my hand on her bare foot.

We looked directly into each other's eyes for a long time. The dawn silence was strangely complete, as if we were deep in the woods instead of around the corner from Wrigley Field. No honking, no car doors slamming, no shouts—nothing.

I'm not sure where it came from but suddenly I whispered, "Our baby."

Malaika's posture stiffened, then she leaned back and closed her eyes. But tears came anyway, seeping past her long lashes. I leaned forward, but with her eyes still closed, she lifted her hands, motioning for me to let her be.

So I just watched her cry for maybe a full five minutes or so, then it occurred to me that her gesture not to be comforted had a deep resonance, as if this were the beginning of another ceremony, our second ritual of the morning. And I started to cry, too. Gently at first, then more and more forcefully until I was crying like a little child as I lowered my head and pressed my hot, tear-streaked face against the cool tops of her feet and repeated over and over again "Ours…our baby…ours." And, finally, she leaned forward and, caressing the back of my head, whispered, "Yes…yes…yes…"

9

What went wrong next is particularly embarrassing and I apologize, again, if my candor is offensive.

After our little reconciliation in the bathroom, our communication over the next few days took a nosedive. We were both edgy as hell, then one night she asked me, "Do you find pregnant women attractive?"

We were in bed together. She popped this question, then flashed me an impish grin and started to stroke my genitals.

I didn't answer right away. I let out a soft moan and arched my back, unintentionally bringing my gaze to the far corner of the ceiling—then panic struck. I saw the cracked, off-white paint that had recently begun to yellow because of my upstairs neighbor's leaky radiator, and I thought: What am I doing? Living in such a dilapidated apartment—and having a baby? And what about that crummy kitchen, with the dirty, chipped tile and cracked, warped floor? And the cockroaches? I can't have a baby crawling around on that floor with those cockroaches!

Just then Malaika leaned forward and whispered, "I want to take you in my mouth."

This is crazy, I thought. Not oral sex, not now. And, absurdly, I imagined my father standing in the room watching us, watching a little boy about to get a blowjob. And in this crazy fantasy I started to scream that I'm not a little boy now, I'm practically a father myself so he should just get the hell out of here. But then the fantasy broke off and a question, though it arose out of my own panicking mind, startled me: Is oral sex inherently adolescent?

Malaika must have sensed my distraction. "What's happening?" she asked. She always liked to know my weird mental spasms, but I didn't say anything about this one. I just shook my head and smiled. Then she pulled off her big grey T-shirt and pressed her naked breasts against my chest.

I tried but couldn't turn off my racing thoughts. Perhaps she wants me inside her mouth because she wants not just to feel the power of a man's penis—but to have that power *over* me. Yes, my prick as tight as a fist and the dark possibility that she could spit it out or bite it off like a chunk of weird, tasteless meat. Or kiss it and suck it and tease it as if it were not just sexual release but my fate, my destiny, my essence waiting to explode inside her mouth.

She kissed my stomach. I clenched my eyes shut. To fertilize the mouth of a woman, I thought. Absurd. An effort to escape responsibility. It just feels good—lust. That's all. Boyish lust. And I'm a father now. It's all wrong.

"Eli," Malaika whispered.

I didn't answer. I was thinking of the baby. My seed, my generative power, my power of origination. *We are not formed to contain God's truth but to be contained by it...* The phrase jumped into my head. An English theologian, Trench. Must have read it somewhere, I thought. *We are not formed to contain God's truth but to be contained by it...* But what of love? Can love, this lover—Malaika—contain me, receive me, forgive me?

My mind went blank as she took me in her mouth. The room, momentarily, seemed to swirl. I pressed my head down against the worn mattress and held still. The apartment was quiet. I heard the sound of Malaika sucking and kissing and breathing through her nose and, in the far distance, the faint drone of a jet high in the air. Then it seemed to get louder, harder—all of it, the breathing, the kissing, the sucking, the jet's drone roaring now, blasting, my whole body like a fist deep below the muscles of the abdomen, below the pelvis, at the base of the spine—a fist, a giant curled fist like a serpent ready to spring forward...

But I couldn't. I opened my eyes. Malaika's head bobbed up and down, her hair hung in front of her face, her fingers were wrapped around the shaft of my penis. It depressed me. She seemed so intent, so concentrated. Moaning and cooing encouragement. And me? So detached. I couldn't help it. It suddenly seemed so absurd: Why would any woman ever want a man's penis in her mouth?

I leaned back and closed my eyes, and a moment later lost my erection. Neither of us said anything. Malaika lay down beside me. Several minutes passed. She fell asleep, I think. Finally, I raised myself to one elbow and looked at her.

When she opened her eyes, I said, "On Sunday, you'll be meeting my dad for the first time, but I think we ought tell him then that we're going to get married."

Her head lurched forward, goosenecked. "What?"

"I think we should just tell him then that we're going to get married."

"Are…are you…proposing to me?"

Without missing a beat, I slipped off the bed and dropped to my knees. "Malaika, will you marry me?" The sound of my voice startled me. It seemed to be deeper than usual, gravelly, hoarse.

Malaika began to cry. Then she got out of bed and wrapped herself in my robe and paced back and forth. The floorboards creaked. I stayed on my knees, watching her. Puffy bags hung beneath her eyes and her slender neck and high cheekbones seemed to sag with fatigue, and the overwhelming feeling I had at that moment was not exactly joy and excitement but rather a sense of responsibility, a profound sense of personal responsibility—for myself, for the baby, for Malaika's tired drawn features, for all of it.

Finally, she stopped crying and pacing and looked down at me and said yes, she would marry me.

The next day we went to my father's. His fourteen-room house resembles a small European castle. Several acres of lawn, groomed weekly by a Puerto Rican family, stretch out in all four directions, and a medieval-type black iron fence separates the property from the nearest neighbor, who was once the governor of Illinois (Ogilvie). Perched atop this imposing iron fence are the obligatory security cameras. The pool and tennis court, located behind the house, closer to the lakefront, are served by extra security cameras, since daring high school kids have, on occasion, been known to prove their prowess with a quick dip.

On that warm, summer evening, about eight security officers surrounded my car as soon as we pulled into the driveway. There was a blast of static, then, "D-22, D-22——"*crackle, crackle*——"At the toolshed, go ahead…"

"Blue J-4. Negative here. This is his son. Car fits the description. He's comin' to dinner."

It was more than a bit unnerving to have my arrival announced in this manner, but I got the picture. Cops and robbers, the real thing.

My dad stepped onto the porch and waved at us with a broad smile. As we approached the bottom of the huge front stairway, his gold-rimmed spectacles caught a glint from the bright porch light. He looked good, with his full head of grey hair and his well-trimmed, salt-and-pepper mustache. Also, his lean, elegant frame radiated power, accented by the hand-tailored clothes he wore: dark cuffed pants with a matching vest; a maroon shirt open around the collar;

and a white silk kerchief tied around his neck. Although he didn't know that I was bringing Malaika, he showed no signs of being surprised.

"Hello," he said in his clear, deep voice as she walked up the porch stairs. "I'm Eli's father." He extended his hand.

Malaika—who I have to point out looked absolutely fantastic that night, wearing an off-white strapless dress that complimented not just her great figure but also the deep, rich complexion of her gorgeous skin—she took his hand and said, "It's a pleasure to meet you, Mr—"

"Please, Jacob. Call me Jacob. And it's my pleasure to meet you." Then he kissed her hand. "Miss...?"

"Malaika, if we're using first names."

"What a lovely name it is." He gave her hand another squeeze.

Then he turned to me. I avoided his eyes. A tightness gripped my neck and scalp.

"Eli, good to see you, son. Thanks for coming."

We shook hands firmly.

"Hi, Dad, hi."

"Please, let's have a drink." He turned quickly back to Malaika and ushered her toward the door. I just stood there, watching.

"Are you from Chicago?" he said.

"No. California."

"Oh really? What brought you here?"

"The theater community, mostly. I'm studying acting."

"How nice! We should have more beautiful actresses move from California to Chicago. I'm under the impression that usually the migration goes the other way around." He laughed, that deep husky laugh of his, which trailed out of earshot as they stepped inside.

There he goes, I thought. The charmer. Mr. Smooth. It sickened me. I couldn't go inside. I paced back and forth, watching them through the porch windows. Malaika on the leather couch, my father on a high-backed antique chair. Then the housekeeper, a strongly built black woman whom I'd never even seen before, set a platter of hors d'oeuvres on the coffee table.

They must have thought I'd just gone to the bathroom or something because for a few minutes they chatted. But when the housekeeper returned with the drinks, my father stood up.

That's when I sat down on the porch steps. The gusting night air was soothing. I closed my eyes and listened to the lapping of the waves in the distance, punctured now and then by the muffled crackle of walkie-talkie static.

Then the front door swung open.

"Eli?" My father stepped outside.

I stood up. "Look, why don't you tell me right now what you did wrong, so I can just stop thinking about it, OK?"

He frowned, then looked back over his shoulder. "Don't you think this is a little rude? Your friend—about whom, by the way, you could have—"

"She's not just a friend," I said quickly. "We're getting married."

His mouth parted slightly, and his eyes widened—but he didn't speak. He just swallowed hard and, maintaining control, said, "Well, congratulations. You've picked quite an interesting way to tell me."

"I guess we're keeping a lot of secrets from each other these days, aren't we?"

He nodded slowly. "I'm going to tell you everything, Eli. Everything I can. You want me to talk here on the porch while your...your fiancée sits alone in the living room? Or you want to come in and have a drink, and I'll tell both of you? Whatever you want—you're the boss."

"Right. I'm the boss."

"Look, take it easy, Eli. I'm the one in trouble, here. Not you."

As he said this, he lowered his voice and stepped forward into the porch light, and I saw that the lines of his face were creased with tension.

I suddenly felt like apologizing, or giving him a hug, but instead I just said coolly, "Let's go inside. I want Malaika to hear it too."

I sat down next to her on the leather couch and popped an hors d'oeuvre into my mouth. My father reached into his vest pocket and handed me a single sheet of paper.

"Here," he said. "Read this."

UNITED STATES DISTRICT COURT
NORTHERN DISTRICT OF ILLINOIS, EASTERN DIVISION

UNITED STATES OF AMERICA INDICTMENT
91 Cr.

-v-

JACOB SHAFFNER,
Defendant.

The Special June 2002 Grand Jury charges:

On or about April 21, 2002 in the Northern District of Chicago, JACOB SHAFFNER, the defendant, being an officer, director, employee, agent or attorney of a financial institution to wit, State National Bank of Evanston, unlawfully, wilfully, and knowingly, did corruptly solicit and demand for the benefit of himself, and did corruptly accept a thing of value from a person, to wit, two hundred dollars in United States currency, intending to be influenced and rewarded in connection with a business or transaction of such institution. (Title 18, United States Code, Section 215 (a) (2).)

Scott R. Lassar
United States Attorney

I read the document twice through, then handed it to Malaika.

"This is how it all began," my father said. "I did a favor for an old friend, and he gave me two hundred dollars." He paused and took a sip of his drink. "It involved letting someone whom I didn't know very well—but who was a friend of a friend of mine—do some business at the bank. What I did was simply approve the establishment of a corporate account. Now, this gets a little complicated, and I don't need to bore you with all the details, but, basically, it was a young African-American man whom my friend wanted to help, which he did by asking me to approve this account without going through the usual procedure of checking references and getting various papers together with their corporate seal and certificate of corporation and so on and so forth. Instead, I just approved it, for which my friend insisted on paying me." He shrugged, then put down his drink and adjusted his silver cufflinks. "It turns out, however, that this young black man whom my friend wanted to help was, in fact, setting up a phony company, and my friend knew about it the whole time."

"He told you?"

My father looked directly at me and said, "Yes. He told me. And I shouldn't have gone ahead with it. It was wrong, Eli. It's illegal for a bank to allow someone to set up a corporate account for a company that doesn't exist, but I did it because I owed this man, my friend, a favor. Now, maybe you're not experienced enough in this sort of thing to understand what it means, in this context, to owe someone a favor. But I did it as an act of loyalty—not for my personal gain."

I nodded. "Who is——"

"I can't tell you who it is," he said, shaking his head. "Not with the investigation going on…" He reached for his drink.

I glanced at Malaika, whose calm and serene expression I found deeply soothing.

My father took a long slow gulp of his scotch, then said, "But in the name of total and complete candor with you—with both of you…"

He looked at Malaika and suddenly, in a different tone, said, "My goodness! Forgive me! Congratulations to you! Eli told me you're to be married!" And he quickly stood up and started to head out of the room. "This calls for champagne, doesn't it?" he called loudly. "Ms. Oakley! Ms. Oakley…?"

"Oh, it's really not necessary," Malaika said, then whispered to me, "You told him?"

I stood up and started after him. "Please, Dad. Not now. Really, I'd rather just continue——"

"Don't be silly! My son's engagement calls for champagne," he said, now halfway down the hall. "Ms. Oakley…?"

"No it doesn't," I said. But he ignored me. "Dad," I shouted, "we don't want champagne."

He stopped and, slowly, turned around.

"We don't want it," I repeated.

Just then Ms. Oakley came around the corner.

"Sir?" she said.

"We just want to…talk to you," I said quietly.

"OK," he said, nodding. "I understand." Then he smiled and, with that elegant composure of his, turned to Ms. Oakley and said, "It's nothing. I'm sorry to have disturbed you." He gave her a small bow.

Then we sat back down.

"Well," he said, sighing deeply, "Of course all of this is just between us, as family— " He stopped himself. "And, really, my deepest congratulations…" He raised his glass toward Malaika. "Although I can't tell you the names of anyone who's involved, I can tell you this…" He paused, then added in a low tone, "this is to be kept completely confidential. Strictly within the family. The press, if they knew what I'm about to tell you, it would be very problematic."

Malaika and I glanced at each other. Then I looked directly at my father and said, "Yes, of course."

"It was city officials," he said slowly, "who came up with the idea, the illegal idea, mind you, to set up this fake company, of which the one at my bank was only the first. Eventually, there were several. Four construction companies, I believe, and three insurance companies. It was all completely fake." He paused, as if to let this sink in. "A scheme to make money by taking advantage of the new minority set-aside laws," he continued, "although, actually, it doesn't depend on those laws but was just an opportunity, since so many new companies were being formed…"

He paused again, and I was struck by his calmness. I know now that he was lying through his teeth. Not about the basic scam, which he was, indeed, describing accurately. What he lied about was his role, insisting he never made another penny after that initial $200 "gift."

But that night I just listened closely as my father explained in great detail how these fake companies knew that city auditors don't actually go out and look at every single job to see if the sidewalk or road or whatever has actually been repaired. Instead, the auditors simply make sure the amount paid matches the invoice submitted.

Malaika, I could tell, wasn't following the whole process, but she nodded politely whenever my father looked to her for acknowledgement. I, too, mostly just nodded politely, but inside I was thinking that it sounded to me like the missing Bill Greengoss—and my father—had to be deeply, deeply involved. But whenever I pressed my father on this "loyalty" issue, he clammed-up, insisting that the one thing he couldn't do is discuss the people in city government who were involved. Eventually, about halfway through another round of drinks, it occurred to me that perhaps Bill Greengoss had chosen not to be quite as "loyal," and that's why he was missing.

I sat with this horrifying notion for a few minutes before I said anything. I remember looking around the large, elegant, thick-carpeted living room. It was filled with artwork my mother had picked out—African masks, Oriental vases, an original de Kooning she'd bought at an auction in Paris. So worldly, so cultivated. It disgusted me.

"Bill Greengoss," I blurted out suddenly, interrupting my father in the middle of his efforts to explain the relationship between the city's chief and junior auditors.

"Hmm?"

"What happened to Mr. Greengoss?"

"Oh, Bill's in Mexico, vacationing."

"Vacationing?"

"Yes. Well, sort of."

"What do you mean?"

My father took off his glasses and pinched the bridge of his nose. I remember this gesture precisely because later I wondered whether my father would have been able to lie to me if he'd been looking at me as he spoke.

"Even though we never made any money on this, and it was all just a favor for an old friend—Bill was nervous," my father said.

"Nervous? About what?"

He laughed, then pulled a small handkerchief out of his vest pocket and began polishing his glasses. "Being investigated by the U.S. Attorney's office is no picnic," he said. "They subpoenaed all of our new account records for the past five years, and they—well, it's partly an attitude. They're an intimidating group of lawyers. I can't say I blame Bill. He doesn't have to be involved in any of this. It's my signature on all of the documents."

"But he knows everything, right?"

"What do you mean 'knows everything?'"

"The city officials who are involved."

My dad shook his head. "Not really. No, Bill doesn't know all that much. He's going to be all right, you'll see. A couple of months in the sun is what Bill needs."

Then my dad put his glasses back on and said, "But look, I want to tell you exactly what I'm planning to tell the jury, if it comes to that. I'm going to tell them that when this young black man came in and said he was starting his own business, I wanted to help him out. So, yes, I let him open up the account without the proper papers in order and, yes, I took two hundred dollars as a token of his appreciation. That was wrong, I shouldn't have done it. But he was an impressive young man, and he pulled one over on me. Now that we know his company ended up being a fake, and he ripped off the city and made a pile of money, I will cooperate as fully as I can in helping the authorities locate him."

"Where is he?" Malaika asked.

"We're not sure," my dad said. "The investigation has tracked him to a post office box in Detroit, and I understand there's a fingerprint search going on. They'll find him, eventually."

"But even if they find him," I said, "he was working for one of the city officials, right?"

"I don't know exactly for whom he worked."

"But you're not going to say anything about the city being involved?"

He shook his head. "It's not necessary. And it's not my place."

"Not your place? They were ripping off the taxpayers——"

"The only thing I did that was wrong, Eli, was take two hundred dollars for that account——"

"I think you're drawing a pretty small circle of responsibility for yourself. If you knew that city officials were involved, then your ethical obligation is——"

My father stood up. "My 'circle of responsibility' and my ethical obligation are up to me to decide." He paused and looked directly at me. "Now, I think I've told you everything I can. Shall we have dinner?"

I glanced at Malaika. Her gaze was lowered, fixed on her glass of wine. I turned back to my father.

"Why do you need all those security guards out there?"

"They have nothing to do with all of this," he said, and then he looked at me with an impressive stillness, as if his physical calm mirrored his inner confidence.

"There was a burglary attempt a few weeks ago," he said. "That's all." Then he added, in a different tone, "So, shall we eat? You haven't tasted anything quite like Ms. Oakley's swordfish with pesto sauce. Out of this world!"

"I don't think so, Pop," I said, setting my glass down on the coffee table. "I think we ought to be going." I reached for Malaika's hand.

My father stepped forward. "Please, Eli. I've been so looking forward to our having dinner."

"I'm sorry. But I just don't feel——"

"But I've told you exactly——"

"What you haven't told me is——"

"Dammit, Eli!" he suddenly shouted. "There are some very powerful people involved here. You don't understand——you don't understand at all. What I'm not telling you is for your own good."

He was breathing heavily, his composure having finally cracked. And then mine did, too. I started to cry. "I want to believe you. I do, Dad. I want to believe you...but I just—— "

I rushed off toward the bathroom. Meanwhile, Malaika correctly intuited what I most needed at that moment and went and got the car. By the time I pulled myself together, my father had "retired," as Ms. Oakley put it. She met me in the hallway and politely explained that my father had gone upstairs.

"He asked me to tell you," Ms. Oakley began, "that he wishes all the best for you and your fiancée and that he hopes to see you again soon under less stressful circumstances. He also said…" she paused, and I remember that as she turned her head and lowered her gaze, the strong, dark, classically African features of her face struck me as extraordinarily beautiful. Then, in her soft, drawling, deferential tone, she continued, "He said to please tell you that you should not hesitate to call if, as you're making plans for the wedding, you need some help. Financial, he said, or otherwise. He was quite strong about it. If you need help with anything, with anything at all, just call him."

"Thank you," I said. "Tell him I appreciate it. Thank you very much."

But as I shook Ms. Oakley's warm, strong hand I knew that the last thing I wanted was to ask my father for help. With anything.

10

Later that night, I was brooding by myself in the kitchen when Malaika came in and announced that she wanted to read something to me from her diary.

"I hope this won't scare you," she said, pulling out a maroon leather folder decorated with a Save-the-Whales sticker. She cleared her throat.

"*Met the strangest man today,*" she began, then looked up at me. "This is my diary entry from the day we met."

I nodded.

"*He was obviously infatuated with me,*" she read. "*I could feel him staring at me from the moment I came out of the dressing room. Or at my body, I should say.*" She flipped through the notebook. I looked at her out of the corner of my eye. She was still wearing that strapless dress.

"Here, this part," she said, "this is the part I want to read." And she continued:

"*Fear. That's what it was. At first I was simply frightened of this guy. The way he flirted with me with the Shakespeare stuff. So sophisticated, I thought. And it's embarrassing to admit it, but I thought right away—just something about him—that he was probably a Jew. Which means Mom will hate him...But why am I talking about introducing him to Mom? We just met. He could turn out to be a monster. But so what if he is—I'd still like to be the wife of a rich Jewish man. Would even the score somehow.*"

She stopped reading, and I could feel her gazing at me even though I stared straight ahead, my eyes fixed on a cockroach crawling out of the sink.

"I've been wanting to tell you this for a long time," she said, quietly. Then she added, "Try to understand me. Please."

I sat there for a minute, then leapt up and shot my palm forward, squashing the cockroach with my bare hand.

What I needed to understand was Malaika's problems with her father. She explained it all to me that night. How her dad had worked as a bartender at a predominantly Jewish country club in Santa Barbara, where he felt "snubbed." He considered himself a skilled expert in a very difficult field, which happened to be tending bar. But the "rich arrogant Jewish bastards" didn't respect him. So he screwed as many of the country club wives as he could get his hands on, and drank as much whiskey as he could hold.

Malaika's mother put up with it, put up with a lot more than she should have, by the sound of it. Malaika described it as "one soap opera episode after another" while her mother and father drifted in and out of treatment programs and therapies of one variety or another until, all at once, on the morning of Malaika's fifteenth birthday, it ended. Her father woke up, got into his car and drove to Mexico. And never came back.

Eventually, he wrote. Said he had a job "in sales" and would send money soon. It was over a year before an international money order for $750 arrived. Malaika's mother tore it up.

"He's dead," her mother said, slowly tossing the tiny pieces of the check into the garbage. "His body may be alive, but his soul is dead. God took his soul away to teach us a lesson. A lesson that we may not—in this world—ever understand."

Her mother had found religion, Malaika explained. And it worked. Sprinkling that torn-up check over the garbage was her way of burying the dead.

But the burial was less complete for Malaika.

"I was a textbook case of—what's that word?" she paused, biting her lip. Then she suddenly snapped her fingers and said, "Promiscuous! I was a textbook case of 'teenage promiscuity,' but I never caught anything. STDs, I mean. I would have told you if I had anything—you know, when we talked about that stuff."

I didn't say anything. I just nodded as a weird chill clasped my ankles, rising up from the sticky tile floor of that crummy kitchen.

She kept talking. She went on into the wee hours explaining how much was at stake for her in this move to Chicago. She said she wanted to finally stop trading on her looks and develop herself as a serious performer; to commit to her yoga practice and deepen her spiritual life; to quit looking for self-approval from men and start finding it in herself; and, finally, she said that she wanted, once and for all, to let go of her anger toward her father, which she felt she used as a crutch by telling herself that whenever anything went wrong, she couldn't really be blamed because, after all, she'd had this terrible father.

That's where we connected. And the message was simple: forgive the fathers, and get on with our lives.

I appreciated what she was saying, though that first bit about marrying a rich Jew was haunting. In any case, we were both exhausted and crept into bed. It was dawn. The morning's first grey light shone through the holes in our tattered window shades. She pointed out how beautifully the thin shafts gleamed in the darkness. And then we fell asleep holding hands.

The next morning, I woke up worried about money. So I got to the club early and found Jeremie, the head pro, bent over the stringing machine. He was working on a new graphite racket with a rich royal blue frame that highlighted his pale blue eyes. He once made a weird crack about his eyes. I'll never forget it. In that obnoxious nasal voice of his, talking about how he wanted to make a move on Gloria Greenstein, he said, "Hey, you never know. She might want to fuck a nice, blue-eyed, Jew-devil like me."

This guy was, truly, a world-class creep. During my job interview, he said to me, "Eli, there are two kinds of people who belong to this club. Rich, obnoxious Jews, and very rich, obnoxious Jews." His contempt disgusted me, though at the time I hardly understood my own reaction to it.

Anyway, that morning I could see from where I was standing in the doorway that the racket he was trying to string wasn't braced properly. Jeremie, on top of all his other loathsome qualities, was simply incompetent.

"What are you doing here?" he said, without looking up. "D'you come in early just to say hello to Gloria?" He winked, then gave his crotch a couple of short, quick grabs. I'd been giving Gloria Greenstein private lessons.

I looked away, straightening the hangers on a rack of tennis shirts.

"If you get her into the office," Jeremie continued, "push the desk in front of the windows, and I think there's room on the floor." He laughed, a throaty, guttural laugh.

"Look, Jeremie," I said, taking a step toward him, "I've really got to talk to you."

"Just don't let her husband find out. I hear he's Mafia." He laughed loudly, then said suddenly, "Goddamn it! This demanding bitch insisted I string this racket today or she was going to the manager."

"Whose racket is it?"

"Mrs. Weiner. She says I've been 'mistreating' her. That I always give her the worst court. What kind of bullshit is that? The worst court? The woman has a goddamn persecution complex—so what am I supposed to do about it? Put her on court one every day?"

"Here," I said, "I'll string it for you." I stepped forward. "And then can we get a minute together? There's something important I have to ask you."

"Sure, Eli. No problem. I'll be in the office." He started to walk away, then turned around and looked me squarely in the eyes. "Thanks. You're a much better stringer than me anyway."

I didn't say anything. This moment of straightforward sincerity threw me. I remember almost resenting it—the simple, unaffected appreciation I saw in his sleepy blue eyes.

"You string OK," I said, lying.

He shrugged, then headed for his office in the back of the shop. I watched him for a minute. He looked like he was putting on weight. Small rolls of fat hung over the sides of his shorts.

I strung the racket thinking about how lonely Jeremie probably was, how he probably went home every night and sat around by himself eating too much. It depressed me. The way he was always trying to make it with one of the members while at the same talking about how much he despised her.

About twenty minutes later, I went to give Mrs. Weiner her racket. The clubhouse smelled of carpet cleaner. A soapy, lemon odor—the members had begun to complain that the smell was ruining their meals. Of course, as an assistant pro, I wasn't even allowed to eat in the dining room. But I always liked having an excuse to go in there. It had huge windows with a great view of the golf course.

I couldn't find Mrs. Weiner, but Gloria Greenstein was sitting at a table in the corner, staring blankly out the window. Though it was only 11 a.m., she had an empty cocktail glass in front of her.

I looked at her closely, trying to see if she had one or two martini-olives on the toothpick sticking out of her empty glass. I'd once had a discussion with the club's bartender, an enormous guy from Puerto Rico named Artie, about how some of the members really chewed him out if they got only one olive in their martini.

Just then, Gloria spotted me and waved. I waved back, and she smiled and pointed to her empty martini glass. So I went to the bar.

Artie had been watching. He was leaning back on his heels, his arms crossed in front of his enormous chest. A frown creased his dark-complexioned face.

"Hey, Artie."

"One word, Eli," he said, in a soft growl. "Poison."

"What are you talking about?"

He stuck his tongue in his cheek and looked away. "Elijah the prophet."

"What? I'm just bringing her a drink."

"We've got waiters."

"Yeah, but she asked me. What am I supposed to do—ignore her?"

"She's poison."

"Come on, Artie. I'm just bringing her a drink."

He didn't say anything. It has since occurred to me that maybe Artie himself had a thing for Gloria. But he just looked at me, his dark eyes gleaming as if he were about to punch me. Then with one hand he reached quickly for a glass while his other hand grabbed a bottle, and, simultaneously, a soft whistle slipped through his teeth. Then a moment later, he set down a martini complete with three olives on a red plastic toothpick, spear-shaped.

I tucked Mrs. Weiner's racket under one arm and picked up the drink. "Thanks," I said, but he'd already turned away.

As I set Gloria's drink down in front of her, I noticed the sunlight falling on her bare shoulders. She looked terrific for a woman her age, which, I later learned, was fifty-three. Grey hairs streaked her brown hair, and wrinkles and deep lines circled her eyes. But I liked the way she made no attempt to hide behind make-up.

"Can you join me?" she said.

Standing over her—I admit—I was enjoying the view I had of her full breasts. She wore one of those Italian low-cut tennis dresses Jeremie sold in the shop.

"I'm really not supposed to sit in here," I said, looking around for Mr. Ferrari, the manager.

"Come on, please." She motioned for me to sit.

"Well, maybe just for a minute."

She smiled and took a sip of her martini. "This is my last one."

I sat down, and a moment later a perky blonde-haired waitress who looked as if she might still be in high school bounced up to the table and said, with a phony-looking smile on her face, "I'm sorry. You're one of the tennis pros, aren't you?"

"Yes."

"I'm really sorry, really. But you're not supposed to sit here." Her eyes darted from side to side.

"What are you talking about?" Gloria jumped in. "I invited him to sit down."

"I'm sorry, ma'am. But Mr. Ferrari——"

"Where is Mr. Ferrari?"

The girl looked around. Her face turned red. Gloria repeated the question, this time a little too loudly. The young waitress stepped back, clutching her stack of checks to her chest. She looked as if she thought Gloria were going to hit her. Gloria raised her voice again. "I invited him to sit here," she said. And then the whole dining room became quiet. The hum of voices, the scraping of silverware, the clinking of glasses——everything stopped.

"I'm sorry, ma'am," the waitress squeaked.

"Forget it," Gloria said. "Just forget it." And then she reached across the table and squeezed my hand. "I'm sorry, Eli. Please forgive me. The rules at this club are grotesque."

I nodded and shrugged, trying to communicate that she didn't need to apologize to me. But I'm not sure the message got across. Gloria kept squeezing my hand, her glassy eyes swollen with emotion.

Finally, I said, in a whisper, "It's OK, Gloria. It's OK." And I stood up, tucking Mrs. Weiner's newly-strung racket tightly under my arm.

Outside, the hot muggy air was soothing. I hurried down the winding brick path from the clubhouse to the Pro Shop. The path was lined with small purple and yellow flowers set in teak flower boxes. Each morning these small boxes of sweet-smelling flowers were hung from the path's brass handrail. When I reached the bottom of the path, Jeremie was waiting for me.

"What happened?" He yanked the racket out of my hands.

"She wasn't there."

"That bitch. First she says she needs the racket right away, and then she goes home and forgets all about it?" He stomped back into the shop, then stood near a rack of women's dresses flipping angrily through the hangers. "So you want to talk?"

"Well, yeah——unless this is a bad time for you," I said.

"No, go ahead. Talk."

I cleared my throat. "I won't give you the whole long story, but what it comes down to is——"

"More hours, right?"

"What?"

"You and everybody else. I told you when I hired you that there wasn't a lot of money to make here."

"But Jeremie——"

"I've got three assistant pros, and you've already got more hours than both of them put together."

"But——"

"Forget it, Eli. You're wasting your breath."

He waved his hand in the air, knocking a skirt off the rack. I was silent. I looked at Jeremie's fat legs. They bulged like sausages in his tight shorts.

"Truth is, you know, you're lucky to have what you've got," he continued. "With clubs closing all over the place, the North Shore's crawling with pros screaming for more hours."

He moved to the shoe display, a waist-high slanted counter. I watched him straighten the row of shoes, meticulously adjusting and readjusting the spaces between each shoe by absurd fractions of an inch.

"Look, Jeremie," I said, "my girlfriend's pregnant."

He froze, his hand poised over a pair of women's Tretorns, the canvas ones with the pale blue stripe on the side. His hand hovered there like a pianist about to strike a chord. Then, slowly, he turned around and stepped toward me.

"Your girlfriend's pregnant?" he whispered.

I nodded, then stood there feeling stupid. The way I had blurted this out almost immediately struck me as a mistake. Jeremie seemed genuinely shook up. He stood there whispering "Jesus" and rubbing the back of his neck. His big, round face was drained of its color. Whitened, his complexion revealed a trace of acne.

"Do you know how much you need?"

"Another twenty hours would bring in eight hundred a week."

Jeremie jerked his head back, as if he'd been poked in the eye. "What!"

"We've got to move," I started to explain. "The place we're living in now is a wreck. No place for a kid. And my girlfriend, well, she doesn't have any money, not really. She had some, but——she's an actress. She'll try to do commercials now, but, well——"

I took a breath, trying to slow my thoughts. Also, Jeremie seemed to space out. I felt like he was looking at something behind me. Then he put his hand to his mouth. "I was in this situation once," he said, quietly. "But we didn't have the courage."

"Courage?"

"To—you know, I thought you just needed money for—you know."

I nodded. Jeremie wiped the corners of his mouth.

"I don't know if it's really so much courage," I said. "I mean—"

"Jesus. I'm sorry for giving you all that shit about Gloria. I was just fucking around, you know. Being a jerk."

He stepped toward me, and I had a weird vision of him trying to hug me.

"Forget it," I said. "Don't worry about it. It's not important."

I stepped away from him. Then the air conditioner kicked in, a whirring rattle. The silence lengthened. "The thing is," I said, "what's important, I mean, is this money."

"What about your old man?" Jeremie asked.

"What?"

"Your father. You told me once he's loaded. Won't he help you out?"

"My father?" I knew I was getting ready to lie. I could feel it beginning to form in the pit of my stomach, a cold, achy tightness. "He won't give me any money."

"Not even a short-term loan? I thought you said he—"

"Look, Jeremie, I'd rather not talk about my father. What I want to know is if I can get some more hours."

Maybe the way I cut him off made him angry. His shoulders hunched up and his head jutted forward, like a bull about to charge. "Eli," he began, "it's brave as hell that you're going to be a father and all that, but—"

"How about if I drum up some business on my own. Group lessons, Sunday night drill classes. I'll give you a cut of everything."

"I can't do that."

"Why not?"

"You know it's three assistant pros with fifteen hours each—and that's the club's policy, not mine."

"Let me talk to Ferrari."

"No."

"Why—"

"Because the first thing he's going to find out is that you're already teaching twenty hours—which I'm only letting you do because Gloria Greenstein thinks she can't live without you."

"Gloria doesn't have anything to do with this."

"Five fucking lessons a week—"

"Gloria's just one person. I can tell Ferrari that a lot of members have been requesting lessons with me. That will get you off the hook."

"Right, great." Jeremie stepped away, then pulled a men's warm-up suit from a rack and checked the price tag, then put it back and pulled out another. "That's a great idea, Eli. That makes me look great. Like the whole club's lining up to take lessons with you. While me, the head pro, is Mr. Unpopular."

He picked up the racket I'd strung for him and bounced the strings hard against the heel of his palm. Neither of us spoke. I listened to the *ping, ping, ping* of the racket hitting Jeremie's palm.

"Jeremie," I said, finally, "think about it for a minute. You know I could work another 20 hours—Ferrari doesn't even have to know. It can all be off the books. Cash. The members don't care. I'll give you ten percent of everything I earn."

"It's not the money. It's the principle of the thing."

"That you're the head pro and I'd be giving more lessons? It doesn't undermine your authority. I'm out there sweating my ass off on the court while you're in here being in charge. That's the way it would look. Like it is: that I work for you. In fact, it makes lessons with you seem even more exclusive."

He stopped bouncing the racket on his palm and looked down at the strings, squeezing and adjusting them thoughtfully. "You've got a point," he said, without looking up. "But I don't think I can do it. Not for ten percent."

"But you just said the money isn't the point."

He kept his head buried in the strings, the oldest tennis trick in the book for trying to maintain—or fake—concentration. Then he fired away. "Fifty percent is my cut, cash, everything off the books—and you've got a deal."

His fat neck stretched out until the tan line below his collar was visible as he leaned even closer now to the racket, his face inches from the strings. I figured he was afraid to look me in the eye.

"You're a son-of-a-bitch, Jeremie."

"Watch it, Eli."

"Why you don't go fuck yourself?"

He looked up. "Is that a counter offer?"

"You're serious, aren't you?"

"Fifty percent, cash, off the books, and we've got a deal."

I paused and looked into his blue eyes. Neither of us blinked. Then I said, slowly, "If I only take home fifty percent, then I can't—"

"There are plenty of pros in the area, you know, who'd line up for this deal."

"Then why don't you just get rid of me? Why don't you just fire me?"

A quick squint, almost a twitch, revealed a trace of genuine surprise in his eyes. I'd thrown him off balance, which gave me a certain momentum, I guess, to follow the flow of my anger.

"But you can't just get rid of me, can you?" I continued. "Because then you'd really have problems."

"I would?"

"That's right. You'd have big problems. Because the truth is everyone *is* lining up for lessons with me."

He shook his head and laughed. "You're a great negotiator, Eli. Insult me at just the moment you want me to do something for you."

"I don't want you to do anything for me."

"Fine, I won't."

"In fact, I'm not sure I even want to be here anymore."

"That sounds even better. And I've got news for you, the members are not going to drop to their knees and weep over your sudden departure. You arrogant little twit."

When I heard this, I stepped forward and, without knowing exactly what I was doing, grabbed Jeremie by the arm. The pink, fleshy flab I expected turned out to be a firm, solid mass of muscle. Jeremie, I realized, could kick my ass.

But it didn't come to that. Far from it. "Let go of my arm," he said, quietly. "Then get your shit out of the office and don't come back. You're fired."

11

Just like that—I was out of a job. I slammed the pro shop door, then took a deep breath and walked directly into the members' dining room. Gloria was eating lunch with Mrs. Schwartz, a large dark-haired woman who, I recall, couldn't hit a backhand to save her life.

"Gloria," I said loudly. "May I speak with you for a moment, in private?"

She looked up at me. The whole dining room seemed to pause in mid-chew. I stood there with a pounding in my chest. Gloria carefully laid down her salad fork, setting it exactly in its place.

"Excuse me," she whispered to her lunchmate. Then she smoothed the pleats of her short tennis dress and straightened her necklace, which I hadn't noticed before—a small, gold Star of David.

Without saying a word, we walked down the long, red-carpeted entrance hall to the club's front door. Outside, I followed her toward her car as the heat of the parking lot's black asphalt rose up through the bottom of my tennis shoes. A sheen of sweat formed on the back of her neck. The club's car-parker, a skinny, blond-haired kid everyone called Flip, came out of his shack running full-speed. But Gloria waved him off.

Her shiny Mercedes was parked right next to my little Toyota. Our cars being right next to each other was, of course, a mere coincidence. But it felt significant.

"So," she said, turning around to face me. "That was bold." Her sweaty, reddened cheeks gave her face a youthful glow.

"I didn't mean to embarrass you."

"*Au contraire*—I'm flattered." She fingered her gold star. "Of course, you know we will now be the subject of terrific gossip."

"Well, I'm leaving the club anyway. That's what I want to talk to you about. I was thinking that you might be able to help me."

"Me? How? You mean you're leaving the club now, at the peak of the season?"

"It's a long story, but, basically, I'm going out on my own and—well, you have a private court, right?"

She looked down and brushed her foot in a little semi-circle of gravelly asphalt. It was a pleasing, childlike gesture. "Yes," she said, quietly. "I have a court at my home." Then she smiled and carelessly ran her hand through her hair, leaving a single grey-streaked strand sticking up like a little wind-blown winter twig. "And I'd love to help you, Eli, in whatever way I can."

Call it a lapse of judgement, but I thought I had a damn good plan. After my talk with Gloria, I raced home to tell Malaika all about it.

"Start packing!" I yelled, opening the front door. "We're outta here!"

She was in the kitchen mashing garbanzo beans with the back of a cracked wooden spoon. "He gave you more hours?"

"Uh, not exactly."

"A raise?"

"Well…not really."

"What—you bought the club?"

She laughed, which gave me a moment to collect myself. I set Gloria's check next to the bowl of beans. Malaika picked it up.

"Jesus! Twenty-five hundred dollars? Who's Gloria Greenstein?"

"A club member. I'm going to be her private coach."

She looked up at me, drew a quick breath, and said, "Are you fucking her?"

This is classic, vintage Malaika. Dramatic candor. Exactly what I most loved about her because I was convinced that Heidi, with her intellectual complexity, wasn't capable of it. I thrived on Malaika's boldness. But I also resisted it.

"Hey," I said, stepping toward her, "slow down."

She backed away, putting a corner of the table between us. Then she lowered the wooden spoon to the side of her leg, clenching it like a weapon.

"Will you take it easy?"

"That depends," she said, barely moving her lips. "Are you fucking her?"

I turned away, throwing my hands up in exasperation. "No, I'm not."

"Look me in the eye and say that."

I turned and faced her. She took a step toward me, still squeezing that wooden spoon so hard I could see the veins in her forearm bulging. Our eyes met.

"I—am—not—sleeping with——"

"Fucking," she interrupted.

"This is ridiculous."

"Just say it."

"No."

"Why not?"

"Because——"

"If it's not true, then just——"

"No, because I refuse to…to…to dignify your accusation by even——"

"I'm not accusing you. I'm just asking——"

"Look, you know what this is really about? I'll tell you what this is really about. It's about you projecting your experience onto me."

"What?"

"Your experience of being, what you called, 'a sex object.' I mean, listen, I'm not going to get into this——"

"Get into what?"

"I'm not posing nude for anyone, OK?"

There was a pause. The threat of tears glazed her eyes, and I suppose at some level I must have known I'd said something cruel. But I finished my riff anyway before acknowledging the pain I was inflicting. A brutal pain, indeed. I look back on this little speech as one of the high points of my being a complete jerk.

"As terrible as I know it was for you to feel so objectified by that old man," I went on, "I'm not going to take responsibility for it——or turn it into some eternally neurotic game between us."

I grabbed the spoon from her hand, then said, "Gloria Greenstein is a very rich lady with a very bad tennis elbow. The two thousand five hundred dollars is an advance on the twenty-five two-hour lessons I'm going to give her over the next five weeks——at fifty bucks an hour, which is more money than I could ever possibly earn if I stayed at the club. She has a private court, and she has a lot of rich friends, so I expect to give more lessons there."

Malaika blinked, clearing the hurtful look in her eyes. "At her home," she said.

"On her tennis court, yes. Now I'm going to say this once, and only once. There never has been and there never will be anything sexual between Gloria Greenstein and me."

Malaika nodded.

I dropped the wooden spoon into the big bowl of partially mashed garbanzo beans and turned away. "I thought you'd be happy about this. I wanted…I don't know…to celebrate. I love you, Malaika. You know that."

She stepped forward and, slowly, took my hand. Then she looked at me with an eerie calmness in her eyes. "I know you love me," she said, in a whisper. "I love you, too." She paused and moistened her lips, and I remember thinking she was going to kiss me. But instead she squared her shoulders and set her jaw and, in that same eerie whisper, said, "And maybe you're right, Eli. Maybe I'm just 'projecting' my experience onto you and just *assuming* this woman wants to fuck you. But if anything…if anything ever——ever—— happens between you and this rich lady with the bad elbow, you won't be able to hide it from me. I'll know it, Eli. I'll be able to tell. And I won't even say anything to you about it. I won't confront you or argue or anything. I'll just leave——and you won't see or hear from me ever again."

There was a long pause. Then Malaika grabbed the back of my neck and kissed me hard. And we made love. Right on the floor of that cramped and disgusting kitchen, with the glare from the naked bulb hanging down from the cracked ceiling, and the briny pungency of our hot bodies mixing with the smell of freshly boiled beans. It was urgent and passionate and afterward I had that fleeting experience athletes live for: the in-your-bones feeling that no matter what you do, you can't miss. A drop-shot from behind the baseline, a flat second serve down the middle. It doesn't matter. You're in the zone, out of your head, and you can't miss.

I felt sure my scheme with Gloria was a winner.

12

For the rest of that summer I didn't once speak to either Heidi or my father. Occasionally, an article appeared in the paper, but the investigation was slow-moving, and I never did more than wonder about it.

I was too busy with Gloria—and her husband.

"A gangster with his head up his ass." That's what Gloria once called him. All day long he wore a maroon silk robe over his pajamas and drank scotch while sitting in a big leather chair in his sun-roofed study, the "plant room." It had a wide-screen TV like the kind you find in sports bars, except that Mr. Greenstein, every time I saw him at least, had the TV tuned to stock reports. He was worth a fortune. A king looking over his kingdom.

One day he asked, "How's her elbow coming?"

I joked with him. "Her elbow is coming along fine and her other vital signs are holding steady."

He turned to me. The grey pallor of his face was frightening. His skin resembled the color of wet clay, illuminated weirdly by the bluish glow of the huge TV. He opened his mouth with a faint sucking sound, like an old person checking their dentures. Then he slowly licked his lips.

"Vital signs?" he said. "What are you—a doctor?"

I shook my head.

"She has a doctor," he went on, "the orthopedic guy for the Bulls. He says a couple shots of cortisone and she'd be fine."

"Yes, yes. She told me."

"But she thinks she needs a private tennis pro to fix her strokes. Says the cortisone will wear off and then what?"

"Well," I said, "she may have a point. Cortisone will reduce the inflammation but——"

"You just be sure she's happy, understand?"

"Happy?"

"You heard me." His voice rattled from somewhere deep in his chest.

"Yes, sir," I answered.

He looked at me for a moment, then blinked so slowly that his hooded, grey eyes reminded me of a reptile's. Finally, he swivelled his head back to the television, dismissing me.

About a week later, it became clear that making Gloria "happy" had indeed become my job.

I remember the day precisely. It was a horrible, muggy morning, with enormous, grey clouds hanging low in a somber, breezeless sky. Just walking from the driveway to the court made me break into a sweat. Out back, I was touching my toes when Gloria showed up. I looked between my legs at her upside-down figure as she waved and opened the metal gate.

"You really shouldn't bend over like that," she yelled, as I straightened up.

"Why?" I smiled, sensing a joke in the air.

"Your ass in the air like that..."

"Yeah?" I looked at her, maintaining my smile, which quickly began to feel forced. She smiled back, but something wasn't right. Her face seemed to hang in the air in front of me, cheshire-style: middle-aged jowls caked with rouge, smacking waxy-red lips, a gleaming eye heavy with purple eye-shadow, winking, opening and closing with a glint.

Make-up? Never before. Had she worn it for me?

She looked at me for a moment longer, then seemed to grow nervous and quickly took off her racket cover and turned around, heading for the baseline.

I pulled the cart of tennis balls to the service line on my side of the net and hit her some warm-up shots. As usual, she swung awkwardly, leading with her elbow, rotating her hips too early, out of synchrony with her shoulders. She also kept her weight on her back foot and ended up snapping her wrist at the last instant. Three shots in a row went into the net.

She dropped her racket, dejected, and approached.

I waved at her. "Stay there. We're just warming up. Take a few more swings."

She continued toward me, her head lowered. She took small steps, fingering the edges of a short pink skirt, a $200 item I recognized from Jeremie's shop. I stepped forward too, and we reached the net at the same time.

"Oh, Eli." She sighed and crossed her arms in front of her. I was still thrown off by the make-up, but I looked at her closely and found the features of her face more interesting than ever before. The rouge accented the sharp angle created by her wide cheeks and pointy chin, like one of Picasso's women, with streaks of purple shadowing her eyes, a patch of sunburnt skin on the long narrow triangle of her nose.

"I can't hit a ball," she said. "Everything is off. I don't have any confidence."

"You only took a few swings, Gloria. Let's try a few more."

"I just feel like I'm getting worse and worse and worse."

"You're making some fundamental changes. It takes time."

She locked her gaze on me, leaning on the net. "But I'm not criticizing you. I like you. You know that."

Her purple-shaded eyes blinked at me, and I tried to escape her gaze by looking just beyond her into the empty court. White lines, boxes, squares, self-contained divisions, boundaries within boundaries——I felt suddenly short of breath.

"Look, Gloria——"

"I'm trying to change my grip, you know. Like you said."

"Yes, well these things take time. Why don't you get your racket and let me take a look at the way you're——"

"Dammit, Eli, I don't want complicated instructions." She looked down at her feet. "I just want my confidence back," she said. And then she started to cry, the tears making small, white streaks through her make-up. I put my hand on her shoulder.

"I don't know what I'm doing anymore," she said. "My elbow's killing me and——I don't know. I'm frustrated. I'm tired and angry and frustrated."

By this time, I knew something about Gloria's frustrations. Standing there with my hand on her shoulder, I thought back to the previous week, when she had told me about a big party she and her husband were going to the upcoming weekend.

"Yes, lots of famous people, politicians and that sort of thing," she had said. "And I'll get drunk and flirt as much as I can, and my husband won't notice." She laughed, then added, "Children, Eli. That's the key. Have children or you'll grow tired of each other in ten years. After ten years you know each other's likes and dislikes and opinions and prejudices and you've been to the world's great cities and seen the great art and eaten in the best restaurants and there's just not that much more to say to each other." She paused and took a sip of her lemonade, then pinched her brow. "Maybe if you're married to a professor or something, it's different. Someone who's always probing or whatever. But if your husband is—I mean, I don't understand it. He buys and sells stock and bonds and things like that, but we don't ever talk about it. It's all just numbers. Maybe it's my fault. Maybe I should really try to understand it better?" She looked at me as if this were a question I should answer.

"But if we had children…" she continued, in a low voice, "if we had children, then we would have something we really shared. Because the children would be *ours*. Not his, not mine—*ours*."

She took a big gulp of her lemonade. "That's sick, isn't it?" she said, rather loudly. "I wish I had a kid so I'd have something to talk about with my husband." She shook her head and gave out a snort-like laugh.

The question I wanted to ask, of course, was: Why no kids? But I assumed that if she had wanted me to know, she would have told me. So I just joined her laughter with a little forced chuckle of my own, and soon we finished our lemonade and went back to the court.

But when she started to cry that morning I knew it wasn't just tennis bothering her. "How about something to drink?"

She nodded, and I climbed over the net, and together we headed for the patio.

"I'm sorry," she said, as we sat down. She took out a Kleenex and blew her nose.

"The game is frustrating," I said. "If it weren't, I wouldn't have a job."

She managed a small smile, then poured out two glasses of lemonade. We were sitting on the patio, shaded by a huge weeping willow tree.

"To you," she said, raising her glass.

"Me?"

"And the eventual return of my confidence." She took a small sip.

I smiled. "You know, I don't have your confidence. It's not mine to give back."

"Oh, you know what I mean. Just spending time with you helps." She laughed, then said suddenly, "Do you enjoy spending time with me?"

"Of course."

"I'm not a very good student, though, am I?"

"That's not true. You're an excellent student."

"I sometimes worry that if I don't improve, you'll get frustrated and leave."

"Gloria, the important thing is that you not become too frustrated. I'm here to help you—not the other way around. You don't have to worry about me."

"But I want to please you," she said.

I laughed, nervously.

"I mean it," she went on. "I want to give you pleasure."

Without missing a beat I answered, "Now that sounds rather suggestive, doesn't it?" And I thought to myself, *There! It's out in the open.* But she refused to acknowledge it.

"Suggestive?"

"Our relationship. The boundaries. They're clear, I hope."

She nodded yes, but then said, "I'm not sure I understand what you're getting at." And I remember the incongruity between her words and her nodding.

I suppose that's partly why I blurted, "The first thing Malaika said to me is that you agreed to this whole deal because you're—well, interested in me. Sexually, I mean. I just want to be clear that you understand I'm not here for that."

There was a long pause, during which I became acutely aware of the awkwardness of what I'd just said. I felt it as a physical clumsiness, a sudden heaviness in my arms and legs, like hitting an off-balance shot. No timing.

Finally, Gloria said, "The girl you got pregnant?"

"What?"

"The girl you got pregnant—that's who said that, right?"

I couldn't believe my ears. The girl I got pregnant? She knew Malaika's name. I'd talked about her dozens of times.

"Malaika," I said. "Her name's Malaika."

"Yes, that's right. I remember. Well, she's just being silly, that's all. Excuse me, I have to go to the bathroom." She got up quickly and disappeared into the house.

I sat there angry and confused. *The girl you got pregnant.* It was an insult. It made me want to walk off the job. But even if I'd had the nerve, I couldn't have quit because by this time I owed Gloria Greenstein either 250 hours of tennis lessons or $12,500. You see, I'd continued to take advances. It was Gloria's idea. "Money is a tool," she said, "use it to build your life." So Malaika and I had put $10,000 down and moved into a little house in Wicker Park. Meanwhile, Gloria and I had increased our schedule to include strategy, stretching, and strengthening. A total of four hours a day. Unfortunately, nobody else had lined up for lessons.

I sat there out on the patio for almost an hour waiting for her to return. Finally, I went inside the house to look for her.

"Gloria?" I called out. "Mr. Greenstein?"

There was a loud thump from upstairs, and then Gloria let out a shriek I'll never forget. A rattling, throaty high-pitched scream.

I went to the foot of the stairs. "Gloria? Mr. Greenstein?"

Suddenly Mr. Greenstein appeared, panting, his big shoulders rising and falling. He extended a shaky hand to the bannister. His maroon silk robe flapped open, revealing a hairy, white leg and the bottom edge of his light blue boxer shorts. He came down the stairs in slow, heavy strides, his labored breathing punctuated by the heel of his brown leather slippers softly slapping each carpeted step.

When he reached the bottom, he said something to me which I recognized was in Yiddish. But I couldn't make it out, then he looked at me and added, "You enter it living and come out a corpse."

I just stood there, waiting for I don't know what—instructions of some sort, I guess. But he just lowered his puffy red face and shuffled past me, moving slowly down the hall and into the living room. I heard him open the liquor cabinet.

Then Gloria called out, "Eli? Eli, are you still here?" She came to the top of the stairs. "Oh, good," she said, catching her breath. "I was afraid you'd left. I'm sorry."

"Are you OK?"

"Yes, fine." She looked away. "I mean—no. I'm not OK. As you can see, I'm having a very bad morning."

"Maybe we should just skip it today."

"Yes, my arm is very sore."

"So you'll put some ice on it, and I'll come by tomorrow. Or even the next day. Give it a rest for a couple of days."

"But we could just talk, couldn't we?"

She waved for me to come up the stairs. Then, as if on cue, Mr. Greenstein stepped into the hallway. His breathing had steadied, and the grey pallor of his face had returned. He held an oversized brandy snifter in one hand.

"Gloria would like to talk with me," I said, pointing up the stairs.

He nodded without the faintest trace of any expression on his face, the same blank gaze with which he stared at the stock reports. Then he silently lifted his glass, as if offering me a toast.

She led me to a small alcove in the master bedroom. It had three large windows overlooking the tennis court. She pulled the curtains open wide, and the summer sunlight poured over two reclining leather chairs.

"Well," Gloria said, sitting down. Then her eyes suddenly widened. "I know!" She hopped out of the chair and disappeared down the hall.

I stood there looking at the Greensteins' canopied antique bed.

"This is just the thing," she called out. And she returned carrying two shot glasses and a small bottle with no label. "From an authentic potato farmer somewhere near Kiev—one of my husband's business associates."

I must have had a blank look on my face. She waved the bottle. "Vodka?"

"It's a little early for me, Gloria."

"Nonsense," she said, and she poured two glasses. "To your…future wife." She finished hers in a gulp. I took a small sip and started to cough.

"So tell me about her," she said.

"Hmm?"

"Your fiancée. Do you have a picture of her?"

"No, not with me."

"Tssss. Shame on you." She leaned forward and poured herself another drink. I took another small sip of mine, this time managing not to cough. "Then describe her to me," she said, and she knocked back shot number two. "Come on. I'm sure you can do it."

She sounded like a coach admonishing a lazy player. I recognized the tone and—well, I not only described Malaika but then went ahead and told Gloria all about how different Malaika was from my "old girlfriend." (As if Heidi could ever be reduced to such a simple label!)

Why did I do it? Why did I open up to a depressed, alcoholic housewife? A basic need to try to change things by making sense of things. Telling it all to Gloria, you see, was a way of organizing my struggles and finding some meaning in them. The stories lives tell. And she was exactly the right audience—for a simple, twisted reason: she was Jewish and rich and talking to her brought me right back to Heidi and my father and everything I was trying to get away from.

At one point I said to her, "Well, Heidi doesn't think I should really make a career out of tennis. She thinks I'm avoiding doing something more important——"

"But your being a tennis pro is exactly what makes you so irresistible," Gloria said quickly. "You're not really such a heady, bookish, nice Jewish boy… " And she threw her head back and actually slapped her knee as she laughed. Then, reaching for her vodka, she said, "Doesn't this Heidi think you look sexy in tennis clothes?"

"Sexy?"

She leaned forward and whispered, drunkenly, "Sexy."

"Well…" I shrugged.

"I'll bet your exotic, lovely, little Malaika"—and she added a little "H" sound *Malaheeka!*—"I'll bet she thinks these outfits are sexy and isn't afraid to admit it."

I laughed. "Yes. That's true."

"And so do I!" she said. "And I'm not afraid to admit it either." There was a long, uncomfortable pause, which I filled by sipping my vodka.

Then, as if she'd been contemplating it for a long time, Gloria said slowly, "What you are, Eli, is a contradiction." Her tone was of a doctor who'd finally reached a definitive diagnosis. "You're not just a good boy. You're also a bad boy. That's really what makes you so attractive. And dangerous. Heidi's probably afraid of it. Contradictions, opposites, ambiguity—they frighten people who want things to be orderly."

She spoke looking at me directly while I sat there as dumb as a rock.

"My husband, for example, he likes things to be orderly. He must be the most orderly—and predictable—man in the world. Of course, I don't really know what I have to complain about. Because I can have anything I want—anything. Absolutely anything. In terms of my marriage, for example, there are no restrictions. None. Not a single one. I can even sleep with other men."

All at once there was a hammering in my head, and the bitter, burped-up taste of vodka burned in my chest. She was still looking directly at me. I just nodded. I didn't know what else to do.

"It started years ago," she went on, "because my husband was having an affair with someone in Hong Kong, and someone else in Tokyo, and another woman in South Africa, and I think later there was one in Argentina, too. He used to do a lot of travelling for business, you see. The exotic turned him on. Whatever exotic really is, I don't know. Maybe you can tell me. Seems to be your taste, too. No accounting for taste, though, is there?" She paused, and her head trembled. Then she wet her lips and steadied herself and said, "Would you sleep with me?"

I was silent.

She looked away, back toward the window. Then she went on, talking so fast it seemed as though she didn't even breathe. It was just one hysterical, drunken exhale of words. "I don't mean will you—I mean would you. I mean, am I attractive enough? I once was, I know I once was, when I was younger I was a real head-turner, believe me, I know it, a real head-turner, I could feel it, walking into a restaurant or whatever, the eyes on me. I loved that feeling.

Pure egotism, maybe, but who cares, I loved it. But now, I mean, the question is do I still look good enough? Do you find me attractive? That's what I want to know. Am I attractive?"

She hiccuped, then turned away, as if she were straining to look out the window at something in the yard. And then she covered her face with her hands and broke into tears.

After a moment, I stood up and reached for the bottle. "Gloria," I said. "Let me take this away, OK?"

"No," she snapped, and turned around. Her eyes were puffy. The purple eye shadow had smeared. "Please, Eli, don't be that way."

"I'm just trying to help you."

"I don't want that kind of help."

"But maybe——"

"I'm a big girl and can decide whether or not it's OK for me to get drunk." She paused and reached for the bottle, which I was still holding. "Today it is OK. Today I decided it is OK for me to get drunk. So give me the bottle."

"You know what we talk about on the tennis court: balance? Balance is all?" I tried to say this with a breezy tone in my voice. But she just nodded impatiently and stretched her hand out toward the bottle. I gave it to her.

"Thank you," she said. "And thank you for talking with me. I'll see you tomorrow."

"Right, tomorrow," I said, and as I turned around I heard the sound of the cap being unscrewed. Then, just as I reached the door of the bedroom, there was the pop of lips smacking and a loud sigh, and she called out, "Wait, Eli. I have a joke for you to tell your jealous girlfriend."

I stopped, but I didn't turn around. I just waited, silently. While up to this point I'd felt there was some genuine, if perhaps perverse, intimacy between us, I now began to feel like I was merely a toy she was playing with.

"It's the only joke I know," she mumbled, "the only one I can ever remember anyway——I always screw up jokes." I heard her take another swallow of her vodka. I kept my back to her. "It's the true story of what happened when Moses first received the Ten Commandments," she went on. "He came down from the mountain and gathered everyone together and said, 'I've got some good news and some bad news.'"

She paused again, then shouted at me, "Turn around, will you?"

I did as she asked.

She laughed, spraying saliva from her sputtering lips. " 'The good news,' Moses says, 'is that I negotiated God down from twelve commandments to ten. The bad news is that Thou Shalt Not Commit Adultery is still in.'"

I didn't even try to smile. The silence between us lasted only a few seconds, then she said, "Are you going to be one of those husbands who really and truly doesn't ever sleep with another woman as long as he lives?"

"I hope so."

"You hope so, but you're not sure?"

"Gloria, I'm going to leave now."

"If I asked you to sleep with me and then told you that if you refused, I was going to make you return all that money I gave you, what would you do?"

"What?"

"If I asked you to sleep with me and then told you that if you refused——"

I took a step forward, trying to interrupt her. But our dialogue just overlapped. "Gloria, you've had too much to drink——"

"——and if you didn't give me the money I'd tell my husband to get some of his big, mean friends——"

I pointed my finger at her and shouted, "Gloria! Stop it!"

She smiled, a crooked impish grin. "You're angry. I've made you angry."

"Look, Gloria, I think I should leave."

"I've never seen you lose your temper before."

"I'm sorry. I didn't mean to shout at you."

She nodded, accepting my apology. Then her smile slowly faded and she took another swallow of vodka. "Next month," she said, in the flat tone now of one making an announcement. "Next month, my husband is going away. Going away to fuck his foreigners." She paused and looked at me. I met her gaze as evenly as I could.

"I hate to stay in this big house all alone while he's over there." She leaned forward, steadying herself now by grabbing the arms of her chair, and then she stood up. The sunlight pouring through the alcove's windows struck her face, and she squinted, then waved her hand at the window and lamely reached for the curtains.

"Will you stay with me next month, Eli? You can bring your pregnant girlfriend, too, if you want and the three of us can stay together, there's plenty of room, obviously, or you can, if you want, if you really want to, like you said, since you said you do find me attractive, if you really want to you could just come by yourself and I won't tell anyone because I can keep a secret, I can, I can keep a secret so good, because I am a secret, I am a secret, and nobody knows, and I won't ever tell anyone I promise…"

She turned from the windows and took an unsteady step toward me, then lost her balance and started to fall. But I moved forward and—just the way I'm sure she wanted—I caught her in my arms.

13

She said she felt sick, so I took her to the toilet and held her forehead while she puked. Then I helped her to bed, propped her head up on a pillow, and waited for her to pass out.

When I left, I told myself that she didn't mean that crazy business about forcing me either to sleep with her or to come up with the $12,500 she'd given me. She was just drunk, I thought. The best thing is to ignore it.

That night I didn't know how to explain any of this to Malaika, so I didn't say anything. She was enjoying her picture of me as a hardworking family man. Everything, she thought, was working out. I kept up the pretense, telling myself that in a way it is working out—and I'll get a different job as soon as I square away the debt with Gloria.

But the next day Gloria didn't let up. At our first break, she asked, "Did you give any more thought to next month?"

I played dumb. "Next month?"

"While my husband is out of town. Have you given any more thought to staying with me while my husband is out of town?"

"Oh, that. I've thought you probably didn't mean it."

"Why would you think that?"

I looked her squarely in the eye, but I didn't know what to say.

"Eli, do you want to keep working for me?"

"Yes, I want to keep giving you tennis lessons."

She shook her head. "What about being my friend?"

"Your friend?"

"I really do like you, Eli—as a friend. I feel very close to you. You've helped me by being so honest. If it makes you uncomfortable to stay in the house with me, I can understand that. Just keep being honest with me, OK?"

"Well, it does make me uncomfortable. That's the truth."

"Of course. I understand. Forget I said anything about that. It was silly of me." Then she leaned forward and kissed me on the cheek. I jerked back. "Isn't that allowed?" she said, then laughed. "OK, here I'll wipe it off."

I stepped away from her.

"Take it easy. It was just a little kiss. I promise I won't tell anyone. Besides, why should a friendly little kiss set you off?" She shifted her weight from one hip to the other, brushing her hair away from her face in a gesture that made her seem like she was about sixteen years old. "I mean, the least you could do is help me get over it." She looked up at me. "The rejection. You are rejecting me, aren't you?"

"I guess so, in a way."

"Oh, Eli. You are definitely rejecting me, but it will all be fine as long as you just keep being honest with me, OK?"

"OK," I said.

And in this manner—with my strange mandate to be nothing but honest—the next couple weeks unfolded with Gloria and me spending more and more time upstairs in her room talking and less and less time on the tennis court trying to fix her strokes.

I told myself we were working on the "spiritual potential" of tennis, which was not altogether untrue. I was assigning books to read. *Zen Mind, Beginners Mind, Man and His Symbols,* and, of course, Timothy Gallwey's *The Inner Game of Tennis.*

One morning our topic was the psychology of competition. Over coffee and muffins, I explained, "The challenge is to find what Gallwey calls 'a game worth playing.' But to do that we have to re-evaluate some basic assumptions about competition and performance, particularly the whole notion that a person is good and worthy of respect only if he or she does things successfully."

She nodded, looking at me intently.

"There are some large issues here," I went on, "because if respect is linked to performing well, then every activity becomes a criterion for judging one's self-worth. For example, take tennis. If I'm caught up in this whole ego-thing, then being a crummy tennis player means I'm somehow less worthy of respect—my own, or the respect of others—than if I were a good tennis player. You see what I mean?"

Again she nodded. I definitely got a charge from the way she seemed to hang on my every word.

"Now, when it's 'just a game,'" I continued, "we can see the absurdity of linking our self-worth to how well we perform. But it's really the same basic dynamic that leads all of us into thinking—sometimes really believing—that intelligent, beautiful, competent people are really *better* people."

She laughed. "Aren't we?"

"Yes, of course. Long live elitism!"

"Or why not try a return to feudalism," she said, giggling. "It might be fun."

"Except, of course, for the peasants," I said. "Which is what we'd be."

"Hmm?"

"Peasants. The Jews, I mean. We were peasants in Russia, at least my grandparents were."

"Oh, yes," she said. "Mine were too, in Poland."

There was a pause. For some reason, the mention of this common ancestry struck an awkward note.

"Anyway," I said, "to find a game worth playing begins by acknowledging that the value of a human being cannot be determined by performance—or by any other arbitrary measurement."

"Which is like what you were saying before about your old girlfriend, the Jewish one, and your dad and everything—how they all want you to be this big success and think you're wasting your time on the tennis court."

"Yes, exactly. Success, to them, means winning the 'outer game,' while to me the 'inner game' is the only one worth playing."

She nodded. "The inner game is superior to the outer one?"

I shrugged. "I wouldn't say 'superior.'"

"But you just said 'it's the only one worth playing.'"

"Yes, well—"

"But you can't have it both ways, can you?"

I took a few deep breaths. This sort of subtle argumentation made me uneasy. In those days, I liked to think I had an answer for all of these little objections.

"Well," I said, "let's use tennis as an example. All I used to care about was winning. That was it. Winning. And it drove me crazy until, slowly, I started to realize that what I wanted—even more than winning—was to overcome the nervousness that prevented me from playing my best. That is, I wanted to overcome the inner obstacles, which is what Gallwey calls playing the inner game, or finding a game worth playing."

Gloria's expression darkened. "I know exactly what you mean," she said, solemnly. "Exactly—that's all I really want, too." She paused, then quietly added. "I just want to overcome the inner obstacles."

I didn't understand why she had suddenly become so pensive, but I had an intuition that it was better not to ask. "It all has to do with competition," I said quickly, "because if competition—measuring your self-worth by performance—is used as a means of creating a self-image, then you're stuck in the outer game. For example, I used to feel that if I lost a match to a poor player, I was somehow less of a person. This meant every game was an absurd test of my very being."

"And now…?"

"Well, I don't want to say that I'm 'above all that,' but I have a different awareness of it all. That's the point. To be aware of the ego-trap."

"Yes," she said. "The ego-trap. I think I understand. The trap involves measuring ourselves by arbitrary abilities like how smart we are or how beautiful we look or how we hit a tennis ball—instead of appreciating the true and measureless value of each individual."

She was reciting from Gallwey's book almost word for word. Had she been memorizing it? The sudden regurgitation made me uncomfortable. But I didn't know how to object.

"Exactly," I said, hesitantly. "You've got it."

She smiled innocently.

But a few days later things weren't so innocent. It started with a *Cosmopolitan* magazine sitting on the small coffee table in the alcove. On the cover, there was a blurb for an article: "Twenty-five Ways to Please Your Lover," or some such thing.

Gloria pointed to the blurb and said, "That's how it all fell apart."

I wasn't sure what she was talking about. It was cool and rainy that morning, and I was preoccupied with a full cup of hot mint tea, holding both the cup and saucer very carefully. As usual, the dishes were exquisite—handmade ceramic, a blue and white flower pattern around the edge. From Italy, she explained.

Then she pointed again to the magazine. "Don't ever get involved with this type of thing. Tips. This is what happened to my husband and me."

I nodded and took a nervous sip of my tea. "Does it make you uncomfortable to talk about this?" she asked. "I'm really curious, in a way, to get your perspective. As a younger man about to be married."

I shook my head. "My perspective on…?"

"Sex."

"Big subject."

"Really big?" She flashed me that sideways smile of hers and widened her eyes. "My mind is in the gutter, isn't it?" Then she said, "You know why I'm always hitting the ball too far behind me?"

"Excuse me?"

"On the court. You know how you're always telling me that I should meet the ball twelve to eighteen inches in front of the foot I step with?"

"The point of contact, yes."

She held her two index fingers about an inch apart. "Well, my problem is that all my life men have been telling me this is seven inches."

She laughed, then quickly grabbed the magazine and started reading. *"In the first year of marriage, couples that had not been living together report they make love three to five times a week. In the second year, however, there's a 50 percent drop."*

She looked at me. "What do you think of that?"

I shrugged.

She went on, "Do you worry about keeping your sexual relationship with your wife—future wife—exciting? I assume it is exciting now."

"Uh, well, I don't—I don't know, I love her."

"Yeah, well...let me tell you, don't underestimate..." But she swallowed her words and her voice trailed off as she turned toward the window. There was a long silence. A gust of wind whistled. She put her finger to the window and traced the raindrops zigzagging down the glass pane. I could feel the gloom of the dreary morning coming over her. The silence lengthened.

"He started to buy manuals," she said, finally, still looking out the window. "Manuals. I couldn't believe it. The 'Joys' and 'More Joys' and I don't even remember the titles. I just remember trying to follow some of these dry clinical directions..." She shook her head. "Curiosity," she said, quietly. "The real source of sexual power is curiosity."

I didn't say anything. We both sat there for a while gazing at the rain, which fell in a steady drizzle. Then I finished my tea and said, "I don't think it's going to let up. I'll see you tomorrow, OK?"

"No, don't go, please. I don't mean to get too personal. I'm sorry. It's just that the more I explore my tennis, the more I see that it carries so much psychological baggage for me."

I nodded. I admit that her making these connections pleased me. I enjoyed playing therapist.

"And the main piece of baggage," she went on, "is that my self-image, my sense of myself as an attractive woman—well, I remember playing baseball with my father, but—" She broke off and laughed. "I don't want to get into all that. Talking about my father."

"Of course," I said quietly. "I understand. But it's interesting how deep—once you start to look at it—the little challenge of hitting a tennis ball can be. I mean, you've linked the habit of bending your elbow on that forehand to your anxiety about being attractive, to your experiences with your father. I admire your honesty."

"Just playing the inner game," she said, smiling.

And I didn't think she was mocking me. I believed with all my heart (and would still like to believe) that good things might come from this sort of self-reflection. I also believed that I was truly helping Gloria to see things in herself that could be transforming.

"The thing is," she said, "if I'm really going to explore the spiritual potential of all this and look at the ego-attachments and inner conflicts that make it so difficult for me to relax on the court and let my strokes change, then I must confront my ego-attachment to being sexually attractive."

I nodded. How could I have done anything else? The inner game, ego attachments, spiritual potential—there she was using my own exalted vocabulary!

She looked away, then fiddled nervously with the collar of her tennis dress. "There's a lot that you don't know about me, Eli. A lot nobody knows—even my husband."

I remained composed. Again, I was moved by what appeared to be her candor.

"I haven't..." she began, hesitantly, "I haven't...had an orgasm in...years."

She just sat there for a long moment, looking out the window. How perfect that I'd just been pontificating about the negative aspects of competition, but my main reaction to this sexual confession was pride in Gloria having just told me something even her big, rich, powerful husband didn't know.

"I don't want to be too dramatic about this," she continued, "but it all goes back to Houston, where I led a kind of double life."

I was under the impression she'd lived in Houston only as a child. "A double life?" I asked.

"When I was nineteen, my parents lost all their money. That's when it all started. I came home from college for the summer, and my father—he was a surgeon, pretty well known in Houston because in 1950-something he was the first Jewish doctor on staff at one of the big university hospitals there.

Anyway, I'd just come home from college and he sat down and told my brothers and me that we could no longer afford lots of things we were all used to having, including our home, our cars, and my tuition for college. Bad investments, he said, and some kind of malpractice suit that I never did exactly understand."

She stood up suddenly. "You don't ever smoke, do you? I suddenly have a terrible craving for a cigarette."

I shook my head. "No, I don't smoke."

"I shouldn't either. Another vice." She sat back down, then took a deep breath. "Money had never been discussed in our home before," she went on. "Never. I mean, I'd always assumed that it would just, you know, be there. Sort of like it is here—not an issue."

She waved her hand vaguely.

"Spoiled," she said, "doesn't begin to describe the way I grew up. I am the original Jewish American Princess." She laughed. "But suddenly there I was, home for the summer, driving around the suburbs of Houston, looking for a job making hamburgers."

She hit the "b" in burgers so hard a little saliva flew from her lips.

"And a job like that," she continued, her energy rising, "it was just—I did it for about three weeks. Until one day this old high school friend of mine who was totally wild and very into the drug scene comes into the burger joint and, yelling right over the counter, says she thinks I ought to quit the job and work as a topless dancer."

Gloria paused. I just looked at her, not sure whether to say anything, not sure if I had even heard her right.

"So I did. I worked at a place called Dream Girls—can you believe that name? Give me a break. But it's still around. One of the oldest and most established 'gentleman's clubs' in Houston, famous now, I understand, because a number of *Penthouse Pets* were discovered there."

My concentration left me. This was all a little too much. In fact, had Gloria not been talking in such an unaffected, clear, animated manner, I would have thought she was lying.

"The strange thing," she said, quietly, "is how much I liked it. Sure, I was frightened at first—in fact, in the middle of my first dance I got my period, two weeks early. But once you really see what's going on in these clubs—the inner game, you could say—you see that it isn't just about men gaping at beautiful, semi-nude women. What it's about is power. Each dance is a battle for control between the dancer and the customer."

She looked at me with what I remember was an absolutely amazing steadiness in her eyes, a Malaika-like stillness.

"The way I thought about it," she continued, "is that customers in these places are paying for a fantasy, for a few moments of escape from their ordinary lives. And what's the matter with that? Movies make millions because people need to escape. It's really not that different. Watching dancers offers an array of constantly changing images. Every eight to ten minutes a new girl takes her dress off." She paused. "But from the standpoint of the dancer, it's very different. The thrill is that you shape men's desires."

She gazed at me with an intensity that seemed to be a challenge of some sort, as if she wanted me to argue with her. But I said nothing, clinging instead to my silent, noncommittal, little nods.

"Of course," she said quietly, lowering her gaze, "it screwed me up. After I started dancing, whenever I met an appealing man in my real life, say at the community college in Houston, where I was taking some classes—well, I was afraid to tell him what I did for a living. A nice Jewish girl like me?"

She smiled coyly. "The thing is that unless I was trying to seduce the guy, I didn't know how to act. At the same time, sometimes when I was at the club I'd get into a conversation with a customer and for a minute forget that I was there to sell this guy a fantasy. Not to really care about him—but just to make him think I really cared."

She broke off, and I watched her eyes well up with tears. But she didn't stop talking, and I just sat there taking it all in with my "nonjudgmental awareness." She went on to describe her rhinestone-covered G-string, and how each dancer carried a plastic identification card and swiped it through a bar code machine each time she entered and exited the club. Contract labor, she called it. The dancers actually paid the club a fee to dance there, and then got to keep only eighty percent of all their tips.

I kept wondering how she met her husband and if he knew all of this, but since I was playing the role of passive listener, I felt I had no right to ask. Besides, I was rather hung up on other sorts of details, like the way the club's management felt bruised kneecaps were the mark of a good dancer.

"It showed you were working hard," she said. "Crawling around on stage, your ass facing the audience."

I couldn't help myself—when Gloria said this, I shot a quick look at her knees.

"It was a long time ago," she said. "Mine are all healed up." She laughed, but then, within a moment or two, the laughter turned to tears.

That's when I finally spoke. I seized on the idea that all of this was, indeed, a long time ago. "It's OK, Gloria. It's over. You can let it all go now. You can let it go."

She looked up at me. "Yes," she said. "With your help, I can let it go." And then she squeezed my hand and said through her tears, "Now be a darling, will you? And bring me a cigarette from downstairs?"

14

I brought her a package of cigarettes, even lit one for her. I'm not exactly proud of it, but at this point Gloria had won my extreme sympathy and compassion. I thought, here's a lonely woman who has had a crazy, screwed-up life. She needs help—I'll help her. That was the main thing. I was convinced that I'd penetrated her unhappiness and touched the truth of her sadness and was now going to ride in on my white horse and lead her out of the darkness. A rescue mission, plain and simple.

Meanwhile, things with Malaika started to deteriorate. One night around this time, we tried to discuss our future. We still hadn't planned a wedding, but she was thinking ahead much further than that.

"I've been wondering," Malaika began, "about raising a kid in the city, you know?"

"Yeah?"

"For the first few years, I don't really see any problem, but later, when they're in school—and then teenagers? Oy!"

I laughed, enjoying the way Malaika had picked up some Yiddish expressions. But my light mood quickly vanished.

"What are you going to do when you can't teach tennis anymore?" she said.

I put down my fork and looked at her. "What do you mean?"

"Are you, like, part of a union with a pension or something?"

"A union? What are you talking about?"

"I mean like when you're fifty years old—you don't see a lot of fifty-year-old tennis pros. Physically, it's just—your back, your elbow."

"There are fifty-year-old tennis pros. Plenty of them."

She shrugged, then looked down at her plate of food. I had fixed dinner that night: brown rice, steamed broccoli, and tofu sauteed in a ginger sauce. She pushed a piece of broccoli back and forth with the tip of her fork.

"That cooked enough for you?"

"Oh, yes," she said, spearing the broccoli and popping it into her mouth. "So there's not really a union, huh?" she said, between chews.

"There's a professional association, but it's not really a union."

"They have health insurance?"

"We have health insurance."

"But we pay an awful lot for it, don't we? And what are we going to do when we retire?"

I pushed my chair away from the table. "What's really bothering you, Malaika?"

"Hmm? What do you mean? Nothing's bothering me. I'm just, you know, I'm just asking." She reached across the table to clear my plate.

"I'll get it," I said quickly, standing up.

"Thanks. I'd rather stay off my feet." She was referring to one of her pregnancy side effects: swollen ankles.

I carried the dishes to the sink.

"How about opening a pro shop?" she said. "Do pro shops make any money?"

"Pro shops?" I turned on the water and started doing the dishes. "I think I'd hate running a pro shop," I said. "Worrying about what kind of dresses to sell? Those half-socks with the little pink balls on the back? No thanks."

A couple of minutes passed, then Malaika came up behind me. I turned off the water and gave her a hug.

"What's all this worrying?" I said, softly. "You're starting to sound like my father, you know? Have a little faith. Come on. Get off your feet. I'll lie down with you. Let's be nice to each other, OK?"

I could feel the stiffness in her arms around my waist, signalling, I knew, that she wasn't drifting into the affectionate mood I was trying for. But I pushed it anyway. "Come on, let's go now. To the couch, pronto."

She stepped away. "I think I'd rather just go to sleep," she said. "I'm exhausted."

She gave me a kiss on the cheek, then went to bed. I finished the dishes and stayed up watching TV by myself, and before going to bed fought off a weird yearning to call Heidi——the one person, I thought, who might understand my fears.

The next day, Gloria turned up the heat. Again we were upstairs. "I have an idea that I think might help us both," she said. It was late morning. She was already sipping a martini.

"Yes?"

"Erotic literature."

I coughed, though I was only drinking coffee.

"Erotic literature," she repeated. "We could read to each other."

She was serious. I shook my head.

"Why not?" she asked. "If the first step toward making a change is accepting what *is*, then we have to accept, first of all, the sort of desires that we have. Right?"

Here she was again, regurgitating exactly the kind of lingo I'd been using.

"Yes," I said. "But——"

"So as long as we're afraid of our desires," she continued, "as long as we're denying them and trying—for example, the way I've been trying ever since I left Houston, trying to be good, trying to fit in, trying to meet other people's expectations, trying to talk away the passions that are, what? Unacceptable…are they unacceptable to you? Do you, Eli, think I'm somehow less worthy of respect——"

"Gloria, I'm not talking about——"

"Let me finish," she snapped. "Do you think I'm somehow less worthy of respect because I enjoyed dancing?"

I just looked at her.

"In fact, I like pornography," she said, defiantly. "I really like it. Am I supposed to be ashamed of myself for that?"

"No."

She paused. "Let me ask you a question…has Malaika put on weight?"

"What?"

"Has she gained weight during the pregnancy?"

I shrugged. "Sure."

"Is she walking with a little waddle?"

"What are you getting at?"

"Are you shamed of yourself for wishing she still had her lean legs and her nice, firm ass?"

I stood up and turned toward the window, looking out at the tennis court down below.

"I'm not trying to upset you," Gloria said, calmly. "I'm just trying——"

"I know what you're trying to do." I turned and faced her.

She smiled, then shook her head. "Oh, Eli. Give me a little more credit than that. I'm not suggesting we read to each other with the goal of becoming sexually excited. That would be playing to win the 'outer game.' Jesus Christ, really, that makes me angry. That you think I'm just sitting here not taking any of this seriously. When, in fact, I'm completely serious. What I want isn't to fuck you but to make it conscious. Everything. The guilt, the shame, the unacceptable desires. Whatever it is that needs to be accepted in order to accept the 'reality of the present,' this crummy present, instead of—how did you once put it?—'allowing our minds to yearn for some un-reality of the past or future.'"

She paused and looked into her martini glass, then finished it off in one quick gulp. "That you think I just want to get laid—for chrissake. If you're not going to take this seriously, Eli, if you're not going to take me seriously, then why don't you just leave. Go on," she said, her energy rising. "Leave. Right now. Because I don't need this. I don't need another man to mock me."

She swung her martini glass against the edge of the coffee table, shattering the top of the glass, leaving just the stem in her hand. Then she sat there, looking down at the shards and slivers of glass in her lap.

I didn't leave. It was a moment I'll never forget. Gloria's smashing that glass not only perfectly punctuated her bitter speech but, more importantly, it convinced me that she was being sincere. The way her anger slowly emerged, building on itself as she spoke—it seemed to have such an unrehearsed spontaneity.

I just took what seemed at the time like the natural next step. I agreed to read erotic literature with her.

We went downstairs. Mr. Greenstein, rarely out of the house, was at a meeting in the Loop, so Gloria and I set ourselves up in their living room, which had the biggest damn couch I've ever seen. Leather pillows the size of small tables, that couch filled one whole side of the huge, carpeted room. I sat in a cushioned rocking chair. Between Gloria and me stood a glass coffee table filled with chunks of black bread, pickled herring, caviar, fresh fruit, and two or three kinds of cheese. She'd asked the housekeeper to "fix a little something."

As soon as I sat down, I shovelled some of the oily little pieces of herring onto that thick black bread and stuffed a sandwich into my mouth, then I stabbed a few chunks of cheese and, before swallowing, crammed those in also. Pure nervous energy. What could I do? Under my arm was a copy of *Delta of Venus* by Anais Nin.

Gloria picked out a passage for me to read:

He crouched over her like a giant cat, and his penis went into her. He gave Mathilde what he would not give his wife. His weight finally made her sink down and sprawl on the rug. He raised her ass with his two hands and fell on her again and again. His penis seemed made of hot iron. It was long and narrow, and he moved it in all directions, and leaped inside of her with an agility she had never known. He quickened his gestures even more and said hoarsely, "Come now, come now, come, I tell you. Give it all to me, now. Give it to me. Give yourself now." At these words she began to fling herself against him, furiously, and the orgasm came like lightning striking them together.

"Like 'lightning striking them together'...give me a break," Gloria said. She'd been sitting directly in front of me on the couch, but now she got up to fix herself a drink. She called out from the liquor cabinet. "The other part, though, I like that. The description that 'his penis seemed made of hot iron.'"

"What about what's going on between the characters?"

"Oh, you're so intellectual——I love it. I'm fixing you a martini."

"No, please. I'm fine."

She came back with two martinis. "What about them?" she said. "They're fucking."

"And?"

"And nothing——I don't get it, professor. "

"Well, you know, in terms of ego-attachment?"

She nodded. Then she lay down on the couch——backwards. Her head hung off the edge, her feet propped up against the back cushions.

"For example," I continued, "does either of them seem to be trying to prove their self-worth by...well, you know, performing?"

She didn't say anything for a second, and I wasn't sure she'd been listening. Then all at once she lifted her legs from the back cushion and raised them straight into the air. Her dress flopped over, revealing her frilly, pink and white tennis panties. Then she swivelled around in the couch and lowered her legs in one impressively smooth spin. A trace of that crooked grin hovered near the corners of her lips.

"You sweet boy," she said in a breathy tone. "Now I understand."

"You understand what?"

"What I'm so attracted to in you is that——" She broke off and stood up excitedly. "When you make love, are you...?" She hesitated. "I'm sorry, I shouldn't ask this, should I? We're just trying to make conscious the forbiddenness of our fantasies, right? I shouldn't actually ask this."

"Probably not," I said, and then I quickly grabbed a handful of green grapes.

"Most men are brutes in bed, you know that?" she said.

"Are you asking me?"

"No. I mean, I don't know. I don't know what I'm saying." She sat back down, carefully smoothing the pleats of her tennis dress. "Maybe you can help me here," she said. "I feel incredibly guilty——typical Jewish guilt, I suppose. You know, my good fortune. All this." She glanced around the room and rolled her eyes. "Sometimes I think I really don't deserve it, and I also don't deserve the affection of a good, gentle man. In fact, I don't deserve affection——or, rather, sexual satisfaction at all." She paused, but didn't look up. "You know who I sometimes wish I were?" she continued.

"Who?"

"My grandmother."

"You admired her?"

She shook her head. "Not really. I hardly knew her. I just wish I were fleeing the pogroms in Poland." She polished off her drink and reached quickly for mine, which I hadn't touched. "Is that sick or what?" she went on. Then she laughed and took a gulp of my martini. "A rich, American Jew like me wishing I were in Poland," she said. "Wasting my good fortune——just like your Heidi."

This threw me. That she suddenly tossed Heidi into her depressing scenario. "What does Heidi have to do with it?"

She finished the drink, then sighed loudly and got up, heading for more booze. "Right. I'm sure your Heidi believes she can make a big, big difference."

"She probably can," I said. "She's very talented."

"Yes, yes. God bless the talented." She hiccuped, then stumbled just before reaching the liquor cabinet.

"What does that mean?'"

"Damn it," she said, loudly. "We're out of vermouth. Do you mind straight gin?"

"I'm not drinking, Gloria."

"Yes, well…" she said. "I mind straight gin. Would you check the cellar for——"

"Maybe two martinis this early in the——"

"Don't start that, Eli. Don't start. I don't want to hear your little rules and restrictions——"

"Not rules, I'm just suggesting that you slow down——"

"I don't want to hear it. Just stop." She picked up the empty bottle of vermouth and pointed it at me, holding it at her hip, as if it were a gun. Then she started to laugh. "Look at us," she said, "bickering like an old married couple."

She turned around and finished making the drinks, again fixing one for me.

"All I'm saying is God bless the talented because they have something to offer society, while me——" She was walking slowly, carefully holding the two drinks, both of which were filled so close to the brim that they were splashing onto the carpet. She stopped and took a sip from each, then made a bitter face. "I just know there's a bottle of vermouth in the cellar."

I ignored her. She put the drinks down. Then suddenly she threw her head back and let out a little bark of laughter, a wild, chesty laugh. "I know," she said. "I should open a dance school. Or...or maybe," she leaned forward, gesticulating with her hands like a comedian trying to quiet the audience. "Maybe I could be...a volunteer." She hit the last word with a deep mocking tone in her voice.

And that's when I asked—completely unaware that asking this question was going to throw me back in time, back to the moment so many months before when I myself had been asked exactly the same question by Heidi—I asked Gloria, just as Heidi had asked me, "But why do you say it that way? Why make fun of trying to help people?"

Gloria looked at me, then lowered her hands. "You don't get it, Eli. You don't see what I'm saying at all, do you? I am not one of those Jews on some sort of mission to——"

I stood up suddenly. The experience of déjà vu, I later learned, can be so intense it's dangerous. Shock, dizziness, even fits of convulsions have been linked to the phenomenon. I grew panicky. My first impulse was to leave.

"Eli? What is it? Where are you going?"

I was short of breath. I started to cough.

"Are you OK?"

"Yes," I said. "Yes. I'm fine."

"You're choking...here."

She started to come toward me, but I backed away.

"No, I'm fine," I gasped. "I'm fine."

120

"I'll get you some water."

"No. I think I should leave."

"Leave? What is it Eli? I didn't mean to—well, I didn't mean to say that everyone who, you know—I didn't mean to say *those Jews*. It was just a generalization."

That's when it clicked. My memory of that night with Heidi and her father. The whole crazy scene, the banter about Saul Bellow, Heidi's comments about yoga, my big ideas about the gaps in Western civilization—and how it all reached a terrible crescendo with my grand declaration: *"I'm my own person and who I am doesn't have a goddamn thing to do with you and your guilty feelings about being rich Jews!"*

Recalling the scene quelled my anxiety. I sat down on the couch. Gradually, my breathing returned to normal. Then I said, "Gloria, do you have any bourbon?"

She smiled broadly. "Now you're talking. I didn't know you liked bourbon!"

As she hurried off to the liquor cabinet, I just sat there, overwhelmed, sinking into the huge, soft leather couch.

"I'm really sorry, Eli, if I offended you. I don't really mean that all the Jews who are trying to help people are—what's the word?—egotists? That's ridiculous, of course. What I meant is that for me to do something like, say, to volunteer—well, it would just be absurd."

She handed me my glass of bourbon, and I took a long, deep gulp.

"That's OK," I said. "Don't worry about it. I know exactly what you mean."

"You do?"

"Yes. That's what—I once had a horrible fight with Heidi and her father about this kind of thing."

She looked at me, that crooked smile beginning to play across her face. Then she kneeled on the floor at the side of the couch and leaned toward me, the top of her dress exposing the dark cleft of her breasts.

"They don't understand you, do they?" she said. "They don't understand that you're just trying to live your life in accordance with your own true nature."

I nodded. "I guess so, yes. Although sometimes I'm not sure what that really means: 'true nature.'"

"Bullshit," she said. "You know exactly what it means." And she put her hand on the middle of my thigh. "This is why we need each other, Eli. To throw off the guilt. To bear witness to each other's intentions, the deeper intentions, which are…" But then she suddenly took her hand off of my thigh and stood up. "Yet it's all quite unsentimental and unromantic—don't you agree?"

I shook my head, bewildered. "What is?"

"Us. You and me. The deeper intention of this relationship, which is not to mourn some imagined paradise of the past—youth, right? When I was a carefree dancer, and you were…what? Happy with Heidi? Not burdened by Malaika's pregnancy?"

"I'm not burdened by it. That's not what I said—"

"The point is we're not here together trying to regain something we've lost. We're here to cultivate something we've found. And you know what I mean, Eli." She paused, staring at me with that unblinking intensity. "You understand me, Eli, just like I understand you. Isn't that so?"

"In a way, yes."

"But what does it mean?" she continued. "That we have this…this connection doesn't mean that we lose ourselves in each other the way someone gazing at the stars loses themselves in the bliss of it all…No, it doesn't mean that. Because it's all quite unsentimental and unromantic with us, isn't it? The point is not the feelings between us, but what those feelings enable us to do…which is to participate more fully in life," she said, firmly. "Even though, what is participation to us looks like running away from it all to them."

She made this pronouncement with a great sense of finality, as if the entire morning had been carefully orchestrated to lead us to this precise point. She even turned and walked slowly toward the edge of the room, which I took as a subtle cue that she felt finished for the day and wanted me to leave.

I stood up. The bourbon had gone to my head immediately. "Yes, well, that's an interesting way to put it," I said. And then I left, feeling vaguely confused but uplifted nevertheless by Gloria's grand conclusion: the exalted struggle of *us* against *them*.

15

That moment of déjà vu had shaken me up. Also, I was a bit too rattled by the strangely deepening connection between Gloria and me to drive straight home, so instead I headed down to Mr. K's office in the Loop. I had a stupid notion that if I spotted him—and maybe even Heidi or my dad—then I'd be instantly reconnected to my former life.

So I made my way through the choke of rush hour traffic, then found a parking place right in front of Mr. K's building on Wabash Avenue. I sat there in my car enjoying the traffic's dark, noxious odors and the roar of the El trains overhead and the throngs of pedestrians hurrying across the big chunks of cracked sidewalk. The messy, unpleasant randomness of it all felt just right. But after half an hour, still buzzed on bourbon, I started to cry. I wanted to apologize for everything. I wanted to reach out to Mr. K and my dad and Heidi and say I was sorry—but of course there was no sign of them. And I lacked the clarity—and courage—to even get out of the car.

For the next few weeks, usually in the afternoon, after we'd spent the morning on the court, I read Anais Nin stories to Gloria. Malaika knew about none of this.

Then one morning I went to work as usual and Gloria overslept. I was out back watching the Korean gardener pull weeds from in between the patio bricks.

Then Gloria leaned out the window with her arms crossed over her bare breasts. "Eli, I'm sorry," she yelled, "I just woke up."

"It's OK," I said. "Take your time." And I quickly turned away.

Then for some reason she adopted a weirdly mixed-up Southern accent and called out, "Be a dahlin' will ya dahlin' and brang me a cup of coe-fee?"

I tried to enlist the help of one of her housekeepers. But I couldn't find anyone, so I fixed her the coffee myself, then headed upstairs. The bedroom door was closed.

"Gloria?" I called. "I'll leave the coffee out here on the little bookshelf and meet you downstairs whenever you're ready, OK?"

"You'll do no such thing. Bring that coffee in here right this minute or I'll scream."

I opened the door and found her sitting in the alcove. She wore a red silk robe that reached to the middle of her thighs.

"Here you are," I said, standing a few feet from her.

"Will you bring it to me, please? Or do I have to get up?"

I put the coffee down in front of her.

"None for you?" she said.

"No thanks." I remained standing.

She took a sip. "Hmmm, perfect. Thank you. Sit down, will you? You know I woke up thinking about the amazing conversations we've had—particularly yesterday."

I smiled, sitting on the edge of the chair across from her.

"And you're so right that the way one hits a tennis ball cannot be separated from other aspects of one's life," she went on. "Last night I couldn't stop thinking about your example of someone who's ambivalent about being aggressive—how they'll probably have great difficulty with the overhead and the serve."

"Yes, well, those are the two most aggressive shots."

"Although other things might come into it, too," she said. "Because the serve, for example, the serve starts the point, so it's also related to being in control, to the way one initiates things, right?"

"I guess so," I said.

She smiled. "I have been so open with you, Eli—it's like therapy, except that because you're not a doctor, with all that authority, I think I've been even more open with you than I ever could be with a therapist. And that you and I are together here in my home and on the tennis court and that it's for so many hours every week—"

She stopped suddenly. Then she looked me in the eye and leaned forward. The top of her red silk robe slid to the side, revealing one bare shoulder.

And just then a spasm of pain gripped my lower back. I took a quick breath and stiffened.

"What is it?" she said, alarmed.

"Nothing. Just my back."

"You OK?"

"Just a twinge, I think."

"Do you want to lie down?"

"No, that's OK."

"How about some ice? Would you like me to get you some?"

I didn't answer. I just got up and hobbled around the room massaging my back and buttocks, while the pain tingled down my legs.

"I'll be OK," I said. "This has happened before. My sacroiliac joint suddenly goes out of whack. Must have been sitting in a funny position."

"Is there anything I can do? A massage? I could give you a massage."

There was a long silence. I could feel her eyes following me as I paced. I didn't say anything. Then she got up and came toward me, but I turned to the window. I didn't want to see her in that little silk robe. Instead, I looked out at the tennis court.

"Well...?" she said. "Do you want a massage?"

I continued to look out the window.

She cleared her throat.

"I'm fine," I said, and again I didn't move.

Then she sighed loudly. "Eli——"

"In a moment."

"Eli——"

"Please, Gloria, just give me a moment."

I suddenly felt hot, like I was going to break out into a sweat. I leaned closer to the window, craving the coolness of the glass pane. During the long silence I noticed all kinds of faint sounds coming from the neighborhood: a lawn-mower whirring, a dog barking, a car door somewhere slamming shut.

Then laughter. Directly behind me, a low growling sort of laughter. "Eli," she said. "I know what you want."

I still didn't turn around. I just looked down at the empty tennis court. My racket was leaning up against the netpost and the full cart of tennis balls was standing at the service line, like props on the set of a play. Then behind me Gloria stepped close enough for me to smell the odor of coffee on her breath and to hear the soft sound of silk-on-silk as she took off her robe and let it drop to the floor.

Then, finally, I turned around and looked at her standing in front of me completely nude.

"Gloria, please!" I said, and hurried out of the room, down the stairs, and out of the house.

Once I got outside, I didn't know what to do with myself. I was standing around on the tennis court, warmed now by the morning sun, when Mr. Greenstein came out of the house. He wore his usual outfit: house slippers, robe, pajama bottoms. He pointed at me, then slowly curled his long bony finger, motioning for me to come to him.

I walked across the court and joined him on the patio. He stood in the shadow of the willow tree. "How's my wife, Eli?"

I strained to see the expression on his face, hidden by the tree's thick shade.

"Actually—I'm just waiting for her."

"Sit down," he said.

I hesitated.

"Go on, sit. I'm not going to hurt you."

I laughed, then said nervously: "It's not that, sir, it's just that—I mean, why would you hurt me?"

"Because you're screwing my wife."

"Oh no, sir. You don't understand."

He stepped out of the shadow, then grabbed a wooden patio chair by its arms and slowly lowered his big frame into the seat. "I don't understand?" he asked, looking up at me. Then, in a tired voice, he said, "Go tell the gardener to bring us a couple of scotches. Not too much ice in mine."

As I went to look for the gardener, I thought about making a run for it. But I knew that would only have made me look guilty. So instead I ordered the drinks and returned to the patio, where Mr. Greenstein had pulled his chair up to the redwood picnic table. He was sitting there picking his teeth with an ivory toothpick.

"He's bringing the drinks," I said, still standing. "Is there anything else, sir?"

"Sit down. I want to talk to you." He wrapped the toothpick in a silk handkerchief and put it in his robe pocket. "You know who Arnold Rothstein is?"

"The name's familiar. Is he a club member?"

"No. He's the man who fixed the 1919 World Series, the Black Sox. A New Yorker, started off as an errand boy working for Big Tim Sullivan, then worked his way up by translating Yiddish—nobody in Sullivan's organization, you see, could understand the Jews. This was the Lower East Side, around 1900."

He paused but didn't look at me, for which I was grateful. I was bewildered by this sudden history lesson.

"Rothstein, Monk Eastmen, Isaac Zuker—Zuker headed a Jewish arson ring, eventually did thirty-six years in a federal prison. And there was Sophie Lyons, Nathan Kaplan, Little Kishky—all just names to you, right?"

"Yes, I'm afraid so."

"And what's the point, you ask. What's the point? The point is that these people—they understood the close relationship between right and wrong. They weren't always good people, not always. But they had—not necessarily what you would call an education—but what I would call wisdom. They knew that right and wrong must learn to live with each other." He paused. "Do you follow me?"

Just then the gardener approached carrying a ceramic tray with our drinks. He set them down. Mr. Greenstein nodded, then looked closely at his drink and reached into his glass and pulled out one of the ice cubes, throwing it over his shoulder. Then he stuck his finger into his glass and stirred the remaining cubes. I just sat there watching him until, finally, he pulled his finger out of the glass and put it into his mouth, sucking off the whiskey with a little popping sound.

"I love my wife," he said, "I love her very much."

He paused. With that coarse, gravelly quality in his voice, he sounded surprisingly genuine. "And she's a part of my life," he continued, "which is complicated, very complicated—for both of us. Being an important man is not the same thing as being a happy man. Remember that."

He looked at me intently. I nodded.

"Still," he continued, "I understand that my wife needs things, other things. Things that... I cannot directly provide. But there are situations where she's a part of my life and I need her. So—enough said."

He fished another ice cube out of his drink.

"I've tried," he went on, "to help her in whatever way I can. Doctors, psychiatrists, whatever. For a long time now, she hasn't been well. Not happy. You know what I mean, yes? I think you know what I mean."

"Yes, I think so," I offered.

"But now she's happy. She tells me that. With you, now, she's happy. And that's a good thing. That means I'm doing something right."

He took a small sip of his drink, looking at me over the rim of his glass as he swallowed.

"But it's wrong," he said, quietly. "For you to have...sexual relations with my wife—it's wrong."

"Mr. Greenstein, you don't understand——"

"Except that she's happy," he cut me off. "That she's happy…this makes it right. This is my whole point. Do you follow me?"

"Mr. Greenstein, Gloria isn't telling you the truth."

As soon as I said this, I knew I was in trouble. Mr. Greenstein stared at me with the heavy, grey lids of his eyes half-closed. "Eli," he whispered. "Are you calling my wife a liar?"

"No. I mean, I don't mean to be disrespectful, but you've got to——"

He slammed his hand down hard on the picnic table. The drinks splashed. I watched him. He seemed to be looking sadly at the wasted whiskey seeping into the wooden table. Then he looked up at me. "Eli," he said. "I have never hurt anyone who did not first do to me, personally, something that was wrong. As long as my wife is happy, you are not doing anything wrong. Do you understand?"

I didn't say anything.

"I think you understand. So——enough said."

He lifted his glass and gestured for me to do the same. "*Lacheiem*," he said, and finished his drink in a quick, noisy gulp.

16

The next day I was determined to put a stop to this. After waiting on the court for over an hour, I went and knocked on Gloria's bedroom door.

"Come in," she said.

I opened the door just a crack, saw she wasn't dressed, and quickly slammed the door shut again. She giggled. "Oh, stop it," she called.

"Gloria," I said, through the door. "I need to talk to you about something very important. Would you please get——"

"You come in here right this minute."

I didn't answer.

"Eli...?"

"Put on some clothes, Gloria. Please. Then I'll come in."

"No."

"Gloria, I'm serious."

"You are making Mommy angry."

I leaned closer to the door. "Gloria, I'm serious. We need to talk."

But she wouldn't let up. "You do as Mommy says," she answered. "And come in here right this minute, like a good little boy."

And then, all at once, I lost it. I kicked open the door and shouted, "Goddamn it——you are not my mother, and I am not your little boy. So just shut the fuck up and put some clothes on."

She looked at me, startled. Her eyes widened as her neck straightened into an unnaturally erect posture. But then quickly she regained her composure and stood up.

"How dare you talk to me that way," she said quietly. And she stood there nude looking at me with an eerie calmness, her arms hanging limply at her sides. The pose was itself a powerful rebuke. Finally, she spoke. "Get out of here," she said, hurriedly. "And wait for me in the living room."

Downstairs, I sat on the edge of the big couch. A few moments later, she entered wearing black sweatpants and a grey T-shirt, which was just about the most ordinary outfit I'd ever seen her in.

"Well," she said, and she smiled. "I forgive you. I know you didn't mean it. And forgiveness——well, one takes such pleasure in forgiveness, don't you think? It so strengthens the bond between people, reminding us what a treasured possession a special person really is…"

I nodded. "I suppose so."

"And you are, to me, a treasured possession. My most treasured possession."

She stood there looking at me, then slipped her thumbs under the elastic waist of the sweatpants. A peculiar gesture. It reminded me of a gunfighter in an old western.

"Gloria, there's a big problem here. We are walking right into——"

"Yes, yes, yes," she said quickly, cutting me off. "You mean my calling you a possession, a thing. Something that I——my ego——owns. Yes, of course. I see exactly what you mean. But our cherished yogic notion of non-attachment doesn't mean we don't fight for what we love or believe in, does it?"

I didn't say anything. The energy in her voice and quickness of her replies made me very nervous. I was in no way in control of this conversation, and I knew it.

She walked toward me. "Fix me a drink, will you please?"

I looked at my watch.

"Please? I'm asking you nicely." She put her hand on my shoulder. "You don't want me to be unhappy, do you?"

I looked at her and nodded, then went to the liquor cabinet.

"Very dry," she called out, settling into the couch. "Very, very dry."

I brought her a martini, then sat down on the rocking chair across from her.

"Before you tell me what is so deeply and urgently troubling you, causing you to turn so sour and humorless and nearly kick the hinges off my bedroom door——there's something I must tell you." She took a sip, then looked away from me. "I realized yesterday that I'm being horribly mistreated."

"You are? By whom?"

"You, Eli. You. And please don't act so innocent, although it is, indeed, an act you do very well."

"What? What are you talking about Gloria?"

"What are you talking about Gloria?" she mimicked. "What I'm talking about is something that I wish I weren't talking about, something that I wish

didn't have to be said at all. But it's my responsibility, I believe. My responsibility as your—well, what am I? Let's just say I'm…your…your older woman."

She got up from the couch and walked slowly toward the liquor cabinet. But her glass, I noted, was still half full. "Yes," she said quietly, stopping in the middle of the room. "I'm definitely your older woman."

"Gloria, I really don't know what you're talking about, but I'm sorry if you feel that I've somehow——"

"Shut up," she said. "I'm talking now, and I'll tell you when I'm finished, OK?"

I just nodded.

"What I need to say to you, Eli, what you need to hear is this… ready?" She paused dramatically, then said, "You mistreat women. Not just me, but Heidi and Malaika, too—if I can be so bold as to claim that my advanced years offer me a degree of insight into those situations…"

Her inflated diction reminded me of the lawyerly, academic tone that I so strongly connected with Heidi.

"The way you mistreat us," she continued, "isn't simple, but it can perhaps best be summed up by saying that you pretend to be something that you're not. In other words, my dear, sweet boy, you're a fake—a gorgeous fake, a sort of planetarium ceiling. But a fake nonetheless. When the lights come up, it's over…"

She looked directly at me, her grey-streaked hair sticking out on one side as if she were a mad professor delivering an impassioned lecture, martini in hand.

"Yes," she continued. "You interpret my calling you 'a treasured possession' as an ego-trap—but, in fact, Eli, the reason you are so preoccupied with pointing out ego-traps everywhere is precisely because you yourself are such an incredible egotist. You don't see it, of course. An egotist never does. I've known others like you—talented, good-looking young men who believe they're somehow unusual, gifted, special. Artistic, or vaguely spiritually inclined, claiming to be selfless or striving for some kind of authenticity without ever seeing that 'selflessness' and 'authenticity' are their *schtick*.

"Which is what it is with you, Eli—*schtick*. A tennis guru, a therapist, a teacher of the 'inner game.' Give me a break. I know exactly what you've really wanted all this time."

I practically leapt in the air as I shouted, "What? Are you trying to say that——"

"Control yourself," she said, cutting me off. "Or I'll call someone to control you for me."

The way she said this—so matter-of-factly, without any hesitation. I sat back down.

"Just wait a minute, Gloria. I never——"

"Oh, you practically raped me," she said.

"You can't be serious."

"Symbolically, I mean. Symbolically…" She said the word slowly, somewhat grandly, as if it somehow clarified everything. "I mean the way you forced yourself into my psyche."

"Forced myself into your——"

"With your aggressive questions. You remember asking me, don't you, why I was so 'hung up' on being sexually attractive? Of course you remember—and I fell for it, the way you seemed to be so innocent about it, so pure, asking just for my own benefit, and always—always, always, always—pretending to be so concerned about our boundaries."

"I wasn't pretending."

"No?"

"No," I said quickly. "I'm still concerned about it. In fact, that's what I'm here for Gloria—to tell you that——"

"It's quite beside the point," she said, walking quickly to the liquor cabinet. "It's quite beside the point because it's not me that I'm worried about. I'll be OK. I've been through far worse, believe me. It's the other women—Malaika and Heidi. They're the ones that I'm quite sure you've hurt terribly with your pseudo-spiritual psychobabble."

An empty, light-headed feeling of fear passed over me when she said this. And it must have shown, because Gloria smiled, that evil little sideways smile of hers, then said, "Sure you don't want a drink?"

I didn't say anything. I was busy trying to recall exactly what I'd told Gloria about my relationships with Malaika and Heidi, and as I thought back on it I realized that I'd told her practically everything. I closed my eyes in horror. The panicked feeling was like being on an El train car when it fails to stop at the correct station. What to do? How to go backward when the whole complicated massive structure just speeds forward, cruelly?

Then Gloria spoke. "Sit down," she said, firmly. "Let's start with Heidi, OK? The nice Jewish girl, right? The one who sees through all of your bullshit and knows that while you claim to be this and that—serving some sort of higher values—you're really just stalling, drifting, avoiding responsibility. "

She stopped and looked at me. I was standing again. "I said, sit down," she repeated. I did as I was told. "If Heidi is your good girl," she continued, "bookish, moral...to sum her up in a word, 'civilized'—then Malaika is your..." She gazed up at the ceiling. "Your...'noble savage.'" She said the words slowly, which at the time I took to be a natural dramatic effect.

"Yes, your 'noble savage,'" she repeated. "It's too bad, isn't it, that she's not more Black than Chinese, then you'd have an even greater time projecting onto her your ridiculously cliched fantasies."

I must have involuntarily leaned forward, revealing that I objected to this racial slur. She added quickly, "Oh don't accuse me of being racist—you're the one, Eli. You're the one with the not-so-secret antisemitic tendencies. You told me yourself—how Heidi's 'too Jewish.' And nice Jewish girls don't do the sorts of things Malaika does—like talking dirty? Posing nude for money? Heidi would never do that, would she?"

Gloria stepped toward me, her energy rising. "Would she? No, she wouldn't—at least not in your innocent little imagination. Your paltry, puny imagination. But what about me? What about me, Eli? I'm not like either of them, am I? Or I'm like both of them—with one big difference. I'm not apologizing for it. I'm not ashamed of who I am. Not like they are. Malaika—she's ashamed of it, isn't she? Ashamed of where she comes from, of what she's done. Her dream—she told you herself, she wants to marry a rich Jewish man. Improve her position in the world. Which is what Heidi's already ashamed of. Being rich and privileged—with her it's a debt, a burden she'll never be free from. Just like you said, Eli, she'll spend her whole life feeling guilty. But not me, Eli, not me. I'm as privileged as Heidi and as slutty as Malaika—and I'm not sorry for any of it."

She was breathing wildly, her chest rising and falling. It occurred to me that she might be on the verge of an asthma attack. "I think I see now why you've come here to break things off with me," she continued, heading for more booze. "But I forgive you. I forgive you for all of it, for everything." She continued to mutter to herself as she fixed herself another drink. "No doubt you have, indeed, hurt Heidi and Malaika, hurt them terribly. And you will hurt them even more terribly by continuing to see me, but you cannot hurt me, you will not hurt me even though you think you want to, because I understand you Eli, and I forgive you."

She came toward me as I stood up quickly, bumping her arm. Her drink spilled over the back cushion of the rocking chair. Then we both started talking at once.

"Damn it," she said. "Get me a towel."

"Gloria, we have to stop this whole thing."

"I said get me a towel——"

"I owe you money, I know that. But I'll pay you back, I promise. I just need a little time to——"

"The money isn't the point."

"No, of course not. But I want to pay back what——"

"Just get me a towel. We're not discussing this——"

"But we have to discuss it. Because I can't keep seeing you. Malaika said from the beginning that——"

"Malaika and you aren't going to last, Eli, and you know it."

"You can't say that——"

"It's a fantasy with her—with both of you. She wants a rich Jewish husband, and you want a sexy little——"

"Gloria!" I shouted. "Stop it, just stop it."

But she ignored me. "Fine," she yelled, "Fine, fine, fine—I don't give a damn...I don't give a damn, Eli. Sleep with Malaika, sleep with Heidi, sleep with whoever you want, but you will not—you will not..." She looked away suddenly, then pulled at the collar of her sweatshirt as if she were about to choke. "You will not break things off with me, do you understand? You will not. I will not permit it."

She covered her face with her hands and looked down at the floor.

"I have to Gloria. We can't continue. It's wrong—the whole thing's wrong. I'm sorry."

"No," she said. "No, no, no no..." She started to cry, still holding her hands over her face, as I just kept repeating, "I'm sorry, Gloria. I'm sorry," and slowly backed out of the room, wondering whether I'd just put myself in real, physical danger.

17

As soon as I got in my car, I had a weird vision of Mr. Greenstein sending a thug after me—and the thug looking like my dad.

This association was spooky enough to make me feel like I desperately needed to talk to someone. And the first person who came to mind was Artie, the bartender. I figured since he'd been tending bar at the club forever he would be able to tell me whether or not I really had anything to fear.

I called him on my cell phone. He didn't seem surprised to hear from me, but nothing ever seemed to surprise Artie. I tried to explain the situation to him.

"I'd really like to talk to you," I began, "because I'm dealing with a sort of ambiguity that I'm not sure I really understand because, you see, there's a vagueness involved that I'm not quite sure I've grasped all that clearly."

He didn't say anything. Through the light crackle of phone silence I heard the sound of his breathing, a nasal-whistle rumored to be from a cocaine phase he'd passed through many years ago.

"You in trouble?" he asked, finally.

"Well, yes. That's right, I'm in trouble."

"With Gloria?"

"Yes, with Gloria."

Another pause, another whistling breath, then Artie named a greasy spoon and told me to meet him there in forty-five minutes.

I got there first. While I was waiting, I thought about how much I liked Artie. His no-nonsense, boil-it-down style struck me as distinctly military in nature. A model of self-control, saying little, moving with the quiet confidence of a predator, never acting merely to reassure himself he is as powerful as he hopes he is—Artie the bartender suddenly seemed to be a man who truly knew himself. And then Yul Brynner's character in the movie *The Magnificent*

Seven came to mind. The perfect warrior. Yes, I thought, that's Artie. And I wondered, how would I hold up in a war?

Just then Artie walked in. The top button of his shirt was open, and his loosened tie hung casually around the middle of his enormous chest. Although it was unbuttoned, his shirt collar still seemed too tight for his big neck. He looked uncomfortable, crouching slightly as if he were in back pain as he glanced up and down at the crowd hunched over sandwiches at the counter. Then he spotted me in the booth and nodded without smiling. I watched his tremendous shoulders carry him forward. He held a folded-up newspaper in one hand.

"You eating?" he said, before sitting down.

I shrugged. "Sure."

"They don't like two in a booth unless you're eating."

I nodded. "OK, I'll eat."

He sat down. "The gyros plate's good. Best thing on the menu."

I nodded. Then, much more forcefully than I thought necessary, as if he were angry at something, Artie grabbed two menus out from behind the sugar container. He snapped open one menu and handed me the closed one. A moment later, a slim-hipped waitress with dirty blonde hair appeared. She didn't say anything. She just stood there chewing her pen and looking down at the floor. Something about her got to me. She had this body of an undeveloped teenager but a worn and wrinkled face that suggested, in that moment, the profound unhappiness of a long adult life filled with many regrets.

Artie looked up at me. "Two gyros plates?"

"Great," I said.

The waitress grunted. "To drink?"

"Coke," Artie said.

"Me, too."

When the waitress left, I had a weird impulse to call after her just to try to say something nice, but then Artie leaned forward, putting both elbows on the table. "What happened?" he said.

"Hmmm?"

"With Gloria."

"Well, it's kind of complicated." I looked around, suddenly terribly thirsty. "You think I could get a glass of water?"

"You ordered a Coke."

"Don't restaurants just give you water anymore? It's not like we've got a water shortage here in Chicago. And it's also not like our conserving water helps the folks in California. That's like the old bit about finishing everything on your plate because there are kids starving in India. But these things are a question of distribution, which is a political issue not an ecological one. Hunger, for example——"

"Hey!" Artie barked. "Get a fucking grip on yourself, will you?"

I looked at him. Bushy, dark eyebrows perfectly framed his square forehead. The symmetry was soothing. Square forehead, square jaw, round eyes, small nose, thick lips——it all added up.

"Did you fuck her?" he said.

I shook my head, startled.

"No?" he asked.

"No."

"But she wants you to fuck her——and now you want out, right? But she won't let you."

"How did you——"

He silenced me with a wave of his hand. "Just walk away from it, Eli." He tapped his forehead with two fingers. "She's so out of her mind she's dangerous."

"How dangerous?"

"You don't want to know."

"That's exactly what I want to know."

"I'm telling you to walk away from her."

Artie leaned back and looked over his shoulder, and I thought maybe he was going to motion for the waitress. But then he leaned forward and said, "She hurts people."

I felt a panic hit me like a dark blow to the chest. "Hurts people? What do you mean?"

Just then the waitress came with our food: two steaming plates of thinly sliced beef on a pita covered with onions and a white sauce. The sauce smelled faintly of dill. She put the food in front of us without a word and turned away.

"And two Cokes," Artie called after her, but she didn't turn around.

I looked at my plate and pushed it a couple of inches toward the center of the table. The sight of it nauseated me, but I didn't want to offend Artie, who immediately began eating. I watched him. He took a large, deliberate bite and wiped the corners of his mouth with his paper napkin. A well-mannered eater, except that the tip of his tie was resting on the table. I thought for sure at any moment a glob of that sauce would splash onto his tie and really piss him off. But I wasn't sure he'd appreciate me saying anything.

He ate half his sandwich, then spoke. "A few years ago, a waiter was sleeping with Gloria. And he borrowed all kinds of money from her—for new clothes, plane tickets, all kinds of bullshit. Then they had some kind of argument, and the next day a couple of guys showed up at his apartment and broke his arm."

"The next day?"

Artie shrugged. "Maybe it was a couple of days, I don't know. But what I heard is that the real issue was the money. Because Mr. G doesn't give a shit about who she sleeps with. But his money—"

Artie stopped himself. He must have read the fear in my face. He paused in mid-chew and looked directly at me, his jowls full. It was the most intense gaze we'd exchanged, and I felt at that moment that Artie was the only friend I had. Slowly, he started to chew again, then he swallowed. Meanwhile, the waitress came with our Cokes, disappearing again without a word.

"You owe her money?" he asked.

I nodded. He looked at me as if expecting me to say more. Finally, he said, "How much?"

"About twelve thousand."

He shook his head and reached for his Coke. I watched him take a gulp, carefully negotiating a large ice cube into his mouth. He chewed the ice in such a way that I couldn't really tell whether he was smiling cruelly at my predicament or shivering from the cold.

"What I'd do if I were you is come up with the money and get it to Mr. Greenstein right away. If you don't owe him money, and you're not still fucking his wife—"

"I was never—"

"Just think of it as a bill. You've got to pay your bill, and once you pay it, that's it. Then Gloria Greenstein doesn't exist anymore. That's all I can tell you."

He picked up the rest of his sandwich and took a large, hurried bite out of it. One chunk of meat didn't quite make it, and he sucked it in as if it were a piece of spaghetti. Then, with his mouth still full, he said, "You gonna eat that?" And he pointed to the untouched food on my plate.

I shook my head.

"Mind?" He leaned across the table and picked up my sandwich. The white sauce oozed out between the slices of beef as he lifted the stuffed pita from my plate. "You'll be fine as long as you come up with the money," he added.

I didn't say anything. I was watching the sauce from my sandwich drip onto the tip of Artie's tie. He didn't notice. He just picked up his newspaper and propped it up against his glass of Coke. We sat there in silence. I watched him read the paper and considered asking if he too had once been involved with Gloria. It's something I still sometimes wonder about.

"Artie?" I said, finally.

He didn't look up from the paper. "Hmm?"

"What if I can't come up with the money?"

"Oh, Christ!" he said, still looking at the paper. "That's the stupidest fucking thing I've ever heard."

"But I don't have——"

"The Cubs are thinking about trading the only goddamn pitcher they've got."

He pointed to the newspaper.

"Look, Artie, I know you warned me from the beginning. I should have listened to you. But…is there any way you could loan me the money? Just to get me out of this mess, then I'll pay you back as soon as I can."

There was a pause, during which Artie seemed to be holding his breath, then slowly he pushed away the paper and looked down at his food.

"I can't help you, Eli."

"Talk to her for me. Tell her I need a little time."

He shook his head. "I can't get involved that way. Club politics are too risky."

"Then what about Mr. Greenstein? He knows you, doesn't he? We could send him a letter explaining——"

"Forget it, Eli."

"Just tell him that I'll pay him, but I need a little time."

"Look, Eli, what do you want from me? I'm not your goddamn father."

I looked away. I remember consciously trying to tune out the force of Artie's comment by concentrating on that slim-hipped waitress taking someone's order at a table directly across from me. She was laughing at something the customer had said. But in my paranoid state I thought she might have been laughing at me. I could only see her from the back, but there she was in that red and white uniform hanging straight off her shapeless frame as if it were still on a hanger and her shoulders bounced up and down and her head shook side to side and she was laughing and laughing and laughing, not giggling but truly laughing in a deep, soft, easy way, laughing,

I thought, with her sad old woman's face stuck on her little girl's body, laughing so deeply and softly and easily, without a doubt, at me.

18

Artie's crack about not being my father was no doubt right on the mark, but my dad was the one person I was determined to avoid. How could I possibly go to him now? I thought. What was I supposed to tell him?

The soul reduced to a balance sheet. That's the phrase which came into my head as I walked out of the diner, thinking about how, according to Artie, everything hinged on coming up with cold, hard cash.

This was an impossible reality to accept. Where's spirit in this? I thought, as I got into my car. Where's passion? Where's intention? Where's the deeper truth? I had no answers. I headed into the traffic looking over my shoulder at every red light expecting to find some burly thug's blue-tinted face staring me down with his five o'clock shadow and slow, sick nod signalling that soon my arm would be broken, just like that waiter's.

And so it was in this state of mind that I drove directly to Uncle Max's. Dear Uncle Max. I told myself that I wanted to talk to him because he was a man of great intellect and spirit who would penetrate my egocentric veneer of panic and appreciate the true depth of my predicament, thereby illuminating the proper course of action. True, I also wanted twelve thousand dollars from him.

Immediately we plunged into conversation. I told him the whole breathless tale while he sipped one of his bitter-smelling medicinal teas and sat in a sagging, green easy chair with a ripped cushion. Finally, I got to the part about the erotic literature and now owing Gloria the money.

His eyes widened, giving his whole oblong face a troubled expression of profound disapproval. It made me think of that most revered of the ancient Jewish elite: the rabbis. That's the group no doubt Max would have run with had he himself not been so secularized. He definitely has the look, with intense features that are still intimidating in spite of the yellowy mucous that occasionally forms in the corners of his eyes; and his long, white beard, getting thicker and thicker with age; and the limp, too. That old war wound gives him an added air of authority, the way he always neatly pins up his empty pant leg, making sure the well-ironed crease hangs straight.

"So this whole problem gets up and walks away just like that with twelve thousand dollars? Poof! Everything's fixed." He made a sputtering noise with his dry, cracked lips and shook his head.

"I guess so," I said.

"Well."

We sat in silence. I knew I was disappointing him. For such a story as I was telling, complete with my commentary on Gloria's "bourgeois" values and my fear of embracing them, as well as my various theories about my father's corruption and my need to avoid that world as completely as possible—for all of this to build to a climax of twelve thousand dollars was, in Uncle Max's eyes, a serious moral failure.

But I didn't know what to do about it. I just sat there in that stuffy little room and listened to the labored sound of Max's asthmatic breathing. With his mouth closed, he inhaled through his long nose, his chest expanding until it pulled the fabric across the chest of his plain button-down-the-front white shirt, the only kind of shirt in all my life I've ever seen Uncle Max wear. The man lives in a realm oblivious to the temporal reality of fashion.

To avoid his disapproving gaze, I looked around the tiny, cluttered room. Books, notebooks, magazines, newspapers—they were piled everywhere. But one stack in particular caught my eye: a dozen worn hardcovers, with frayed threads hanging from the bindings. I couldn't make out the titles, but a yellow notepad had been stuffed in the middle of each book, resulting in a crooked column of texts about three feet high that looked like it could be toppled with a sneeze.

I stood up to take a closer look, then Uncle Max spoke. "And does this satisfy you?"

The question confused me. The "and" and the "this" weren't clear, which is a perfect example of what it's like to try to talk to Max. Conversation with him has its own madman continuity. You can be discussing something with him on Yom Kippur and pick up right where you left off seven months later on the first night of Passover.

I looked at him. He propped up his one leg on the brown, folding, metal chair I'd just vacated. Then he seemed to stare straight ahead, at his foot. The shoe he wore, a badly scuffed wingtip in need of a good polishing, was untied.

"If I gave you the twelve thousand dollars," he said, still staring straight ahead, "this would satisfy you. Yes?"

"Satisfy me?" I said. "That seems like sort of a funny way to put it, Uncle Max. I mean, all I know is that I'm afraid there's some guy out there right now just waiting around for the right moment to break my arm."

He nodded. "Of course. That is frightening."

There was a tremor of irony in his voice, a subtle lilt in the way he lengthened the word "is."

"And your fiancée? Malaika it is, right?"

"What about her?"

"You said you've never told her about this…this…other relationship."

"What do you mean 'other relationship'? I worked for Gloria. She knows I worked for her, but of course I haven't told her—well, about reading the erotic stories."

Again he nodded, still staring at his foot, or whatever the hell he was looking at.

"You really never *shtupped* her?" he said.

I didn't say anything. Not only was I incredibly hurt that Max doubted my integrity, I also didn't appreciate his dipping into Yiddish. "You don't believe me?" I walked directly into his line of vision, taking hold of the back of the folding chair.

He stared at me without saying anything, then wiggled his foot. "Would you mind tying that? My back was so stiff this morning, it didn't bend…"

I tied his shoe.

"Of course I believe you. You're my nephew," he said. "But your fiancée, well…I'm just trying to be sure I understand what your plan is. The idea is for me to give you the money—"

"I'm not exactly asking—"

"But you owe this Gloria money?"

"Yes."

"And you believe that if you don't pay her, you will be physically harmed?"

I paused. I'd seen Max do this before, slip into cross-examination mode. Usually, the subject was politics, and the target of the questions was my father. "I told you what the bartender said, Uncle Max. About what happened to the waiter?"

"Yes. And that's the basis of your present choice, right?"

"My 'present choice'?"

"That physical harm must be avoided at all costs."

"You make it sound like that's unreasonable."

"Unreasonable? Why should I think that? I didn't say that. Did I? No, I didn't. But maybe you're right. Do you think it's unreasonable?"

Without even realizing it, I'd begun to squeeze the back of the folding metal chair so tightly that the tips of my fingers ached. I didn't say anything.

After a moment, Max continued, "Maybe it's reasonable, maybe it's not. Whatever. The idea is for me to give you the money and then you pay off your debt and then you're out of physical danger and you look for another job and you never tell Malaika about any of it. Is that right?"

I took a deep breath and exhaled loudly, dramatically. To no effect. Uncle Max just sat there with his one leg resting on the chair in front of me and those dark, mucous-filled eyes fixed on me. In the long silence, I grew dizzy. I hadn't eaten all day.

"Can I sit down?"

Max lifted his leg off the chair, but his gaze remained fixed on me.

"I don't feel so good," I said.

"Sick?"

I nodded. His expression softened, his jaw dropping just enough to slacken the muscles in his face. Then he reached for his crutches and started to get up. "How about a nice hard-boiled egg and a fresh bagel? Charlene brought me half a dozen bagels this morning, still hot. You sit. I'll fix one for you. I don't have any cream cheese. Too rich for me, you know. But a little raspberry jam I have, I think, unless I finished it. It was so delicious. Charlene brought that, too. Homemade, from a cousin of hers in Michigan…or is it Wisconsin?"

He leaned over a rickety card table and opened a refrigerator about the size of a small television. Then he pulled out the hard-boiled egg and the white paper bag filled with bagels.

"Salt?" he looked at me. "With your egg, you want salt?"

"Yes, please."

He again took the lid off a small wicker basket and pulled out the sort of perfectly ordinary salt shaker that I'd just seen in the coffee shop with Artie. A meaningless detail, perhaps, but in my sensitized state these small things felt significant. Pressure from Artie, pressure from Uncle Max, same salt shaker—it proved something.

"Here you go." Uncle Max limped over to me, balancing the plate in the crook of his arm as he negotiated his crutches.

I hated to see him waiting on me like this, but I was too dizzy to get up. In silence, I ate the hard-boiled egg and the bagel with raspberry jam. Then

Max brought me a cup of lukewarm tea that tasted like mint toothpaste. I drank it quickly.

"More?" he asked.

"No thanks."

We stared at each other.

"Sure?"

"Yes, I'm sure. Thanks. It was delicious."

"Good. Never make an important decision on an empty stomach."

I smiled. "Old Jewish proverb?"

"Sure. I just made it up—and I'm an old Jew." He shrugged, then leaned forward. "You know you're in trouble, boychick."

I nodded. "Yeah."

"But you also know what you should do, don't you?"

He paused, but not really long enough for me to respond, which was fine. I didn't have a response.

"What you should do is go home and share your troubles with the woman that you love, and together—together—you decide what to do." He stopped and fiddled with the crease of his empty pant leg.

"But how am I supposed to tell her? Even you don't believe me that nothing happened except for reading those—"

"You tell the truth as simply and clearly as possible," he said, cutting me off.

I stood up. I couldn't help thinking that all of this was easy for Max to say. As far as I knew he'd never been involved with a woman at all. Or, for that matter, a man. What does he know about intimacy, I thought, pacing the room.

"You're afraid, I'm sure," he said.

"It's just that—I don't know how to explain it to you, Uncle Max. But it's not as easy as just 'simply and clearly' telling her the truth."

"Why not?"

"For one thing it's going to hurt her."

"Ah, pain. Yes. Pain hurts. That's what pain does. It hurts."

"But it's like you're saying I should just ignore that!"

He slapped his hand against his thigh. "No! Not ignore it! That's not what I'm saying." He grabbed hold of the arms of the sagging easy chair and pulled himself up. Then he pointed his finger at me, a gesture I'd seen him employ only in his most impassioned arguments with my father. "The nature of pain," he began, "is not recognized by the spirit standing at a distance from it. You cannot *watch* pain's drama unfold and expect to truly recognize it. The man who does this may have all sorts of brilliant thoughts about pain, but he will not recognize the real nature of it. That is done only by the man who casts himself into the depths of real pain, who takes up his abode in the pain and gives himself over to it, permeates it with his spirit until the pain discloses itself to him. Then…then…recognition *may* happen." He paused and took a wheezing breath, then licked his dry lips and swallowed loudly. "And why should you do this? Why? This of course is the question you'll ask."

He lowered his head. The room's yellowish light made the liver-spots on his bald scalp appear deep brown, the color of milk chocolate. I thought about how old Max was, and how much pain——real pain——he had endured. Having a leg blown off. Compared to that, I thought, what the hell do I know about pain?

Then, suddenly, Uncle Max broke into a bad fit of coughing.

"You OK? Uncle Max? Want a glass of water?"

He shook his head, catching his breath. "Not by the stripping off of reality," he said, in a choked voice. "Not by the stripping off of reality, but by the penetration into it, a penetration of such a kind that the nature of pain is exposed in the heart."

He stopped again, still breathing unevenly, wheezing. I went to him and took hold of his shoulders, kneeling directly in front of him.

"Relax," I said. "Don't speak, just take it easy."

But he went on. In a small, squeezed voice, he said, "Such a penetration——" And he stopped again and exhaled, seeming to force the breath out with the muscles of his flushed, reddened face.

I said, "Stop, Uncle Max. Ssshh…please."

But there was no getting through to him. He leaned forward. Our faces were inches apart. Then he took another long, labored breath. "Such a penetration," he said, "we call spiritual." And he exhaled again, this time directly into my face, and I smelled the strange medicinal odor of his tea.

He closed his eyes then, and slowly sat back, lifting my hands from his shoulders, signalling, I knew, that he felt he'd made his point, which, stripped of its rhetoric, I took to be simply this: that anything less than telling Malaika the whole painful truth was pure cowardice.

19

By the time I got home, it was dusk. The streetlamps cast a pale yellow light on a group of kids playing stickball in the shadows. I drove slowly, looking out at the tightly packed houses with their small, square windows. Wicker Park, at that time, had a mostly Mexican population, and a few families were sitting on someone's front steps listening to a Spanish radio station. The tips of their cigarettes glowed faintly.

I parked near four teenagers sitting on the hood of an abandoned car, a stripped-down Pinto that had been decaying near our house since the day we moved in. As I got out, one of these kids shot me a look, his mouth hanging open.

I froze, standing there with one hand still on the car door. Then the kid, who couldn't have been more than about sixteen, jumped off the hood and came toward me, with his three buddies falling in line behind him. They formed a small triangle, with the leader, as I thought of him, pumping his arms as he walked. He wore blue jeans and a tightly fitting, sleeveless T-shirt, which accented his large, intimidating biceps.

The next thing I knew, the boys surrounded me. The leader said, "You Eli?" I nodded, and he punched me in the face, catching the side of my nose. I fell back against the car. He took out an envelope and threw it at me. Then out of nowhere a knife appeared, and he sliced the side of my right arm, just above my elbow.

"Just a warning," he said. "Next time we hurt you."

And then, quickly, they piled into a big car without a muffler, which roared away making an awful racket.

I didn't move. I held my nose. Warm blood trickled through my fingers. I remember thinking: Is that it? Is it over? And slowly I looked around. Apparently, none of my neighbors had seen a thing. I picked up the envelope. It had my name typed on the front. Inside was an ordinary sheet of paper.

Balance due $11,600. Failure to remit promptly will result in further penalties.

The first thing I thought of was that Mr. Greenstein had his math mixed-up, off by $400 dollars. I sat there re-computing the number of lessons I owed Gloria. Then, in another ridiculous distraction from my bleeding and stinging, I thought: those teenage punks—they are Mr. Greenstein's muscle? That big-shot Jewish gangster hired *them*? And I criticized myself for not fighting back. An athlete? I call myself an athlete and just stood there?

Finally, I went inside. Malaika met me in the front hallway.

"Oh my God!" she said. "What happened?"

"I was mugged," I lied.

"Mugged? Just now?"

"Yes, just now."

"You mean right out front?"

"Yes, yes."

She took hold of my cut arm and led me into the kitchen. "We'll call the police," she said. "Also, you may need stitches for this."

"No," I said, panicking as I saw how this lie—like most lies—was quickly taking on a life of its own. "No police."

"Why? Why not? They might catch him. Especially if we report it right away."

"No, no—look, the most important thing is that I'm OK, right? Just get me some ice, please."

"Of course the most important thing is that you're OK, but—"

"Please, Malaika. I don't want to call the police."

She nodded. Then she sat me down and rolled some ice cubes into a moistened dish towel.

"Head back." She put the towel on my nose, which was still bleeding, though more slowly. "Hold this here." Then she soaped up a second towel and began washing the cut on my arm, a long, thin slit like a giant paper cut. Very impressive—and frightening.

"Does it sting?" she asked.

"Yes," I said. "But I don't think it needs stitches."

"Unless it keeps bleeding. What a slice." She paused, then said, "Jesus, mugged right in front of the house. I can't believe it. You must have been scared to death. The guy had a knife, huh? Was he alone and just came up to you?"

"Ummm—not exactly."

"There was more than one person? You didn't try to fight back, did you?"

"Not really—but they just sort of surrounded me. It all happened pretty fast."

"Did they take your wallet?"

"My wallet? No."

"No? Well, that's good." She gave my arm a final wipe, then said, "Let me rinse this out." But before she stood up, she leaned over and kissed the side of my neck. "Thank God you're OK."

I didn't say anything, hoping to avoid any further elaboration of this mugging tale. But to no avail. Over the sound of the running water, she said, "Is this the first time you've ever been mugged? I mean, I think I'd be a nervous wreck. But you just...just seem so calm."

I lowered the packed ice. I knew this wouldn't work—and that if I was ever going to tell her the truth, it had to be now.

"Malaika," I said, softly. "I wasn't mugged."

"What?"

She turned around and squinted at me, confused. In her soapy hands she held the blood-spotted dish towel. It dripped now onto the floor. "What do you mean?"

"I wasn't mugged," I said again.

"You mean they didn't get any money?"

"No," I said. "That's not what I mean."

Her expression darkened, the squint relaxing into a steady, cool gaze. And then she dropped the rag into the sink behind her and wiped her hands on the front of her sweatshirt.

"What are you saying?"

"I just—well, I need to explain it all to you."

"Explain what?"

"What really happened."

"You mean..." she paused. Then she added quietly, "I see. You're lying to me?"

"No—well, yes. I just don't want to upset you. I don't want to hurt you."

She nodded. "Of course. Of course—you don't want to hurt me. So you lie to me."

"Now wait a minute, don't jump—"

"That's the way it always begins."

"You don't understand. I'm not——"

"So you weren't mugged. So what happened?"

I didn't answer right away. It's embarrassing to admit this now, but I was struck by how beautiful she looked at just that moment. Angry beautiful—— her high cheekbones glowing in the bright kitchen light, her small angular jaw betraying an intense determination. This was part of her essence, an aspect too of her spirituality, a clue to what drew me to her so profoundly: the toughness, the hardness, as if she could at any moment stop what she was doing and quickly remind you that the world is a broken place filled with disappointment and loss and the only way to overcome the basic pain of our lives is to take it without flinching.

There was a long moment of stillness, then finally she said, "There's someone else, isn't there?"

"No," I said.

"Please don't lie to me."

"I won't. I will not lie to you. That's the whole point. I want to tell——"

"It always begins with some shit about being honest. It hurts you terribly to have to say this, right?"

"Malaika, give me a chance to——"

"Who attacked you?"

"Just some kid. But he wasn't——I mean, he works for someone else."

"What...?"

"Malaika, I need to explain the whole story. I can't just——"

"Works for someone else?"

"Malaika——"

"Who?"

"Money. It's about money. The whole thing's about——"

"Who wants to have you beat up?"

"I owe someone money...Gloria Greenstein. I owe Gloria money. "

She turned her back on me and leaned over the kitchen sink. Then she sighed, making a little noise like the grunt of someone stubbing their toe. Without turning around, she said, "I know this scene. I know it, and I can't believe it's happening to me again."

"Malaika——"

"OK, fine then be honest with me, but don't tell me it's about money, Eli."

"But it——"

"A rich lady like that doesn't have someone beat up over money."

I pinched my swollen nostril, then stood up and put the letter on the counter next to her.

"What's this?"

"I told you I was taking advances on the lessons I was giving her. Well…it's not working out. I mean, she's not taking lessons anymore."

"Why?"

"Because…well, she's really a little bit nuts, this woman. You've no idea. I mean, I really need to tell you the whole story."

She read the letter, then shook her head. "I don't want to hear the whole story. Just get to the point."

"Malaika, don't. At least let me——"

"You know the only time I've ever hit a man—and I hit him myself, not rich enough, I guess, to hire someone else to do it for me—the only time I ever hit a man was this one time with this guy who fucked me so nicely I thought it had to be love, and when I finally figured out that he didn't give a shit about me…"

She turned away, facing the sink again, and she pressed down hard on the counter. Her shoulders trembled. "I'll pack now and get on the red-eye."

"What?"

"I'm going back to California." And then she walked out of the kitchen.

"Malaika," I called after her. "Wait." I followed her up the creaky stairs. "Look," I said. "I don't care if you want to hear this or not—I want to tell you. Nothing ever happened between Gloria and me. I read to her—that's all I did."

"Read to her?" She stopped, one hand on the bedroom's heavy wooden door.

"Yes. Anais Nin stories."

"Who?"

"Anais Nin," I said. "Erotic stories, which are literature, really. But anyway, it doesn't matter. We just read and talked about sex because she's got a crazy marriage, which she ought to just get the hell out of. We talked about her marriage, and I read these stories to her, and then she wanted to be physical with me—but I said no, and walked off."

"And…?" She leaned into the wooden door.

"And…and now she—or her husband, who's also a nutcase—is trying to get the money back for the lessons I owe her."

"How long has this been going on?"

"How long?"

"Yes."

I paused. "What do you mean how long?"

"How long have you two been reading pornography together?"

"I wouldn't exactly put it that way. It's not pornography. And it's not like we were reading to each other. I was reading to her—that was it."

"I see." She pushed open the door.

I followed her into the bedroom. "OK, yes. I should have told you before. A couple weeks. It's been a couple weeks, but I didn't tell you because I was afraid you'd react exactly the way you're reacting."

She turned around and faced me. "Two weeks?"

"Yeah, I think so. Actually, a little less. About twelve days."

"Give or take a day, but you're not sure, right?" She threw open the closet door with a burst of energy. The hangers rattled. Clothes swayed from the force of the door's breeze.

"Please, Malaika. Let me try to explain. I mean, once I'd gotten into this mess where I owed her the lessons, I didn't know how to get out of it. But nothing ever happened between us. Nothing."

She started to cry, covering her face with her hands. "Nothing? Except that you read pornography to her."

"It's sick, Malaika. It is. I never should have done it. I'm sorry."

I started toward her, but still crying she stepped to the closet and started pulling out clothes. "I've got to get the hell out of here."

"No, Malaika. Please don't leave."

"I thought you were different, but——Jesus. Was it an interesting experience? Did you learn something about yourself? Or did you help her get closer to her 'soul'?"

"Don't say that. You're not even giving me a chance to explain."

"You've had two fucking weeks to explain!" she shouted. Then she turned from her closet and took one strong, quick step toward me and planted her feet firmly and pulled her head back, lifting her chest, assuming that elegant, long-necked posture of a dancer about to leap. She blinked away her tears. "I don't care if you fucked her or not. I really don't," she said, her voice quiet and controlled. "Now we don't have any money, right?"

"I'll get the money."

"Forget it, Eli. I know you. You are just like all the others, and I've had enough. I'm taking my baby, and going back home."

"*Your* baby? What are you saying? The baby's the whole reason——"

But I stopped in mid-sentence. Because she wasn't listening. She had already turned back to the closet and pulled out her suitcase.

20

She didn't leave that same night, and for the next two days I tried to reason with her. But the question of whether or not I'd slept with Gloria quickly became irrelevant, because Malaika spent hours on the phone with her friend Star, who turned the whole conflict into a question of feminist politics.

At one point, Malaika sat me down in the living room and gave me a little lecture, parroting, I'm sure, what Star had said to her. "I'm not sorry this happened," she began, "because genuine independence is the freedom to make choices, and that's what I'm doing. This situation forces me to confront, once and for all, my dependence on men. You see, Eli, for many years I've been duped into thinking that being a liberated woman is mostly about sex, about being able to have sex on my own terms, with no strings attached. But that's not being free. In fact, the 'sexual revolution,' all that hippie bullshit, was started by men. By men! The whole sixties business—rock music, cosmetics, Hugh Hefner, all that crap. It was a revolution stimulated by advertising and the business-as-usual ethics of competition and consumption."

Here, especially, I knew she was just a mouthpiece for Star's ideas. Malaika, with her anxiety about being poorly educated, would never use this kind of jargon. But she was definitely memorizing the lines.

"The first wave of the women's movement just created new markets," she went on. "We were never liberated from our roles, only more objectified. In the sixties, women won the right to wear miniskirts, which made them feel powerful. But come on—miniskirts are not a revolution. Where's economic equality? Where's equal respect for equal contributions? Where is genuine independence?"

These weren't questions for discussion. They were intellectual constructs that made Malaika entirely inaccessible. In fact, that final morning at the airport, she barely spoke to me at all, and she wore sunglasses the whole time. At one point, we were standing in line at the checkpoint for ticketed passengers only. I'd met her there, since she had refused to accept my offer to drive her to the airport.

"How about a cup of coffee?" I asked. "You've got plenty of time."

She adjusted her sunglasses and turned to me. I looked at my distorted reflection in the dark lenses. "Don't do this," she said, quietly.

"Do what?"

"Make a scene."

The line moved forward. I bent down to help with her carry-on bags, but she stepped in front of me and took them herself. "Malaika, do you really think you can just get on a plane and forget about me?"

I thought I saw her lips tremble, as if to fight off tears. "Yes," she said, very quietly. "Yes."

"You're crazy," I said, and grabbed her arm. "We have got to talk!"

This startled her. She glared at me over her shoulder. "Let go of my arm," she whispered, "or I will scream and watch you get arrested."

I hesitated, but I could tell she was serious. Then I saw the guy checking tickets, a security guard, looking at me. So I let go of her arm, and a few minutes later she handed the guard her ticket and passed through the metal detector, and then she turned around and looked at me one final time. She still had those sunglasses on, but she was definitely looking right at me as she pressed her hands together in prayer position and bowed. And that was it. She disappeared around a corner and was gone.

That evening, I decided to see my father.

I found him out back, sitting in the dark in a reclining chair by the pool. Wedged into the plastic slats of the chair next to him was a half pint of Canadian Club. It was empty.

"Dad?" I whispered.

He didn't stir. Out cold, breathing deeply, his mouth was partly open. I leaned over him. A faint smell of whiskey survived the night breeze coming off the lake. I took a step back. I hadn't seen him since that evening months ago with Malaika. He seemed to have lost weight. His bony ankles and skinny wrists stuck out of his worn, pale blue warm-up suit. He also needed a shave. A patchy layer of grey whiskers covered his cheeks and chin, and a few hairs of his untrimmed mustache seemed to be growing upwards, into his nose. The jacket of his warm-up had a frayed sleeve and a rust stain on the elbow.

The whole pathetic picture of him angered me. It was all his fault, I thought.

Everything. All of it.

"Dad," I said, loudly.

His eyes blinked open. He looked around. "What, what? Who is it?"

"It's Eli. I'm right here."

"Eli? You alone? The guards know you're here? They're supposed—" He broke off and reached into the pocket of his warm-up suit. "This goddamn thing." He pulled out a small walkie-talkie and pounded it with the palm of his hand. "It's supposed to beep. They're supposed to beep me if someone…" He stopped again, looking closely at the walkie-talkie, clumsily fiddling with some sort of switch on the top. Then he tried to slip the walkie-talkie back into the pocket of his warm-up suit. But he kept missing. Three or four times he awkwardly swung his hand right past the pocket.

"You're drunk, aren't you?" I said.

He stopped and, holding the walkie-talkie now in one limp hand, waved it at me. "What are you talking about?"

"You're drunk, and I think it's disgusting."

"What?" he grabbed the arms of the chair and pulled himself up. "I had a few drinks, but I'm not drunk." He stood there swaying unsteadily. "I'll show you what a drunk man looks like. Have you ever seen my impression of a drunk man?"

"I don't want to see it."

"Why not? Here. Watch. He walks like this…"

He took a couple of wildly exaggerated, wobbly steps, then I grabbed him. I grabbed him, and I shook him as hard as I could, digging my fingers deep into the soft cartilage of the joint in his shoulder. And I swung his body back and forth in my grip. I'd never before grabbed someone so violently. It was exhilarating. The way his mouth hung open in shock, his lips twisted, a gleam of fear and surprise in his widened eyes. And all because of me. My power. The strength of my youth overwhelming him. We were near the edge of the pool. The pale blue water, illuminated from within, rippled slightly from the steady breeze off the lake behind me. It would have been easy to push him in.

But, suddenly, one of the security guards pulled me away. Before I even knew what had happened, this guy, whose huge arms and thick legs bulged beneath a tight-fitting, black running suit, threw me face down on the gravelly cement near the side of the pool. Then he held me in an armlock while his partner shined a bright flashlight in my face.

"Let him up goddammit, that's my son," my dad said in a hoarse voice, breathing heavily.

The guy holding my arm mumbled something I couldn't make out, and I had an impulse to tell him that I wasn't trying to hurt my father, that I was just upset about a lot of things and had momentarily lost my cool—displaced aggression and all that. But, fortunately, I kept my mouth shut. It was not the time for psychological explanations.

My dad crouched over me. "Are you OK? These guards are fucking maniacs." And he shot *them* a dirty look.

My heart was pounding, and I had the shakes from my surging adrenaline, but I just nodded and said, "Yeah, I'm OK." And then together we walked silently into the house, leaving the guards to disappear into the shadows.

We ended up in the living room, the exact same spot, in fact, where Malaika and I had sat before. The large, elegant, thick-carpeted living room filled with art from around the world—African masks, Oriental vases, the original de Kooning.

My father motioned to the two leather easy chairs in the room's far corner. "I'm going to have another drink," he said, flatly. "Can I fix you one?"

I hesitated, impressed, I must admit, by this deft strategy for putting behind us what had just happened.

"Sure," I said. "Whatever you're having."

"Canadian Club on ice. That OK?" His slow, thick speech betrayed his efforts at sobriety, but I remember thinking at that moment: OK, so he's drunk, so what?

I nodded. "Canadian Club on ice will be fine."

He fixed the drinks, opening a bar hidden in a wooden cabinet near the fireplace, the whistle-clean fireplace which, even to this day, has never been used.

"So," he said, handing me my drink. "What sort of trouble are *you* in?"

The question threw me off. Suddenly, it's as if we were equals: a couple of hard-drinking men sharing their troubles. I wondered if my nose still looked injured.

"What makes you think I'm in trouble?"

He raised his glass in a toast and silently took a long drink, then exhaled loudly, smacking his lips. "I don't know—maybe just because I'm in such deep shit I figure everyone else must be, too."

He laughed. I took a small sip of my whiskey. It tasted cool and sweet, soothing.

"Have you been following it in the papers?" he asked.

"Sort of, but I've been pretty busy."

"Yeah, well, the papers don't know the half of it anyway," he said. "I could give a shit about those asshole newspaper reporters. Bastards. They can all go fuck themselves."

His cursing unnerved me. Where was his cool, calm dignity? His *I'm always in charge* poise? I noticed for the first time how sunburned his unshaved face was. The skin on his nose had peeled, leaving a raw pink patch. I thought about how he must be doing nothing but sitting around all day by the pool.

"I mean really," he said, a little more loudly now. "I don't give a fuck about my reputation—I just don't want to lose all my money!" And he laughed, louder this time, wagging his head back and forth.

I realized then, that during the past several weeks, the pressure had gotten to him. Somehow I hadn't ever thought that was a possibility. My father— Mr. Smooth—crack under pressure?

He plopped himself down in the easy chair next to me and said, "You know, it's the only thing I've ever done with my life."

"What is?"

"Make money."

"Come on, Dad, you can't say that——"

"Not like my brother," he said, cutting me off. "Max was different. Money was irrelevant for Max. He never gave a shit about money. Still doesn't."

He started to hum a tune I vaguely recognized, then sang in a throaty voice:

Arise ye prisoners of starvation,
Arise ye wretched of the earth,
For justice thunders condemnation,
A better world's in birth. . .

He broke off and said loudly, "Yes! Yes! Workers of the World Unite! A better world's in birth!" Then, a little glassy-eyed, he stopped and reached into the torn pocket of his warm-up jacket for a handkerchief. He wiped the corner of his eye. It wasn't a tear but a small, yellowy secretion. Conjunctivitis, I think. Just like Uncle Max.

"The point is, Eli, my life's been about one thing: making a pile of money. That's it. Money."

He looked at me blankly, and I didn't know how to respond. Although in my anger I would have agreed with him completely half an hour earlier, what he was saying now struck me as unmistakably false. I had a confusing impulse to defend the man that moments ago I'd sincerely wanted to hurt.

"Money," he repeated. "The almighty buck. I flirted once with a life of real meaning but traded it in long ago for a life of real comfort." He laughed again.

"That's not true, Dad."

"The fuck it isn't," he said, spitting the words out angrily. He took another gulp of whiskey. "It's a bunch of crap," he said. Then, more quietly now, looking into his glass as if he were studying it, he added. "That's why it was always your mother's values I wanted you to have, not mine. Not my values."

He stood up. I flashed on how my mother had fancied herself as something of an aesthete. The truth is her artistic work never advanced much beyond being a regular in pottery and painting classes at the Evanston Art Center. But she took herself seriously in a way hardly anyone does these days. Partly, it was her therapy. She had a regular on-the-couch analysis, and all that psychological theory seemed to animate her—offering her an enlarged, subtle view of the world, which my father didn't share. He once called psychoanalysis "the greatest scam of the twentieth century."

That's why it surprised me to hear him talk approvingly of my mother's values. I watched him take a few slow steps to a shelf in the far corner of the room, where he picked up a small, green vase. Cut jade. An intricate engraved pattern, circles within circles, mandala-like.

"Very pretty," I said. "You get it last winter in Japan?"

He didn't answer. He just looked closely at the vase, holding it first in one hand, then the other. Finally, he put it down and picked up a small, ivory sculpture of a laughing Buddha. "Yes, Kyoto," he said, quietly, and he stood there looking at the little statue. "Your mother would have——"

He started to cry, turning his back on me. Then I started to cry too, and I remember having a weird flash of concern about those security guards seeing us as I stood up, and my dad turned around, and he came toward me shaking his head side to side, tears streaming down his face, mucous dripping from his nose.

"Oh God," he said. "Oh, God, I never..." He staggered into my arms.

"It's OK, Dad," I said, holding him tight. "Everything is going to be OK. You'll see—it's all going to be OK."

And I wanted so badly to believe this. I wanted at that moment for love to just take over somehow and enlarge us and lift us both out of the mess we were in.

But then, still hugging me tightly, my dad said, "He's dead, Eli. He's dead."

"What? Who?"

"They killed him."

"What are you talking about?"

"Oh Eli..." he said, squeezing me tighter. "They killed Billy."

"Mr. Greengoss?"

Slowly, our embrace loosened. My father stepped away. He didn't look at me. "I can't prove it," he said quietly. "I can't prove it, but I know it's true."

"What are you talking about?"

"Billy, you see, he wanted to——" He swallowed hard, still not looking at me, talking in such a low tone that it was almost as if he were just mumbling to himself. "He was going to testify, you see, against both of them——the mayor and the governor. And that's why they killed him——to scare all the rest of us, all the other bankers. They killed him."

"The mayor and the governor?"

"I can't prove it. I know that I can't prove it, but he's dead... A car accident, they say. Somewhere outside of Mexico City——I know it's not true. I just know it..." He looked up at me and, slurring his words, said, "I have something for you. You should have it, yes. You should..." Then he walked out of the room.

I sat down and tried to pull myself together, thinking about big, fat, jolly Bill Greengoss——gone, dead. Moments later, my dad returned with a suitcase, an old-fashioned metal Samsonite with red brackets reinforcing the corners.

"Here, this is for you." He set the case down at my feet, then stood off to the side. I looked at him, but he avoided my eyes. His gaze was lowered. He twisted his wedding band. "Open it," he said, finally.

I leaned over and popped the suitcase's metal latch and opened the lid. Inside, there were stacks of fifty dollar bills with old, worn rubber bands tied around them. At first, I thought the money looked fake. I counted eight rows across the width of the suitcase, and eight rows up and down the height. I'd never seen so much cash before.

Then my father kneeled beside me and whispered, "Fifty thousand dollars. Please, Eli, take it. It can't be traced."

I shook my head. "What...? Whose——?"

"Yours," he said. "It can't be traced. You take it."

"But I can't——"

He cut me off, gripping my leg tightly. His fingers dug into my thigh. "Please, Eli," he said, tears again glazing his eyes. "Please take the money."

I looked at him, then slowly I unpeeled his grip from my leg and stood up. He remained on his knees, and his hand slid down to my shin, and then my ankle. He squeezed harder. "Please, Eli. Please."

I looked down at him. What was he asking for? My acceptance? My approval? I yanked my leg out from his grasp and walked clear to the other side of the room before I turned around and said, loudly, "You stole that money?"

"No," he whispered hoarsely, still on his knees, his head propped up on his elbows.

"But you just said——"

"But not stolen. That's the wrong word. Just please take it," he repeated. "Please."

He looked at me for a minute, his mouth hanging open, then he raised himself onto all fours and started to crawl toward me.

"What are you doing?" I said.

He ignored me.

"Dad? Dad, get up."

But he continued to crawl toward me, his head hanging forward like an old dog's.

"Dad, don't crawl."

He kept coming, looking up at me now, a sheen of sweat giving his face a sickly flushed pallor.

"Goddammit, Dad! Get up!"

I stepped toward him, but just then he stopped and lowered his head to the floor and vomited. Immediately, the stench burned in my nostrils, but I knelt beside him holding his trembling shoulders.

"Take it easy," I said. "You'll feel better now."

He panted, spitting saliva, then retched again. I put my hand on the back of his sweaty neck. Finally, he said in a low voice, "Help me to the shower, will you?"

"Sure," I said, and I lifted him to his feet. Traces of saliva and vomit covered the front of the warm-up jacket. I unzipped it for him, then I started to take his elbow to lead him upstairs. But he shook his arm free.

"I'm OK," he said.

"I'll turn the water on for you."

He shook his head. "I'll be fine, really." He was looking down at the carpet.

"Don't worry about it," I said. "I'll clean it up. You get in the shower."

He nodded, then turned slowly away, and I watched him shuffle across the room, holding his arms out a little to the side, as if he were balancing himself on a narrow beam.

I finished cleaning up the mess just as he came back downstairs. He thanked me, then pulled the collar of his terry cloth bathrobe snug under his chin and headed for the kitchen. He was struggling, I could tell, to regain his composure. I followed him, trailing the fresh scents of his soap and shampoo.

As he put some water up to boil, he said, "It's been a long time since that's happened." Then he leaned on the counter and stared at the water kettle, a small, blue pot with a chipped spout. My mother had bought it many years ago in Portugal.

In silence, we waited for the water to boil. The house struck me as depressingly large and empty. The hissing of the gas flame seemed the only sound of life.

"Maybe it was something you ate?" I said, finally.

He looked up at me and cracked a small smile. Then the boiling water rattled the pot, and my father reached into the cupboard and pulled out two orange mugs.

"Tea?" he said.

"Sure."

We sat down in the darkened breakfast nook overlooking the swimming pool. Neither of us turned on the light. We just sat there in the dark. Outside, that guard who had thrown me to the ground passed in front of a patio light, then shined his flashlight on us and waved. My father gave him a small nod, a gesture that lifted my spirits, carrying as it did a tiny bit of my dad's old poise and confidence. The OK sign from the man in charge.

"I drank too much—that's why I vomited," he said, quietly. "Not because of something I ate—because I drank too much. Just like yesterday, and the day before that, and the day before that."

"So you've been drinking, it's understandable. You're under a lot of stress."

He ignored this feeble line. Without looking at me, he blew into his cup, cooling his tea. "Eli," he said, slowly, "there's something I want to tell you. It's something I've been wanting to tell you since…I don't know, since these last several months…when we've been out of touch."

I felt my stomach tighten, and a chill gripped me even though I was holding the mug of steaming tea. I looked straight out in front of me at the empty swimming pool.

"What is it, Dad?"

I could feel his gaze locked on me, and in the dark the smell of his soap and shampoo seemed even stronger.

After a moment, he said, quietly, "When you were here that night with Malaika, I lied to you."

I nodded.

"What you have to understand," he went on, "is that there are times when a father feels that he should——"

"I know, Dad. You were just trying to protect me. You don't have to apologize." I stood up quickly and turned on the overhead light. "So what happens now?" I said, as my eyes adjusted to the sudden brightness. "I mean, with Mr. Greengoss and everything."

He squinted into his mug of tea. "Nothing, really. There won't be any investigation into Bill's death and, in terms of everything else, a young guy, one of the auditors——couldn't be more than, well, your age. He's taking the fall."

"You mean that he's the one who——"

"It's all very carefully orchestrated," he interrupted. "He takes the blame, and life goes on."

"And you?"

"Me? I'll follow the program," he said softly. "And I'll be all right." His voice trailed off. Then neither of us spoke for what seemed like a long while. I noticed the sound of those big end-of-the-summer moths bumping against the now brightly lit kitchen window.

"More tea?" he said, finally.

I nodded. "Sure."

"Put the water up, will you? I have to use the toilet." And then he gave my shoulder a gentle squeeze. "A little milk in mine, please," he said, heading out of the kitchen and down the hall.

Several minutes passed. I carried the two fresh mugs of tea into the living room, where I found my dad crouched over the suitcase, closing it up.

He looked at me. "Tea ready?"

"Yeah."

I set the mugs down near the two chairs we'd been sitting in before. My father finished snapping shut the suitcase's latches. Then he said, "I'll be right back." And he picked up the suitcase and went upstairs.

I tried to drink my tea, but the mixture of ammonia and vomit and lemon-scented carpet freshener made me sick to my stomach.

When my father returned, he quickly sat down and took a big gulp. "Ahhhh," he smacked his lips. "Just right. Just exactly the right amount of milk." He smiled, then crossed and re-crossed his legs. I recognized the forced cheerfulness in his manner that I knew as a trait of my own. "So what brought you out here tonight, Eli?"

The question caught me off guard. I suddenly had no idea why I was there.

"I mean, was there anything special?" he asked.

I looked around, and my gaze got stuck on the abstract painting of de Kooning's hanging over the couch. I knew there was a nude woman somewhere in the swirl of color and line and geometric shapes. But at that moment I couldn't isolate the *figure* from the frenetic scheme of the work as a whole. I couldn't *see* what I knew was there, couldn't bring my attention to it—and this inability was frightening. Instead of the painting's unity I experienced the fractured memory of my reflected image in Malaika's sunglasses from earlier that day, and then, flitting back to the present, I took in the dark, natural wood of the picture frame around de Kooning's tangled colors, mixed now with the smell of my father's puke lingering just below the odor of cleaning products, while on another threshold of awareness there drifted this abstract neutral knowledge—facts—of Malaika gone and my mother gone and Gloria gone and Mr. Greengoss gone. And stabbing through the foggy feeling of loss was again and again the question of the figure in the swirling colors. Where was she? Why couldn't I see her? And then my father asked me again why I'd come to visit him, but his voice sounded far away, filtered as it was through my rising anxiety until another voice, my own this time, spoke as if it were calling out from some faraway darkness, a puny, barely audible voice slowing everything down, bringing everything into focus again, the most simple focus. The nude woman. Her breasts were two blue-green circles, with a small red line above them suggesting a smile, and a triangle, dark brown, for a nose.

I turned to my father and said, "I came, Dad, because, in fact, I need some money."

21

So I took it. I took my dad's dirty money and paid off Gloria's husband and then, about four months later, I went to California. It was March. The baby was due.

Of course, I had tried a million times to reach Malaika at a number I had for her mother. Star's number was unlisted. But I did have Star's address, which is where I went directly from the airport.

It was my first time in San Francisco. The roller-coaster streets, houses built at impossible angles, tropical foliage sprouting weirdly out of cement— it felt like a foreign country. Star lived on Vallejo Street in a two-story, pale blue stucco house with a small porch. Directly across from her was a café called Toni's.

After I found the house, I panicked. The thought of actually seeing Malaika was suddenly too much. So instead of parking I drove down to Fisherman's Wharf and joined the crowds wandering through the strips of restaurants and souvenir stands, where I bought a glass mug with a picture of the Golden Gate Bridge etched onto the side. Then I took a trolley ride to a lunch place where the waiter said I could arrange to have San Francisco's famous sourdough bread shipped to me in Chicago.

Finally, at dusk, I headed back to Star's—on foot. I had a map, and I thought it would be fun to walk, but soon I was lost. It got darker. The damp fog grew thicker. And that's when I found myself standing next to a woman who turned out to be Star herself.

She was holding two bags of groceries and waiting patiently at the corner for the light to change, even though no cars were coming. I was busy trying to position my map to pick up the faint yellow light coming from the streetlamps. I sensed she was watching me, so I looked up at her. She had wide, flat features and big, dark eyes. Her skin was a deep golden yellow. Native American, I thought. Also, she wore cowboy boots, blue jeans, and a loose-fitting sweater with an orange and black pattern of pyramid-like geometric shapes. She also wore a wide-brimmed hat made of tightly woven green reeds. She smiled and said, "Are you lost?"

"Yes, I think so." It didn't seem right to give her the exact address, so I tried to explain that I was looking for a coffee shop on Vallejo.

"Toni's," she said quickly. "She roasts her own coffee. It's really the best in the neighborhood. I'm heading that way." She encouraged me with a small rise of her thick eyebrows, a pleasant gesture of attentiveness.

While we walked, she told me the whole history of Toni's café. Apparently, Toni was a good friend of hers. I explained that I was visiting from Chicago, and she laughed and said a good friend of hers just got back from there. But, of course, I made no connection. At this point, I simply thought this was a friendly stranger genuinely trying to be helpful. She was, perhaps, a bit flirtatious, but it was innocent enough.

"Well, here's Toni's," she said, "If you don't mind the sugar buzz, the cannolis are delicious."

We had stopped directly in front of her house, though I didn't yet realize it was hers. I looked at the front porch and felt my chest tighten. Is Malaika really there? On just the other side of that door? What if the baby has already been born?

"Would you mind if I join you?" Star asked, breaking my reverie. "I could use a hit of caffeine." A small smile spread to her thick, flat lips, and, for the first time after all those blocks, she put down her groceries. The bags were filled with bulk-size cartons. White rice, brown rice, black beans, red beans, bran, granola—the cartons were labeled with hand-written white stickers.

"I don't mean to be too forward," she continued, "but I like to make out-of-towners feel welcome. Frankly, you're an attractive and, I presume, a rather interesting man."

I shook my head and laughed softly. "Wow, I'm just caught off guard."

She brushed back a strand of her dark hair, which was bunched up underneath the brim of her hat. "I know, our culture dictates that men are supposed to be the initiators, right?"

I nodded. "Just a social construct, I suppose."

"Exactly." She nodded, a single, firm nod, business-like. "What do you do for a living?" She seemed to glance up and down at my clothes. I was wearing my usual: sneakers, jeans, tennis shirt, and a warm-up jacket.

"I teach tennis."

"Really? That friend of mine, the one just back from Chicago, she almost

166

married a tennis pro."

I froze, smiling, as a pinch grabbed my lower back, and in a moment of horrible intuition I understood this was Star.

She bent down for her groceries. "I live right over here," she said, with a flick of her head. "I'll just put these away and meet you at Toni's, OK?"

"OK," I said, without even thinking, and then I turned around and hurried across the street, and when I reached the curb, I looked back and saw Star carrying the groceries up the porch steps and Malaika, hugely pregnant, opening the front door. She wore dark sweatpants and a shapeless, black sweatshirt. She moved stiffly as she stepped onto the little porch and, after what looked like some sort of friendly bickering, took one of the bags of groceries.

For me just to see Malaika, to know she was there, alive, real—the feeling was like catching a glimpse of a celebrity. Suddenly this untouchable exists in the everyday world.

And then the moment passed, and she was back in the house, and the door closed, and I found myself trying to calculate whether the incredible coincidence of meeting her friend Star worked to my advantage or to my disadvantage.

To collect my thoughts, I went inside the café. Toni's was a basement place with a two-step drop to a cement floor where about a dozen wobbly, wooden tables were crammed together. Almost every table was full. A chalkboard sign in the corner read, THE CANNOLI IS HANDMADE, YOU KNOW? And beneath that was written: YES, YOU CAN SMOKE, BUT WORK IT OUT WITH THOSE SITTING NEAR YOU.

It took a minute for my eyes to adjust to the room's dim lighting. I stood there listening to a Billie Holiday song playing softly over the hum of conversation. Then I watched a small, black cat (named Chino, I later learned, as in cappucino) jump up on a table and sniff a little, metal canister filled with cream. No one seemed to mind.

I sat down at an empty table in the corner. The deep, rich smell of fresh coffee mixed pleasantly with the odor of tobacco. Though I don't smoke, I leaned over to the table next to me and asked a big-bellied man wearing a purple T-shirt if I could bum a cigarette. He gave me one and smiled so warmly that it made me nervous.

I quickly turned away and watched the guy working the espresso machine behind an ornately carved wooden bar. He wore theatrical make-up, white face like a pantomime artist's, and bright red lipstick. He also wore a red beret and a red bow tie. Pretentious as hell, I thought. I hated him. It was totally irrational, but I wanted to punch him, to scrape that make-up off him and beat him into conformity. Meanwhile, he wagged his head in time to the slow, sad music as he poured steamed milk into two tall glass mugs. Then he twisted his red lips and white face until he looked like he was in pain as he mouthed the words to—and I swear to God I'm not making this up—it was Billie Holiday singing, "God bless the child…"

And that's when Star and Malaika walked in.

22

Star came through the door first, then Malaika appeared, wearing a black raincoat draped over her shoulders like a cape. I dropped my unlit cigarette and shot up from my chair like a cowboy in a gunfight. I knew that once the shock of recognition passed, Malaika's reaction would be to turn around and leave.

And that's exactly what happened, and when she did turn around, I started after her, moving so jerkily that I bumped the table next to mine and spilled a half cup of coffee on the book the guy in the purple T-shirt was reading.

"Sorry," I said. "I'm really sorry." And I reached into my pocket for some money. But all I had was fifties—still living on the money I'd taken from my dad. So I threw a fifty dollar bill on his table.

By this time, Malaika and Star were both out the door. I took the two-step rise in a leap and could hear Star saying, "What? What is it? What?"

Malaika's raincoat billowed from her fast strides toward the street. Star, holding her wide-brimmed hat in her hands, lagged behind a step. When they reached the curb, I shouted, "Malaika! Goddammit, stop!"

She turned around. The distance between us was no more than about twenty yards and in the growing darkness, against the backdrop of those pastel-colored houses, she cut an impressive figure in her black attire, even if it was just a sweatshirt, sweatpants, and a baggy, old raincoat. She looked at me and then, in a gesture so wonderfully familiar, she took a long, slow breath, lifting her chest, extending her carriage, head back, neck long—the poised performer, the beautiful dancer, the tough, hard, mysterious woman whose spell, like in some old fairy tale, drove me out of my mind.

We just looked at each other. Then Star spoke. "You two...know each other?"

Malaika remained still. I nodded.

There was a long pause. Behind me, I heard faint voices. Tones of concern, worry. The people in the café, I realized, must have thought I was crazy, throwing that money around, running out of there. They might even have called the police. I suddenly had an urge to explain everything to Star.

"I'm Eli," I blurted. But then I didn't know what to say next.

Star looked at Malaika, whose expression softened, her heavy, swollen face relaxing just the tiniest bit around her mouth and eyes.

"Jesus Christ," Star said, quietly. And she took a step back, out of the line of fire, so to speak.

I stepped forward. "How are you?"

Malaika shook her head. "You shouldn't have come, Eli."

"I wanted to see you how you are. How the baby is."

"I'm fine. The baby's fine."

I waited for her to say more, determined to outlast her in the silence.

Finally, she said, "I don't want you here."

"What do you——"

"You don't belong here."

"This is our baby."

She shook her head. "You're the man who got me pregnant." She paused. "The biological father, that's all."

She paused again, waiting, I suppose, for the hurtfulness of this to set in. I held my silence.

"Plenty of single women out here are raising children," she went on, "and some of them have never even met the biological father. Artificial insemination and——"

"What are you talking about? Artificial insemination! Have you lost your mind? This is our baby, and I——"

But she lifted her hands, silencing me. A dramatic gesture, operatic. Vintage Malaika. She spoke in a low tone, "Listen to me, Eli. Leave us alone. I don't want you to be a part of this——at all. And if you fight me on it, you'll lose. I promise. You will lose."

Slowly, she lowered her hands, and then she turned around and walked across the street.

Star looked at me, obviously shocked at discovering who I was. She held her hat in front of her, nervously sliding the wide brim through her fingers.

"Help me," I said. "Please."

She didn't answer, but before she turned away I felt certain that in her sad and puzzled expression I saw a deep and genuine concern. That was enough to give me hope.

The next morning, I stood on a damp, foggy corner near the house. I got there at 6:30 a.m. and waited for Star to come out. I had no idea what I was doing. I just figured that eventually she'd leave the house, and then I could talk to her.

At eight o'clock she stepped out, and as soon as she saw me, she nodded, almost as if she'd been expecting to find me there. We shook hands like a couple of business partners. Needless to say, gone without a trace was any aspect of her earlier flirtation.

"I want you to know that the reason I'm going to talk to you is not that I give a shit about you but because I care about Malaika," she said.

I nodded.

Then she looked away and, in the cool morning air, blew into her hands. "Also, I want you to know the only reason I talked to you in the first place is because I was horny and you looked like you might be a nice fuck." She paused, but still didn't look at me. Then she said, in a more quiet tone, "Now, however, my meeting you on the street like that was no doubt synchronistic, orchestrated by the universe—so there's an obligation to fulfill."

I still didn't say anything.

She went on, "I feel responsible for Malaika because it's from me that she's gotten most of her ideas. Ideas that now she's…well, come on."

We started to walk. "I assume you've never heard of androcentrism," she said.

"No. I'm not familiar with the term."

"It's the belief that male ideals are universals to which women should conform—the strand of contemporary feminist theory challenging both 'polarization' and 'essentialism.'" She paused, then said, "Listen closely, OK? 'Polarization' is the view that men and women are so different all of society should be organized on the basis of those differences; 'essentialism,' closely related, is the notion that these differences are 'essential,' in other words rooted in anatomy and genetic factors. Malaika, who doesn't really understand these distinctions, is in way over her head."

This sudden intellectual flourish intimidated me. It felt clear that Star wasn't trying to engage me in conversation so much as establish a superior position.

"I don't suppose you've read Sandra Bem or Helen Haste, have you?" she said.

I shook my head. "No, I'm afraid I haven't."

"You ought to. We are living through a revolution in gender roles that may turn out to be one of the most significant transformations in human behavior since history began," she said. "Bem and Haste—they're making important contributions, both of them."

Again, I nodded. Then we walked for several blocks in silence, during which I had serious doubts about whether or not Star was going to be any real help to me at all.

"Malaika's in bad shape," she said, finally, "because, you see, she's a follower not a leader—by which I'm not suggesting anything morally speaking. Not everyone has to be, or should be, a leader. The point is that she's in over her head and her thinking isn't based on anything."

"Anything...political you mean?"

"Political or cultural, it doesn't matter. Even if it were just a great, simple, romanticized love for women—that would be fine, too. But with Malaika it's not even that—it's not a love for anything. The root of it all, of everything she's trying to do, is this incredible anger she has at everyone. Nothing good can come out of that kind of anger, especially in terms of the birth."

I stopped and, without even thinking, took Star's elbow. We were on a crowded corner, near a bus stop. At the end of the block was an entrance to an animal hospital, where, it turned out, Star worked. "What about the birth?" I said.

She lowered her eyes and looked at my hand on her elbow. Then she was silent.

"What about the birth?" I said again.

She lifted my hand off her elbow. "I'm going to be late to work. Meet me tomorrow morning."

The next day, before Star explained the details of the birthing ritual, she told me that her bond to Malaika had its roots in both of them coming from "dysfunctional families." She rolled her eyes as she used the term but went on to tell me how they met in grammar school, were best friends growing up near Santa Barbara, then lost touch for a long while and ran into each other one day at a health food store in San Francisco. They were twenty-three. Star had just moved to the city to be trained as a veterinarian's assistant. Malaika was tending bar. They re-connected at the right time, Star explained, because they had both recently sworn off men. They got close, so close that once they tried to satisfy each other sexually. Star gave me a rather intellectualized description of it. "It was a meditation and physical enactment of erasing biological sex as the core of human identity and sexuality," she said, without a trace of irony. My impression was it left both of them a little embarrassed and disappointed that being gay was not going to be the answer.

Nonetheless, they were "soul mates," and that's why I listened carefully when Star said she feared Malaika was headed for serious trouble, especially in terms of this elaborate birthing ritual.

Malaika had dreamed up the whole thing. It involved seven women being present during the home delivery, each one representing a different goddess from one those pop-psychology books. *The Goddess in Everywoman*, or some such thing.

As Star explained this she reached into her pocket and—with the careful quality of attention I imagined her giving the ailing pets in the hospital where she worked—she slowly unfolded and handed me the xeroxed sheet summarizing who was who:

> *ELLEN: Artemis. Goddess of the hunt and the moon. Personifies the independent achievement-oriented feminine spirit. Qualities often thought of as unfeminine. Beautiful for her strength.*

> *BARB: Athena. Goddess of wisdom and craft. Logical, self-assured. Ruled by her head rather than by her heart. Beautiful for her judgement.*

> *STAR: Hestia. Goddess of the hearth. Patience, steadiness. Finds comfort in solitude. Exudes a feeling of self-containment and wholeness. Beautiful for her wisdom.*

> *JOYCE: Hera. Goddess of marriage. Vulnerable, loyal, committed. Suffers from the distant father (Cronos, who swallowed her at birth) and the powerless mother (unable to defend her). Beautiful for her depth.*

> *MARGARETA: Demeter. Mother goddess. Altruistic, fertile, caring. Beautiful for her generosity.*

> *KARINE: Persephone. Queen of the underworld. Intuitive, receptive, open to change. Beautiful for her vitality.*

CHERYL: Aphrodite. Goddess of love and beauty. Embodies the transformative and creative power of desire. Sensual, spontaneous, engaged with the world. Beautiful for her inspiration.

Along with these seven women/goddesses, Star explained there would also be two flute players, a Native American shamanic healer and, of course, a midwife who specialized in these sort of ritualized births. A sacred wooden tub—sanctified in some way that I couldn't quite follow—was to be filled with warm water, and Malaika would sit in it while actually giving birth to the child, whose transition into the world, so goes the theory, would be made more gentle by going from womb to warm water. Then, with the flutes playing special music and the shamanic healer chanting a blessing and the seven women sprinkling some sort of sacred herbs and flowers over the exhausted mother, the baby—hopefully a girl, I assumed—would be washed in a separate, smaller, wooden tub, while the first wooden tub, hooked up somehow to the sink in the bathroom, would be drained and filled with rain water (very scarce in California, the midwife kept a stash). The rain water, since there was no fireplace, would have to be heated on the stove. Then, finally, mother and child would be reunited, the warm tub of "water-from-the-sky" having been blessed by the shaman and prepared with the proper herbs.

My reaction to all of this? As crazy as it sounded, I accepted it with enthusiasm. Giving birth is an amazing mystery—so why not celebrate it as a spiritual act? My only objection—indicative, I suppose, of the basic egotism I was so mired in—was that *I* wasn't included.

Star, on the other hand, had a much deeper intuition about the whole situation. "It's dangerous," she said simply, in her deep melodic voice. "Because Malaika's anger isn't channelled."

This made sense to me, although it didn't alter my basic resolve just to be there. That's really all I wanted, as if the only thing I got out of Star's whole explanation was that the birth of my child was a great big party to which I hadn't been invited—but was determined to crash.

23

Although it may have been inconsistent with her sophisticated theories about gender identity, Star thought my presence at the birth might somehow help Malaika deal with her anger. Maybe she hoped that in the midst of delivery Malaika would undergo some kind of change if I were there. I'm not sure. But I didn't argue. She agreed to call me when the labor began.

I nearly went crazy waiting. I bought a cell phone and two or three times a day called the hotel desk clerk at the Best Western where I was staying and asked him to phone me, just to be sure I hadn't suffered any sort of technological breakdown. Meanwhile, I was a wreck. I could barely eat and sleep. I spent most of my days at Toni's café. The rest of the time, including half the night, I drove around the neighborhood, listening to the radio.

Which is exactly what I was doing when, at four a.m., I pulled out of the driveway of a gas station where I'd just consumed a six pack of bite-size powdered doughnuts and a cup of coffee—and a fire truck raced by with its siren blaring. I followed it, ghoulishly seeking some middle-of-the-night entertainment.

It never occurred to me, even as we drew closer and closer to Star's house, that I might actually be involved. The emergency was "out there," and my long list of personal concerns, however intense they might be, certainly didn't extend that far. But the fire truck turned onto Vallejo Street and stopped directly in front of Star's and then a second truck roared up the street from the wrong way and as the swirling lights threw streaks of red and white across Star's pale blue stucco house, I saw her porch door had been propped open with a sandbag marked S.F.F.D. in bright orange letters. And then, for some reason, I thought of Gloria—how I'd simply turned around and walked out of her life. I had an impulse to do it again. To drive away. To flee this mad scene the same way I had fled hers.

But, of course, this was different and I pulled up as close as possible to the two fire trucks and got out of my car. From my hours spent at the café, I recognized a few of the people who had come out of their houses and now lined the narrow street, standing in their pajamas. The fat woman with frizzy dark hair who always smoked thin cigarillos—she stood there that night wearing Indian moccasins and an absurdly short nightgown, as if the street were a strobe-lit disco, and she the forlorn dancer, fat and timid. She waved at me, one plump arm swinging slowly across her big frame.

Then a fireman shouted, "Back it up. Get that car the hell out of here."

I turned and saw the sleeve of this enormous black rubber raincoat flapping at me. The fireman, who must have been six-and-a-half feet tall, yelled again, "I said back it up! Let's go!"

"I have to go inside," I shouted.

"What?"

"Inside," I said. "That's my...my girlfriend's house."

He moved toward me with the big, confident strides of a man used to being in charge, wide shoulders swaying with each step. Then he pushed his orange hard hat off his forehead and gave me a closer look.

"What did you say?"

I hesitated, realizing that I might or might not be welcome inside. And something about this fireman's face—his bad acne, hard jaw line, the crease in the skin on his forehead where his hat had been pulled snug—he looked so young, like a big high school kid, captain of the football team. It confused me. My sense of purpose wavered. Tongue-tied, I looked at the fireman's badge and flashed on my father, his trouble with the law, and how I couldn't help him now nor could he help me because I was here and my father was there, back in Chicago, alone, both of us so pathetically alone.

"My girlfriend's in there," I said, finally.

"What? Which one is she?"

"Which one? Uh...she's...she's pregnant."

Almost as soon as I'd gotten the word out, the fireman grabbed my arm and said "Follow me."

He took the porch steps two at a time. The unfastened metal snaps of his heavy boots jangled softly, a gentle sound I'll never forget in that damp pre-dawn darkness otherwise filled with the shrill of those sirens and harshly flashing lights.

I followed him through the door. A tall, fair, blonde-haired woman dressed in something resembling an Indian sari stepped into view at the far end of a long hallway. Her wrap-around dress, or whatever it was, reached to the top of her bare feet. She took small, jerky steps.

The fireman called out, "The father of the baby."

She strained to look more closely at me, leaning forward from the hips. Then she spun on her heels and with her awkward little steps hurried back into the room.

So we started down the hallway. It was lit by an old-fashioned chandelier that had only one dim bulb in it. Hurrying to keep up with the fireman's long strides, I stumbled on a patch of torn carpet and nearly fell. Then several voices, including the deeper pitch of a man's shout, erupted. And, again, a woman stepped out from the room at the end of the hall.

A large woman, with the square-shaped body of a man, she wore black slacks, a peach-colored button-down-the-front shirt, and a silk kerchief around her sizeable neck. I have often wondered, even to this day, what goddess she represented.

"Get him out," she said in a raspy voice. And she raised her hefty arm and pointed at me. "Get him out."

The fireman looked at me, then looked back at her. She met his stare with an impressive poise, then without missing a beat said quickly, "She doesn't want him here."

"It's my baby," I said.

Then Star stepped into the hallway.

"Star!" I shouted. "Tell him. Tell him it's my baby," and I stepped back, motioning to the fireman.

Star hesitated. She'd fixed her hair into two long braids, which she held now in front of her, one in each hand.

"Star!" I repeated. "Tell him!"

She opened her mouth, but before she had a chance to speak another fireman came out of the bedroom. He was a small, tense Asian man with a muscular build. "We can't stop the bleeding," he barked angrily. "And she needs oxygen. You call EMS?"

"Yes," the fireman behind me answered. "They're on their way."

"Good. Radio Billings that we've got a code-blue hemorrhage coming in. Those fuckers should've taken this call anyway."

The Asian man turned away, and I remember reacting even then to the coarseness of his language, which seemed so inappropriate. But then everything started to happen at once. The big woman in the black slacks pointed at me again and shouted, "Get him out! Just get him out!" Then Star began to cry, and I stepped toward the room, and the fireman behind me grabbed my arm. Then I heard Malaika moaning in pain. So I shook free of the fireman and pushed past the big woman and finally reached the doorway. But I couldn't see either Malaika or the baby, both of whom were in the bed surrounded by two more firemen as well as all of the other women, one of whom wore a floor-length black strapless evening gown. Absurd, totally absurd—but at the time it hardly registered, because crumpled on the floor in front of the bed was a blood-soaked sheet. I stared at it, then one of the firemen spoke to Malaika in a low, intense voice. "I'm going to massage your stomach, OK?" he said. "You tell me if it hurts too much now, OK? We're trying to slow the bleeding, but you tell me if it hurts too much. You tell me…OK?"

Malaika groaned, and I wanted to call out to her, but just then the fireman whose grip I'd escaped from—he grabbed me by my neck and shoulders and pulled me out of the room, spinning me around and wedging his forearm under my chin, pinning me against the wall in the hallway. Then he leaned so close to me that I could see the moist whites of his pimples. I could also smell his breath, which reeked of french fries.

"Listen, pal," he said, whispering. "I don't know how you're mixed up in this and I don't want to hear it because I don't have time. You want to help— get in your car and meet us at the hospital. Otherwise get the hell out of here or I'll see to it you spend the night in jail."

"That's my baby in there," I said, hoarsely.

But he just pressed his beefy forearm up into my chin.

I went and stood out on the lawn. About fifteen minutes passed. Two ambulances arrived. Malaika was carried out on a stretcher. Then the fireman who had pinned me to the wall came down the steps of the porch carrying my baby in a little mauve-colored blanket. Malaika went in one ambulance, the baby in the other. Then Star came out. "It's a girl," she said, and told me to stay away from the hospital.

I went anyway. But I only hung around for about four hours, which is how long it took me to understand three basic things: one, that Malaika and the baby were going to be OK; two, that nobody knew exactly why Malaika had hemorrhaged; and three, that Malaika had carefully instructed all of her friends not to let me get near either one of them.

So instead of arguing with them and the hospital administrators and God knows who else, I drove straight to the airport and got on the first flight back to Chicago, peeling off more of my dad's fifties to pay for the ticket.

24

During those first few weeks back home, I left messages on Star's answering machine almost every day. Once, Malaika answered the phone. But when she recognized my voice, she hung up.

I didn't know what to do with myself, so for about six straight weeks I went to the movies almost every day. I guess I was trying to amuse myself to death. Finally, I wrote to Heidi.

> *Dear H,*
> *Something terrible has happened. And I think you may be one of the only people who can understand...Please let me see you.*
>   *— Eli*

That was it. The whole poetic opus. Naturally, she didn't answer. But I wrote again anyway, and then again, and again, and again. Until, finally, this one she couldn't ignore.

> *Heidi:*
> *I don't blame you for not responding to me. I've treated you badly. But I'm as lost now as I've ever been in my life. As that great spirit Jose Ortega put it——*
> *"...this is the simple truth: that to live is to feel oneself lost. He who accepts it has already begun to find himself, to be on firm ground. Instinctively, as do the shipwrecked, he will look round for something to which to cling, and that tragic, ruthless glance, absolutely sincere, because it is a question of his salvation, will cause him to bring order into the chaos of his life. These are the only genuine ideas: the ideas of the shipwrecked..."*
> *Please, Heidi, let me hear from you...I'm shipwrecked. And in*

my "tragic, ruthless glance," it is to you, in absolute sincerity,
that I turn... —— Eli

I later learned that she found my quoting Ortega so pretentious and infuriating that she couldn't resist writing back, just to put me in my place.

> *Dear Eli:*
> *You've always had a gift for self-dramatization, without seeing that for you, at its core, it's basically a form of narcissism.*
> *I don't want to have anything to do with you. The very idea that after all this time you write me letters about how "lost" you are, and then expect me to come running——it's offensive.*
> *My advice: don't romanticize your pain. Do something about it. And if you're harboring illusions about getting back together with me (now that your yoga-fling, or whatever it was is over, I assume), try asking yourself, honestly: How many times can the same two people hurt one another?*
> *We're through, Eli. We have been through for a long time. With your "tragic ruthless glance" take in this basic reality, OK? And please don't write to me again. —— Heidi.*

In this I found hope——just that she'd written back to me at all. Her line about "how many times can the same two people hurt one another?" at least acknowledged the significant history we shared. Also, her advice not to "romanticize my pain" was exactly the kind of thing I needed to hear. A no-nonsense exhortation, it reminded me of how in high school, just before a big tennis match, she once grabbed me by the arm and said, "Respect yourself. Play hard."

I just wanted to see her. So I wrote again:

> *Heidi:*
> *Please don't misunderstand my intention. I don't expect you to come "running." And I don't mean to "romanticize" my pain. The truth is simply that I find myself thinking about you. Does that mean I'm "harboring illusions" of us getting back together? No. At least I don't think so. But I can't say for sure what it means. All I know is that I want to see you.*
> *You ask: "How many times can the same two people hurt one*

another?" The answer: Many times, many, many times.

> *But if the reason you don't want to see me is because you're afraid of us hurting each other, that's cowardice. On the other hand, if you really have no desire to see me, that's another story altogether. My point is just this: Let's be brave, take chances, and follow our desires…*

This put her over the edge. My arrogant, outrageous challenge to her to be "brave" enough to see me—this angered her so much that she was compelled to write again. I think it was supposed to be a short, quick, hate letter. But Heidi isn't someone who hates short and quick. It went on for five pages. With her, strong emotion is automatically linked to analysis and interpretation, a quality of hers I admire. Some people might say she thinks too much, makes things more complicated than necessary. But to me her ability to take a whole and break it into pieces is a way of appreciating subtlety, of seeing clearly and honestly that to grasp the truth of a situation usually requires understanding various components and how they relate to one another.

Anyway, one part of her letter really got to me:

> *The way I see it, Eli, your whole life is about protecting yourself. You take flight. You embrace mystery—as a form of defense. But meanwhile, your isolation grows, and with it you become increasingly desperate for greater and greater "mysteries." So you pick up a woman—terribly sexy and athletic, I presume—at a yoga class.*
>
> *Some men, perhaps, can actually keep their deepest fears and feelings of loneliness at bay by chasing women, but you're far too basically honest and introspective for that. I'm sure about this. And I'm sure that the truth of your isolation will reach you eventually. Perhaps it has hit you now—which is why you feel so "shipwrecked." But regardless of whether it has hit you now or is still to come, the moment you realize your isolation will be the most painful, frightening moment of your life, Eli. And then—it may get even worse. Because in your fear and panic you may withdraw even further into your private world, until eventually the world outside, the common, ordinary world from which you are so isolated, will cease to exist. Your panic and anxiety will disappear*

because the world outside will disappear…

I know, I can hear you clicking your tongue, whispering, "The old insanity bit." So ignore me. That's fine. Because this is the last time you will ever hear from me. Alienation is life's problem, the great problem. And love is the basic reality, the simple answer. But you must participate. You, Eli. You must participate…I can't do it for you, even if I wanted to, which I don't. So DO NOT WRITE TO ME AGAIN. I will consider filing a harassment complaint if you do. I know that sounds hysterically extreme, but, believe me, I'm serious. I'm too busy, and my life right now is filled with too many very important and challenging things for me to lose myself in your melodramatic, immature, self-serving angst…

My initial reaction to this was rage. I stomped around my apartment and cursed her for thinking she knew me so well. Also, I found it outrageous that on the one hand she said I was heading for nothing short of a nervous breakdown, while on the other hand she refused even to speak with me because my suffering was "melodramatic, self-serving angst." I took this inconsistency as evidence of her basically disingenuous intentions. So the hell with her. And the hell with her whole anxiety-ridden world view. "Alienation is life's problem"—fuck that, I thought. That's just more of Heidi's famous fear of being alone.

I decided to tear up the letter and throw it away. But when I stood over the trashcan gripping the pages, these words jumped into my head: *If I killed myself right now, a few people would be upset. But they'd get over it, and that would be that.* I couldn't seem to turn off these thoughts, and suddenly I grew short of breath. Then my neck and scalp tingled and my mouth got dry and a wave of nausea overcame me. I kept thinking, *If I killed myself, would it really matter?* Not that I was about to attempt—it was an anxiety attack, that's all. But these thoughts scared the hell out of me. I had become, just as Heidi had predicted, suddenly aware of the extent to which I was isolated.

Needing "someone to talk to" sounds simple, but it's nothing, I learned, to take too lightly. I got into therapy. Three times a week I talked and talked and talked until, gradually, all that had happened began to feel human, and I began to accept how screwed up my life was and that I'd have to learn to live with the fact that, unless I fought in court, I had fathered a child I might not ever know.

Eventually, I began to move forward until by the end of the following year, I was beginning to make plans to apply to law school, doing some legal secretary type of work in a big Loop firm, and just getting out more in general.

Which is how I finally ran into Heidi. My father and I—back on guarded speaking terms, with the bank investigation inching along—had gone to an art opening at the Nat Weiss art gallery. Mrs. Weiss was an old friend of my mother's. I was nibbling raw carrots and celery and sipping white wine when Mr. Kirschbaum walked in with Heidi at his side.

My dad spotted them first. "Oh, look," he said, smiling. "Irv and Heidi." He gave my shoulder a little pat and began to make his way through the small, crowded room.

I faded into a corner, trying to concentrate intensely on a stark, abstract painting in black and white called *Willem's Excavation, re-visited.* The title referred to a famous Willem de Kooning piece done in the late 1940s. The whole exhibit, in fact, was an homage to de Kooning, who had recently fallen out of favor with some of the art world's more influential critics.

Not that any of this particularly mattered to me in the heat of that very awkward moment. Instead of the jazzed-up grit and intensity of the city (de Kooning's subject during this time, according to Heidi), the painting I was looking at—with its black and white layered lines, jagged cubes, and swirling brush strokes—seemed to portray nothing but my own frayed, out-of-control, burnt-black nerves.

Breathe, I told myself, fearful of an anxiety attack. Just breathe.

Heidi avoided me, which was easy to do since there must have been at least fifty people packed into that tiny room. But soon I heard her talking in a strong, confident voice, explaining how she viewed de Kooning's role in the rise of abstract expressionism. She said it marked "a powerful conflict between the inherited traditions of cubism and surrealism."

I listened closely. Though I usually found Heidi's art talk merely pretentious, at that moment I was struck by the pretension of my calling *her* pretentious.

I turned to look at her. She had her back to me, so I couldn't help but notice right away that she'd gained weight. Her buttocks, hips, and thighs had filled out. But, to the extent that I was on a sexual wavelength at all, I thought she looked great. She wore a brightly-colored, loose-fitting cotton skirt and a worn denim blouse. A casual, early-spring look, accented by a pair of paint-streaked sneakers that made her look more like a starving artist than an academic art historian, a distinction I noted carefully.

I stepped closer. A small cluster of people had gathered around her, including an older woman who had once been a friend of my mother's. I don't recall her name, but she had tan, leathery skin and wore gold hoop earrings and a gold necklace with a pendant shaped like a letter from the Hebrew alphabet. I could smell her flowery perfume from where I was standing. She smiled at me, then said, "Hello, Eli. Come listen to this—it's so interesting."

That's when Heidi turned around.

"Hi," I said, quietly.

She nodded and, without missing a beat, continued, "One way to put it is that de Kooning—unlike Pollack or Rothko—remained interested in the question of what the artist's 'self' can mean within the tradition of painting."

She stepped right past me, and the little group of listeners followed. "You can see here," she said, pointing to a canvas— but then she broke off and, out of nowhere, gave the fellow standing next to me a small wave.

I'll never forget it. This guy was wearing black pants, a black T-shirt, a black jean jacket, black cowboy boots, and dark sunglasses. He was Heidi's new boyfriend, Phil, the rock musician.

Everything about him bothered me—the cocky way he crossed his arms, the "bad-boy" indifference in his long, narrow face, and that he wore those sunglasses inside an art gallery, as if he were some sort of celebrity trying not to be recognized and not just a jerk trying to look cool.

The whole scenario of their relationship came to me as if in a vision: Heidi—the new Heidi, that is, the bohemian artiste in her paint-splattered sneakers—was sleeping with Mr. Cool, whose garage-band rock music, while lacking sophistication, captured the spirit of the people such that together they were uniting ethics and aesthetics and making a truly relevant and authentic cultural statement...blah, blah, blah.

I leaned over to Phil and said, "You know her?"

He didn't answer right away, so I touched his elbow. It was a thin, pointy elbow. Everything about him was thin and pointy. He stood well over six feet, swaying above me like a bamboo stalk.

"Yeah," he said, pushing up the bridge of his sunglasses. "She's brilliant."

I laughed. The idea of this asshole telling me that Heidi—my Heidi, which is, after all, how I couldn't help but think of her—the idea of *him* telling me that she was "brilliant." It was just too absurd.

Still, how I behaved is inexcusable. I leaned over and said, "Yeah, she is brilliant," then added, "how well do you know her?"

To his credit, Phil showed great restraint. He just ran his fingers through his long, straight, black hair, then readjusted his sunglasses and walked away.

But there wasn't much of anywhere for him to go in that tiny gallery. I followed behind and leaned into his ear, his shoulder really, since he was almost a full head taller than me. "She does really understand this stuff, doesn't she?" I said.

He turned around. "Have you got a problem?"

"Me? No. No problem, no problem at all. Nooo prooooblem!" My voice—whiny, high-pitched, suddenly too-loud—attracted Heidi's attention. Quickly, she weaved through the crowd, murmuring, "Excuse me, excuse me." Then she called out, "Phil, Phil!"

He turned around and extended his hand, but I grabbed his opposite shoulder and said, "Wait, Phil."

"Oh for chrissake," Heidi said.

"But we were just chatting," I said. "Weren't we, Phil?" I looked up at him. He strained to keep up the shaded, cool-guy front, but his shoulders were riding high, scrunched up—in a very unhip manner—around his ears.

"You know him?" he said to Heidi.

"Of course we know each other," I said quickly. "And I agree with you completely, Phil..." I looked at Heidi. Her brow and dark eyes twisted her face into a fierce scowl. But I didn't let up. "He thinks you're brilliant, you know that?"

"Jesus, Eli..." she said. But then she didn't say anything more.

"Eli? This is the guy?" Phil said.

Heidi ignored him. "I feel sorry for you," she said to me. "Really. But at least have the dignity to——"

"Dignity?" I interrupted. "But I was just——"

"Come on," she said, grabbing Phil's elbow. "Let's get out of here."

He turned on the heels of his cowboy boots, then gave his jean jacket a little tug on each sleeve and tossed an over-the-shoulder glance in my general direction. I watched them walk out. Then I just stood there feeling the close presence of the paintings and the perfumed air of the gallery and the politely chattering voices of the patrons as if the walls of the whole place were closing around me, squeezing me, making it impossible for me to move. And then I flashed on the blood-soaked sheet from Malaika's birthing ritual. My therapist had explained that these flashes were a common post-traumatic-stress-disorder symptom, so I shouldn't panic. But this time the flash lasted longer than usual, and it shifted from bloody linen to some kind of documentary-type photo of a baby being born, a tiny, blood-and-mucous-sheathed baby flailing its little arms and legs like a frightened insect.

She's leaving, I thought, Heidi's leaving, Heidi is leaving.

And then—well, this will probably sound more grand than I mean it to—but then I felt as if *I* were the baby, the one struggling to be born, with nothing but the instinct to cry and scream.

I took off after them. I bolted out of the gallery and sprinted down the block, with the cool spring air chilling the sweat on the back of my neck as I shouted, "Wait…Heidi, wait!"

When I caught up with them, Phil turned around first. He set his feet as if he thought I were going to slam into him, and he held his ring of keys with the sharp jagged end of each one pointing through his clenched knuckles. Heidi kept her back to me.

"Take it easy," I said to him, panting. "Just take it easy. I'm—I'm not looking for trouble."

He didn't say anything. With his free hand he adjusted his dark glasses, then leaned back a little on his heels. Finally, Heidi turned around.

"Look…" I began, "I'm sorry, OK? Really I am. I mean, I'm just, you know, I'm just being the jealous boyfriend. I mean, excuse me, ex-boyfriend. But I just, you know…"

I was still trying to catch my breath, and my voice trailed off into a long sigh, which is when Heidi saw Phil's fist and laid her hand gently on his arm, lowering it to his side.

"Eli," she said, "what are you trying to prove?"

"Can I just talk to you?"

She didn't answer, but in the yellowish light from the streetlamp I saw that her big, dark eyes were looking directly at me.

"Just for a minute?" I said. "I just…I mean, it's not like we're not ever going to run into each other."

She shook her head, a slow, bitter, sarcastic little shudder. "I've got nothing to say to you."

"Then don't say anything," I said quickly. "That's fine. Just…I don't know, just listen to me, just let me explain—"

"Explain what?"

"I don't know what," I said, softly. "I don't know." There was a pause, then I went on, "You know, you were right about me. In your last letter, I mean."

She glanced at Phil—obviously, she hadn't told him about writing to me. He leaned away from her. "I'll meet you at the car," he said, then started to turn away. But first he slipped his arm around Heidi's waist and pulled her close to him. And she gave him what I knew——and I took a certain sad pleasure in the intimacy of this knowledge——was a distracted and half-hearted little kiss.

Then Phil walked away. Heidi and I just looked at each other as the click of his cowboy boots grew faint. The sound echoed weirdly against the cavernous, red-brick warehouses lining the street. Finally, I stepped toward her.

"Well…" I said. "It's…a…it's good to see you."

She held still, then offered a barely perceptible, noncommittal little nod.

"Your hair——" I began.

"Shorter, yes. I know. Look, have you got something you want to say? Because if not, I feel really bad right now for Phil, who shouldn't have to——"

"You guys been together long?"

She pressed her lips together and looked down at the ground.

"Forget it," I said. "I'm sorry——it's none of my business, I know. I just…well, forget it."

There was another long pause, during which a strong cool breeze blew back the short, dark curls of her hair, and she shivered slightly, hunching her shoulders. I wanted then to reach for her and thought of how powerful it is to know some things about a woman, small things, ordinary comforts, such as exactly the way she likes her shoulders rubbed when she's chilled. But of course I just kept my hands in my pockets, and she crossed her arms tightly across her chest.

"There is something, I guess, that I want to say to you," I began. "It may sound corny, but…well, I guess I just want to say thank you."

"For what?"

The matter-of-factness in her tone I'll never forget. That famous Kirschbaum lawyerly detachment. I recognized it at once. But instead of finding it repulsive, it drew me toward her. She seemed to genuinely want to know what I was thanking her for, and to be reserving judgment until all the facts were in.

"For the letter," I said. "I'm in therapy now, and I really think part of it is because of what you…"

She nodded, and I stopped talking. For the first time I thought I saw the tiniest trace of softness and warmth in her face. But she didn't say anything.

"I mean, I'm OK and everything," I went on, "but, well——it's intense, you know. I'm going three times a week."

Again, she nodded.

"I'm really sorry, too, about those letters," I continued. "I was out of line, I know. In fact, I've been talking to my therapist a lot about—well..." I stopped. I felt myself rushing my words. "About everything I suppose."

She looked once again as if she were about to say something, but then didn't.

I continued, "Well, about my dad, mostly. Finally. Oedipus lives!" I laughed. She offered a small half-smile. "But I guess your father has told you all about——"

"No. Until tonight I hadn't seen or spoken to my father in quite a long time," she said quickly.

"What?"

She turned her head suddenly, looking over her shoulder in the direction that Phil had walked. "Look, Eli, I've got to go. This really isn't fair to Phil."

I nodded. "Right."

But then she turned back to me, and we both just stood there looking at each other. And this moment was one which, later that night, I replayed in my mind over and over again, thinking about how the fullness of her face struck me as so extraordinarily beautiful precisely because of the weight she had gained, as if the added pounds were an expression of her great emotional and intellectual size. A silly, love-struck notion perhaps——but there it is.

"Well, I'm sorry about whatever is going on with you and your father," I said. "Really, I've always thought of——"

"It's no big deal," she said quickly. "It's just that I gave up on the Ph.D. and he got all upset about it and we ended up having a sort of falling out."

She turned away again, looking over her shoulder.

"Your dissertation? You're kidding? How could you——"

"Give me a break, Eli," she cut me off, still not looking at me.

"I'm just surprised, that's all. I mean, after all the work you've done——"

"Look, I've got to go."

She started to step away, but then she hesitated. And when she looked back at me, there were tears in her eyes.

Exactly eight days later (believe me, I counted them), she left a message on my answering machine.

"Eli...? Call me."

That was it——no name, no number. I liked the assumption of intimacy.

But then when I called and left a message for her, she never called again. Three times, I left messages. Finally, I decided she was toying with me, and I told myself to forget about it. Then one night she showed up.

I was living once again in Wrigleyville in a roach-infested studio apartment. True, I still had all that money from my dad, but the crummy apartment provided a way to compromise with my guilt. By this time, I was studying for the LSATs, so I knew all of this was only temporary.

Our first visit that October night was marked by a certain ordinariness, as if she were simply an old friend stopping by for a chat. It was about 11 p.m. when she knocked at the door.

"I hope you don't mind my just coming by like this."

"No, not at all," I said. "Come in. Can I fix you some hot tea?" I asked.

"Tea would be nice." She stepped a bit further into the room. "But if this is a bad time, I don't want to——"

"No, it's fine. Really. I'm glad to see you. " I pointed her toward the tiny alcove which passed for a kitchen. "Just put the water up, would you? I need to use the bathroom."

A few minutes later, as the kettle whistled, I stepped out of the bathroom. Heidi had taken off her coat. She wore loose-fitting blue jeans and a dark sweater. I'd rehearsed this moment a million times, with a million different versions of eloquent apology. But then there she was, and I couldn't find a single word to utter. I just looked at her, watching her pour the steaming water into two mugs.

"I made chamomile," she said, quietly. "Is that OK for you?"

When she looked up at me, I felt myself on the verge of crying. Throat tightening, eyes getting watery——but I didn't want to make some kind of display of "sensitivity." I didn't want that at all.

"Yes," I said, "that's fine." And I turned away, blinking hard and clearing a space for her to sit on a corner of the sofa bed. Then I pulled up a stiff-backed chair for myself. I was grateful that she didn't react to my tearfulness. She just set the mugs of tea on the wooden footstool I used as a makeshift coffee table. That footstool had been in my family for ages.

"Remember this?" I asked, giving the stool a little kick.

She nodded, but didn't smile. She was sitting now with her hands folded in her lap, her gaze lowered. I watched her take a long, deep breath. She seemed to be preparing herself to say something, but then didn't.

We talked about the weather, changes in the neighborhood, the relatively new addition of Wrigley Field's historic night games. Just a couple of old pals shooting the breeze, until all at once we ran out of subjects and there was nothing but awkward silence. Outside, a car door slammed and someone shouted "Fuck you!" Then tires squealed, and several cars honked, and there was another wailing screech. The cruel city, I thought, and I had an impulse in that moment to try to break through all our crap and simply take Heidi in my arms.

Then she said suddenly, "I broke up with Phil tonight."

"You...you did?"

"Yeah. Just before I came over here. I don't really know..." She paused, and I thought she was going to say something about not knowing why she broke up with him, but instead she said, "I don't really know what the hell I'm doing *here*."

"I'm glad you came," I said quickly.

She looked up at me. "Yeah? Why?"

"Because I care about you."

"Right," she said, again lowering her gaze. "Right."

Again, we fell silent. I sipped my tea. She folded her hands in her lap, pressing her thumbs against each other.

"If...If you want to talk about it...I'm...well, no pressure. But I really am glad you came. Regardless of..." I stopped myself, suddenly not sure what I was saying.

"Regardless of what?"

"I don't know. It's just good to see you."

She sighed. "Yeah, well, I guess I ought to be going." She stood up quickly.

"You sure you don't want another cup of tea?"

"No, I really have to get going. I've got a busy day tomorrow, and now, after tonight, well——"

"He doesn't deserve you anyway," I blurted out.

She smiled, then shook her head. "Thanks. You don't know what you're talking about, but thanks."

"What do you mean I don't know what I'm talking about? I sure do. He doesn't deserve you. It's that simple."

"Yeah? Why doesn't he deserve me?"

"Because you're special."

She reached quickly for her coat, and I thought maybe I'd offended her. But then she said, "That must be why I came to see you——because I needed to hear that."

Then she leaned over and kissed me on the cheek. "Thanks for the tea," she said, and left as quickly and strangely as she had come.

25

I told myself whatever happens, happens. Seeing Heidi rekindled my passion for her, but I was determined not to let this passion throw me off the path of what I thought of as my "recovery." So over the next few months, I did nothing to upset the carefully defined relationship we managed to establish. It was our old intellectual connection that did the trick.

Late at night, over tea, usually at a café, we sat at a comfortably Platonic distance from one another and "discussed our lives," exploring subjects like the Jungian concepts of the "anima" and "animus." In fact, it was "this most interesting issue of how one integrates the contrasexual aspect" that led to her telling me all about Phil. First, she said that I'd been right about her wanting to *make* art instead of just write about it. That's what had led to her fascination with Phil, whom she first saw on stage at the No Exit Café in Rogers Park. They started to date and Heidi fell for his line about being an undiscovered Bruce Springsteen, complete with his own gravelly voice and blue-collar roots on Cicero Avenue. Springsteen notwithstanding, Phil failed to impress Heidi's father, who, for all his tolerance, turned out to be rather priggish about Heidi's desire to begin painting and leave behind her work at the prestigious University of Chicago.

"The monster of status reared its ugly head," Heidi said. "And I had no idea, especially in terms of my father, what an ugly monster it is."

This was rather strange for me to hear, because by this time I was quite eagerly seeking some higher status myself, with law school looming larger and larger every day.

After Heidi opened up about Phil and her dad, I knew it was my turn to tell her about Malaika and the baby. But I couldn't. All she knew was that Malaika had gone back to California. That seemed to be enough——for both of us.

But every day we were becoming closer and closer "friends," and then one night we were at my apartment and, just as I was pouring our first mugs of tea, she said. "What do you think, Eli? Do you think we'll ever be sexual again?"

At first I didn't think she meant with each other. We'd both been dating occasionally and talked sometimes about how difficult it seemed to find that spontaneous sexual spark. "Of course we'll be sexual again," I said. "Don't be ridiculous."

"Really?"

Then all at once I understood. "You mean——?" And I spilled hot water on the floor. We ignored it. "Me and you—after…after all this time?"

She laughed. "Far-fetched, huh?"

"I…I think so, don't you?"

"Yeah." She came around to my side of the counter, then crouched down and wiped up the water I'd spilled. "But why? Why shouldn't a good friend make the best possible lover?"

"Well…" I went back to pouring the tea.

"And I don't mean to raise a whole big philosophical thing," she continued. "The dualism of body and spirit and all that. I just mean that if you really trust someone as a friend, shouldn't that make being a lover easier?"

"You could say that trusting your lover might make being a *good* lover easier, but I don't think you can apply trust to one category and then say it helps in the other category."

She looked up at me. "What are you—trying out for the debate team?"

I laughed. "I'm just saying that trust helps, yes. If you're already attracted to the person, trust helps."

"Are you attracted to me?"

The directness of the question startled me. "Yes." I said.

She smiled. Then I said, "And are you——"

"Yes," she cut me off. "Yes, I am still attracted to you." She turned then and tossed the wet paper towels into the trashcan. "But it's a choice. Whether or not to do anything sexual together. It's a choice. Because I'm attracted to a lot of men."

She put one hand on the tiny kitchen counter, her back to me. Neither of us spoke. She shifted her weight from one foot to the other. The floor creaked.

"I guess it's going to get awkward now between us now," she said, slowly. "Isn't it?"

It was, indeed. awkward——because I was still hanging on to my secret. But that night we made love. And a few weeks later, we moved in together.

And still I said nothing. It's amazing how sometimes the past can seem not just far away—but totally irrelevant. For the next few months, on the surface at least, everything was great. Heidi was teaching and back hard at work on her dissertation, while I was waiting to hear from law schools, and making a little money clerking for a pretty major firm. Our relationship, after all we'd been through, seemed solid. We even had a dinner party with Heidi's parents and my dad, and handled it without a wrinkle.

But not telling Heidi about Malaika and the baby still haunted me. In almost every therapy session, I talked about it, and though my therapist remained "nonjudgmental," I felt sure he thought I was a damned coward. Then one freezing winter day the tension got to me. I had stopped at a grocery store on Wells Street, around the corner from where Malaika lived when I first met her. I was picking out some fruit when I saw this little girl, a skinny, curly-haired kid maybe five years old. She wore these cute corduroy overalls and was sitting in the shopping cart. In her tiny hands, she held a banana.

"Mommy?" she said in a sweet little sing-song voice. "Can I peel this and eat it before we pay?"

This struck me as a wonderfully precocious question. I looked at her mother, who had long, painted fingernails and an all-leather dress-suit complete with matching purse, gloves, and shoes. A fur coat hung over one corner of the shopping cart.

"No," she said, and she took the banana out of the kid's hand.

A moment passed. The little girl happened to look up at me, her big, grey eyes, I thought, appealing for help.

Now, I had no right getting involved in this, and I still feel bad about it, wish I could apologize to this innocent mother and poor kid. But the whole question of being a parent—well, I lost control of myself. "Aw, come on," I said. "Give the kid a banana."

"Excuse me?" The woman looked at me, surprised.

"They won't care," I motioned to the check-out aisles.

"Who won't care? About what?" She tightened her frown. Her eyebrows, I noticed, had been plucked.

"The people at the check-out counter," I said. "They won't care if she eats a banana." I held up my bag of bananas.

The woman took a step toward me. "Excuse me," she said, "but I don't think I asked for your opinion."

And this is when I cracked. Before I knew it, I said, "I'm not her parent— right. I'm not. But I could be a parent. I could be!"

I was practically shouting. The little girl started to cry, and her mother became frightened and quickly wheeled her cart down the next aisle. I just stood there, catching my breath. A few customers stared as I put down my bag of bananas and walked out of the store.

This incident truly spooked me. As I got into my car my heart was pounding and there was a strange tingling in my fingers. I pulled out my cell phone and started dialing my therapist. But just before hitting the send button, I had a weird, impulsive idea: to drive out to the cemetery where my mom is buried.

And I don't know why but, fortunately, I didn't question this idea or talk myself out of it by analyzing it to death. Instead, with my heart still pounding, I drove out to Westlawn Cemetery and dusted the snow off my mother's grave and stood there in the freezing slush telling her how much I missed her and loved her and wished she were here to help me. And then, while I was all emotional and crying and carrying on—my mother "answered" me. It was a short answer, sharp and to-the-point, and it was very surprising. She told me that therapy wasn't enough. She said that I needed to see a rabbi.

26

So the next day there I was calling synagogues, trying to remember the name of the guy who performed my mother's funeral service.

"You're not a member of the congregation here, are you?" said one receptionist, an older woman with a deep guttural voice filled with disapproval.

Her attitude angered me. "I'm not a member of the congregation, no," I said. "Or any congregation, or even of any synagogue anywhere—but I'd like to talk to a rabbi. Is that against the law? It's about a personal problem."

She sighed heavily. "I can take your name and phone number, but I can't promise you when the rabbi will be able to get back to you."

I gave her my number, and about fifteen minutes later, while I was still thumbing through the book, the phone rang.

"Mr. Eli Shaffner, please." The voice was high-pitched, nasally.

"This is Eli—who's this?"

"Danny Chernowitz. You called the synagogue?"

"Yes, I called about seeing the rabbi."

"I am the rabbi."

"Excuse me?"

"I'm Rabbi Chernowitz. Danny Chernowitz. You can call me Danny."

"Oh, I'm sorry. Excuse me, Rabbi. I didn't realize— "

I apologized again, and we set up a meeting for the next day at Congregation Ohav Sholaum, which to this day meets in the dank basement of a small, square greystone building out on Diversey Avenue, past Elston. Back in the forties, my parents lived out there. I recognized the blocks and blocks of identical row houses, with their shared front porches and small patches of lawn and nothing but a narrow sidewalk separating one identical unit from another. Uncle Max used to take me on an annual tour of these streets where, as he put it, "the West Side Jewish communists once breathed fire."

Maybe, but Rabbi Danny Chernowitz's congregation now barely breathes at all. The neighborhood is about ninety percent Latino-Catholic and the rabbi explained that his tiny congregation of aging Jews are those for whom the great exodus to the suburbs was a trip they missed. Now, they're too poor or too sick (or both) to do much of anything—except pray. "Every Friday night," he said, unable to contain his excitement, "I get twenty or sometimes thirty people cramming in here, and, let me tell you, this joint is jumping."

The snowy afternoon I showed up, however, the "joint" was deserted. Two of the plastic address numbers hanging over the door were missing, and the walkway needed shovelling. The buzzer, fastened to the rotting wooden door frame with red electrical tape, didn't work. A handwritten note said: SHALOM. SORRY, BUZZER BROKEN. KNOCK HARD. IF NO ONE ANSWERS, KNOCK HARDER. I'M DOWNSTAIRS.

After a couple minutes of making my knuckles sore, the rabbi himself opened the door, and my first thought was that I'd made a big mistake. I don't know what I expected—a wise old man with a white beard, I suppose. But what I got was young, clean-shaven Danny Chernowitz, dressed in a loose-fitting dark suit and tie, his skinny neck swimming in the collar of his plain white shirt. He shot his hand forward and smiled, revealing a full set of braces on his teeth, rubberbands and all.

"Been knocking long?" he asked, in that high-pitched voice of his. "Sorry. The heat just kicked in, and the radiator makes an awful racket. Steam heat, you know. That's why I——" He leaned out the door and pointed at the note. "Oh, good. It's still there. Sometimes the kids come and steal my note." He smiled. "I think they get a kick out of us being in the neighborhood, but they don't know how to express it." His narrow shoulders rose, then fell. "But come in, come in."

I followed the fluttering of his fingertips, and stepped inside.

"Come. We're downstairs."

He gripped the bannister and took each step one at a time, always leading with the same foot. I feared that he'd fall down right in front of me. I peered over him. Books lined the basement's walls, big, thick, dark books sitting on shelves of unfinished wood fastened to the wall with grey, metal L-brackets. When we finally made it to the bottom of the stairs, the rabbi visibly relaxed, moving more smoothly as he settled in behind a big, scratched-up wooden desk.

I sat down directly in front of him on a metal folding chair.

"Well," he said. "I'm glad you've come to talk with me. Our tradition—excuse me, you're Jewish, I presume."

"Yes."

He smiled. "Our tradition has much to offer us, particularly when we face life's unavoidable difficulties and need guidance."

I nodded. "Yes, well, I guess that's what I'm here for."

Again he smiled, and again I found the sight of his braces unnerving. Adults with braces—I flashed on a magazine article that I'd read. Something about the treatment of jaw pain.

Neither of us said anything for a moment, then the heat started again, rattling and hissing. I turned around. The dull winter sunlight, streaming in through the tiny window in the room's corner, cast a faint glow on the clunking, grey radiator. The room felt oppressively warm.

"I've never done this before," I said.

"Never done what?"

"Talked to a rabbi like this."

"Really?"

I faced him directly. "Yeah. I never even had a bar mitzvah."

His expression—lips and jaw relaxed, eyes steady—didn't change. "I see," he said, quietly.

"It's not that I mean to be disrespectful, Rabbi, but I—"

"Call me Danny," he interrupted.

"Danny?"

He nodded. "Let me tell you why," he said. "I ask the members of my congregation to call me by my first name to make a point, which is an important aspect of our tradition: that as a rabbi I'm not any closer to God than you are. I'm not any holier than you or than anyone else. Perhaps more learned, yes. Something of scholar, maybe. Knowledgeable about the tradition, I hope. But it is the tradition which has the wisdom—not me. This, you understand, is the Jewish way." He nodded his head so vigorously that his yarmulke, clipped to the tight curls of his close-cropped black hair, shook. I nodded back.

"So call me Danny, OK?"

"OK, Danny."

He smiled. "Now, if you tell me what's going on, I can maybe help you to make some choices. Like I said, our tradition has much to offer."

I took a deep breath. "The thing is, this 'tradition,' as you put it, is not something that I've ever been very involved with."

"I understand."

There was a long silence. We sat there looking at each other. Three or four minutes must have gone by. I imagined him secretly amusing himself by using his tongue to fiddle with the rubber bands on his braces. Finally, I started to get up. "I think maybe this was a mistake," I said.

"Being Jewish was never important to you," he said quickly, "but you're here. So what made you decide to come?"

"My mother," I said.

"She told you to come?"

"Not exactly." I stood, but just to take off my coat. I was thinking to myself, what the fuck, this young-guy rabbi wants to get into it with me, fine, I'll get into it with him. "You see, Danny, my mother's dead."

"I'm sorry."

"Don't worry, she died a long time ago. But yesterday I went to her grave because I'm having all kinds of trouble with the woman that I'm living with and this other woman that I had a child with and this money that my dad gave me and——well, I imagined my mother telling me to go see a rabbi. So here I am."

He nodded.

"But I've never gone in much for being Jewish, you see? Personally, I've been more into yoga and meditation, Hinduism, Zen, the whole JUBU thing, you know? Jewish Buddhists? For some reason there are a disproportionately high number of Jews, or former Jews or whatever, who now practice Buddhism, or call themselves Buddhists. And there was a group——a Jewish group, mostly rabbis, in fact, they went to see the Dalai Lama——did you hear about this? It was just after the Dalai Lama won the Nobel Peace Prize and he wanted to know about being a spiritual leader in exile and how the Jews have survived all this time while the rabbis wanted to know what is it about Buddhism that makes so many Jews so interested in it."

I could feel myself racing but couldn't seem to slow down. The rabbi nodded and said softly, "Yes, *The Jew and the Lotus*. I read the book. Fascinating."

"Yes, it is, in a way, though I'm not into that too much either, not really. Basically, I guess I just believe in, well——I'm not sure exactly how to describe it. I'm in therapy, and I've come to feel that the unconscious, you know..." My voice trailed off. I'd been talking without breathing and, literally, gasped. Then I tried to take a long, slow inhale. My chest expanded, but I still felt light-headed. "Look," I said, still racing, "It's just that, the way I see it, the values of your basic enlightenment liberalism——you know, the idea of granting rights to individual persons instead of groups?——this idea, which is really a historical breakthrough, this idea, I believe, informs who I am a lot more than Abraham and Isaac or the miraculous parting of the Red Sea." I paused. "Am I making any sense?"

The rabbi hesitated, then leaned forward, resting his elbows on the desktop. "Eli," he began, "you don't have to explain your religious identity or defend yourself for not being 'Jewish enough.'" He made little quote marks with his fingers. "Why don't we leave your beliefs out of it and just talk a little about what's going on right now in your life?" Again he smiled, and this time it impressed me that he seemed to be so relaxed about those braces.

So I started talking, and eventually I told him all about Malaika and the baby and my dad's money and even about Gloria and the Anais Nin stories. He listened intently, nodding, taking notes, occasionally asking for clarification. He was extremely concerned with keeping me focused on the choices I had to make now, instead of allowing me to turn the session into another rumination about the past. I give him a lot of credit for that.

Finally, after I'd spent about an hour explaining the situation, he interrupted and said, "Let me tell you the Jewish way of forgiveness. That's what you seem to need, right? You need to tell Heidi about all of this, and then ask her to forgive you?"

"Yes, I guess so. But I understand, you know, that it's going to be difficult for her because——"

"I know, I know. You've explained how honesty and openness have been the foundation of your relationship all these years, yet all this time you've been holding on to your secrets." He nodded, eyes closed, a surprisingly solemn expression on his thin, young face. "The Jewish way of forgiveness," he said, opening his eyes. "This is what you need to understand."

He cleared his throat. I leaned back in my chair. And though I'm not proud of it, I have to admit that my first thought was: Here it comes, the lecture.

"First, some background. *Ben Adam la-Makom* is what we call an offense committed against God alone but not involving another human being. *Ben Adam la-Havero* is an act against a fellow human being. Now, offenses against God alone may be atoned by"——he counted the steps on his fingers—— "repentance, prayer, the giving of charity, and the proper observance of Yom Kippur."

I leaned forward. "Yom Kippur is a holiday that I've always celebrated.

In fact, Heidi and I have celebrated together, which helped me a lot, particularly back when——"

He waved his hand, silencing me. "Please." The authority in his squeaky voice surprised me.

"Sorry," I said.

"In cases of offense against other people, however, all the above-mentioned steps are inadequate in and of themselves. They must be accompanied by forgiveness granted by the victim. Do you understand?" He looked up at me. "This victim need not forgive, however, unless every effort to correct the situation has been made by the aggressor. Furthermore, and this is a crucial addendum, if a person has sinned with the conscious intention of repenting afterwards——such a sin, in the Jewish tradition, is never forgiven."

He spoke these last words slowly, drawing out the "nnn" in forgiven. The dramatic effect worked on me. I felt spooked. And my defenses were still up. As he pushed his chair away and stood up, I grew more suspicious of his every move. Here he comes, I thought, moving in now for the kill.

He came around now to my side of the desk, where he folded his arms over his chest and stood directly over me. "So why did you break up with Heidi in the first place?" he asked, in a low tone. "Did you think you could just apologize later?"

"No," I said. "No, that isn't it."

"Then why are you so afraid to tell her what's happened?"

The room had grown darker by this time. A shadow fell across Danny Chernowitz's young, clean-shaven face, giving his smooth skin a grey tint.

"I'm ashamed of myself," I whispered.

"I know," he said. "You told me that. But why are you so afraid to tell Heidi about your shame?"

"I don't know," I said, suddenly growing irritable. "I don't know." I started to slide out of my chair, but Danny put his hand on my shoulder. Then he leaned closer, his mouth just inches from my ear. "Eli," he whispered, "from what you've told me, I think you really love Heidi. The two of you have been through a lot together. And you yourself have been, as they say, around the block." He paused. His breath was hot and smelled faintly of pickles. "You don't have to confess to me. That's not how we do it. In Judaism, confession is to God alone, without any human intermediaries or intercessions. But I'm telling you that if you want to act in accordance with the Jewish tradition..." He squeezed my shoulder, then gave it a little pat. "Well, I think you know what to do..." Then he straightened up and walked back around to his side of the desk.

"I'd be happy to talk this over further with you," he said, an official quality now creeping into his squeaky voice. "I'd also be happy to meet with both you and Heidi, if you think that would be helpful. But, unfortunately," he looked at his watch, "I have to get over to Michael Reese Hospital right now. A member of my congregation is recovering from surgery."

I stood up. "Well, thank you for your time," I said, a little distracted by this abrupt finish. "Umm, what do I owe you?"

"Whatever seems appropriate to you."

"Excuse me?"

He smiled, but didn't repeat himself.

"Do you have a standard consultation fee?"

"I leave it up to you," he said, busying himself with a folder on his desk.

"Well, I have my checkbook."

"The synagogue—and we're not the rich Jews, you know, the ones you hear so much about. The synagogue will gratefully accept whatever charitable contribution you might wish to make." He spoke quickly, without looking up. "And, of course, it's tax deductible."

I stood there for a moment, holding my checkbook, and I don't know what got into me. All of the sudden, I felt horribly manipulated. I actually said to myself: Well, he's being a real Jew, isn't he? Knows I feel shitty about my dad's money and everything else in my life and he sees an opportunity to score. Although this line of thinking was completely irrational, I couldn't help it. The surfacing of latent anti-semitism, perhaps. I told myself I'm not going to be suckered. "What do most people pay for something like this?" I asked.

This time he looked up from his desk and said, "Eli, true repentance involves sincere regret for the past act, the undertaking not to repeat it in the future, and the effort to do all that is humanly possible to make amends." He held his hands in the air. "Pay me whatever you feel is appropriate."

"Well," I said, "I appreciate your generosity." And I put away my checkbook.

"Good luck to you," he said, extending his hand. "And don't hesitate to call if you'd like to talk further. I'm sorry to rush off."

This guy's good, I thought. Smooth. And I shook his hand, then—sick bastard that I was at the time—I left without giving him a penny.

But that night I couldn't sleep. And it wasn't just the money. At three in the morning, with Heidi sound asleep next to me, I found myself thinking about Danny Chernowitz. It was the whole idea of talking to a rabbi and how he wanted to know why I'd broken up with Heidi in the first place. A rabbi, of all people—as if I owed him an explanation! And the "Jewish" God? A God of History? Liberation? Justice? What a scam, I thought. A ridiculous idea dreamed up by a bunch of slaves. But then, in spite of myself, I started to cry. Not just because it suddenly seemed so overwhelming to be a Jew but because it seemed overwhelming to be alive at all. And I remember how my tears nearly turned to laughter as I flashed on an idea of Brian Swimme's, his metaphor for comprehending the evolution of the universe: raisin bread. The crucial point, Swimme says, is for humans is to place ourselves *within* the process rather than outside of it. Forget the oven, the loaf's crust, the cabinet with the ingredients. The cosmic process, he says, is like baking raisin bread, and we ourselves are the raisins.

So, yes, in my own twisted, intellectual way, I realized that my life was, indeed, changing—expanding all around me—and that I was about to make a choice with real consequences.

Being careful not to disturb Heidi, I slipped out of bed and wrote a four-page letter explaining to her everything that had happened with Malaika, and Gloria, and my father. Then I wrote a check for $1,000 payable to Congregation Ohav Sholaum.

I left the letter where I knew Heidi would find it in the morning. By the time I woke up, she was sitting at the kitchen table. The letter was in front of her, and next to it was a pack of filterless Camel cigarettes. She looked up at me, then opened the pack and lit one, taking a long, hard drag.

"Good morning," she said. "I'm reading—and smoking."

"Heidi— "

She shook her head. "Please don't lecture me about the effects of tobacco, OK? I'm already informed." She took another puff, inhaling deeply.

"OK," I said. "Let's just take this whole thing one step at a time, OK?"

"Fine," she said, an edge in her voice. "First of all, thanks for the letter. Very informative. I just wish you'd told me all of this before we moved in together."

"I'm sorry, it was wrong—but I was afraid."

"Do you still love her? She had your child? Maybe you can look me in the eye and say you don't love *her*. But what about your child? I don't even want you to look me in the eye and say you don't love your child."

I don't know what possessed me, but I walked over to her and grabbed the burning cigarette out of her hand. "I love *you*, Heidi. I don't know what else to say right now except that I love *you*."

She didn't even blink. She reached for my hand and took back her cigarette, then said, "I'm going to pack up a suitcase and stay at my parents' house for a few days."

And without waiting for me to answer, she got up and walked past me, her arm brushing against mine as she headed for the bedroom. I started to follow her. But she took a few steps, then spun around and faced me. "Don't," she said, pointing her cigarette at me. "Don't even think of trying to stop me."

So I sat down at the kitchen table and held my head in my hands and breathed in the unfamiliar odor of that damn cigarette. And then I heard the creak of the closet door and the plop of her suitcase dropping onto our bed and then the sound of her dresser drawers opening and closing. And opening again, and closing.

27

When Heidi came back a week later, she was a model of self-containment. Calm, clear, cool-headed, she said she wanted to talk about "every detail of this whole situation, so we can get it out of our lives once and for all."

"Maybe we should do this with a therapist?" I suggested.

But she shook her head. "That isn't necessary. Just answer my questions." We sat down on the couch. "First of all, what made you decide to tell me?"

"I figured it would be better," I said.

"But how did you finally decide to...? Why now?"

"Well, I went to see a rabbi."

She blinked, startled. "A rabbi?"

"Yes."

"You're kidding? You went—for advice?"

"Sort of. Well, yes, for advice."

"And what—he told you to write everything out and give it to me?"

"Not really. No. He didn't say anything too specific." I shrugged.

"You went to see a rabbi?" She shook her head. "I can't believe it."

"I just want to be open with you, Heidi. I want you to ask me every question you can think of. I want us to talk about everything—everything!"

So we did. It was a test of our trust, our honesty, our compassion. It was a ritual purification. It was a purging of our souls. But it didn't work.

She moved back in, and we lived as roommates, with me sleeping on the couch. Then, after a couple weeks of this arrangement, she came home one day from the library and said, "Eli, I'd like to take a yoga class with you."

"A yoga class? Really?"

"Yes. I'm curious about it."

I shrugged. "Well, sure. There are lots of places to take yoga, and it would probably be good for my back. Maybe we can——"

But she interrupted me, dropping her backpack to the floor.

"I want to take a class at the same place where you met Malaika."

"You do?"

"The woman had your baby. I want to know the world you and she lived in."

"Right, of course," I said. "Sure."

And a few days later, there we were climbing up the steps of the old yoga studio on Halsted Street, with the scent of incense lingering in the narrow stairwell, and a framed picture on the door of Guru B.K.S. Iyengar performing some impossible pretzel position, which Heidi, I thought, looked at with the same hushed respect I had once felt.

Inside, Shahms, good old two-faced Shahms, greeted us at the door. His appearance hadn't changed a bit: ponytail, tie-dyed T-shirt, he wore some sort of leather necklace strung with seashell beads.

"So here you are!" he said, tugging at the tip of his pointy beard. "I read your name in the book but told myself not to believe it until I saw it. And now I see it."

Smiling, he stepped toward me, his arms open wide. We hugged, but I didn't trust this display of affection. Ever since Malaika had left I'd been out of touch with everyone at the yoga studio, and my silence, I knew, had hurt Shahms' feelings. I also knew that Shahms hated me for stealing Malaika's affection from him.

"And who's your friend?" he said, pulling out of our embrace.

"This is Heidi." I stepped back as they shook hands. "And this is the famous Shahms, who was—or is—my yoga teacher."

"Aaah grahhsshopper," Shahms said, putting a hand on the crown of my head.

Then Heidi spoke. "I love your T-shirts. The ones with the Rumi quotes?"

"Oh, thanks. I haven't made any new ones in a long time."

"I sometimes sleep in those T-shirts."

Shahms's eyebrows seemed to twitch at this comment, which I managed to ignore.

"Well," I said, "those high-class dressing rooms still in the same place?"

"They sure are," Shahms said. "Same old curtains." He looked at Heidi. "But you can use the bathroom if you want more privacy."

She smiled. "No. That's not necessary."

We went to change. I was a nervous wreck as I thought of Heidi behind the same mauve-colored curtain (which still didn't quite reach to the ground) where I'd first fantasized about Malaika.

By the time I stepped out wearing my gym shorts, five or six other students had arrived. They all seemed to know each other. Shahms joked with them. Heidi stood near the windows, looking out at the street.

Then class began. Heidi placed her green mat next to mine, but she barely acknowledged me when I said, "Be sure not to overdo it, OK? You don't want to hurt yourself, you know?"

Just then Shahms announced to the group. "We have two new students today, Eli and Heidi. Or I should say one new student, Heidi. And one little lamb who lost his way."

Everyone laughed, including Heidi, which angered me. But I couldn't think of anything to say, so I just lowered my gaze and concentrated on the first pose.

It was a side stretch—a standing pose where your arms and legs are spread apart, sort of like a jumping jack position, but one knee bends until the thigh is parallel to the floor.

Almost immediately, Shahms came over to help Heidi.

"Try to relax," he said, and he put his hand on her thigh. "If you feel a kind of burning sensation here, that's just the muscle working, and that's a good sign. That means strength is coming."

"Strength," Heidi said, straining. "Oy gvelt."

"That's OK, too," Shahms continued, still pressing his hand down on her shaky leg. "A friend of mine teaches yoga down at a JCC in Miami Beach, where they call it 'stretch and kvetch.'"

Heidi laughed, and so did most of the other students. But I was busy watching the two of them out of the corner of my eye. Shahms' hand, I thought, had been on her thigh just about long enough.

But I didn't say anything. And as the class continued, I told myself that I was being silly, that it had just been my imagination. And I forgot about it.

I really and truly forgot about it until one afternoon a couple of weeks later, when I came home unannounced and—this might seem funny to you, since, in a sense, I totally deserved it—I found Shahms and Heidi in the shower together.

And how did I react? I moved out that same night, and we didn't speak to each other for almost a full year, as I began a period of consciously selective isolation.

It wasn't that I felt Heidi had done something horrible. On the contrary, I told myself Heidi was simply mirroring back to me my own "unintegrated shadow," as my therapist put it. That is, I had been a womanizer with Gloria and a liar to Malaika and an irresponsible father to my unknown child; so I deserved to be cheated on, lied to and disregarded—by everyone. Heidi, Malaika, my father, Shahms, Gloria, Uncle Max, Artie, even Jeremie, the long-lost head pro anti-semite—every single one of them, I felt, had a perfectly legitimate right to despise me. Because I was despicable. Guilty, unlovable, worthless. Period.

My only option, I figured, was to move. Preferably some place very far away. Oregon, Seattle, Hawaii. I also considered Las Vegas, taking some stock in the fact that the gambling business there had sprung from the visions of people like Meyer Lansky and Benjamin "Bugsy" Siegal—bad Jewish boys, all of them. More seriously, however, was the one thing I had going for me: high scores on the LSATs. This, I believed, would be the foundation on which I'd build a new life. A good law school in a far-away city.

Law, I told myself, was an appropriate "path" for my new life precisely because of its strong connection to Judaism. In fact, I talked about this a few times with Danny Chernowitz. I even started to write a personal essay on the subject, in which I tried to develop Hegel's notion of the Jews as the first people in history to lift the deity out of Nature and conceive of Him as an entity above and beyond the universe itself. This, I argued, could be directly linked to the creation of "Jewish Legalism" because only a God above and beyond the universe can sit in judgment of it and create laws.

Such were the big ideas I distracted myself with while the months passed until, finally, the following December, I made a decision. Finished with Heidi, I thought (and of course still without a word from Malaika), I packed up for Boston. I'd been accepted at Harvard. The winter was a crazy time to move, but I was going to take a couple of electives during the winter term. Also, I simply couldn't take it anymore in Chicago. That's it, I thought. I'm out of here. All I'll do is say goodbye to Heidi and my dad—and go.

But a few nights before what was supposed to be our final farewell, I had a long, late goodbye dinner with my father, during which we touched on what has turned out to be one of this situation's most haunting subjects: my family's Jewishness.

"Your grandfather came to this country, you know, because in Russia they were killing the Jews," my dad said, sipping an after-dinner brandy.

I nodded, thinking of the often-told family tale that, just as the boat carrying my grandfather pulled into New York Harbor and the Statue of Liberty came roaring into view, my grandpa's brother, who'd been fighting pneumonia the whole way, died. Looked out at the Statue of Liberty, smiled, and died—right in Grandpa's arms.

But instead of that apocryphal story, my dad said, "The funny thing is that once he got to this country your grandfather didn't give a shit about being a Jew. He just wanted to be a success."

My dad shook his head and laughed. "And now..." he looked around the big living room. But then he didn't say anything more. We both just sat there quietly, sipping our drinks. And somehow the subject was dropped.

Dropped, that is, until I went to say goodbye to Heidi, and we had the most frightening fight of our lives—frightening to me still, because it's the only time in my life I have ever physically attacked a woman.

28

What exactly put me over the edge I can't say. I started out in such a gentle, nostalgic mood. Driving over to Heidi's, thinking about how I'd be in Boston by the first of the year, I began to feel enormously sentimental about everything having to do with Chicago, particularly the weather. It was a freezing December night, with great icy winds blowing sheets of swirling snow sideways across Lake Shore Drive, and I loved it. The famously brutal wind, the subzero temperatures—these, I felt, were precisely what gave Chicago its distinctive moral character: a shrug of contempt for the frivolous; a grunt of gratitude for the necessities.

Which was a distinction much on my mind. From what's frivolous to what's necessary was a sort of conceptual frame of reference for what I felt I was going through—confronting, finally, the necessity of growing up.

But Heidi didn't quite see it that way. She started in on me before I'd even stepped inside. "If you're really just coming to say goodbye to me," she said, one hand still on the doorknob, "I want you to know that I think you're an unbelievable coward."

I was standing on the freezing porch of her old place in Hyde Park, directly across from the University of Chicago. That was the first thing that occurred to me when she brought up cowardice—that I was choosing to leave Chicago, in spite of my love for the city, because I couldn't take being in the same place she lived.

"Well," I said, startled. "I'm...I'm sorry you feel that way. Do you want me to leave?"

She shook her head and made a soft smacking sound with her lips, a hushed little chime of disgust. "Do whatever you want."

I hesitated, really just to collect my thoughts. But then she started to close the door.

"Wait!" I shoved my foot into the opening. "I came all the way down here, didn't I?"

"Just to say goodbye, right, as if goodbye is all that——"

"Well, I am leaving."

"For where? You know you didn't say. What are you—afraid I'll track you down?"

"No, I'm——" I stopped myself, recognizing that I was being drawn into an argument I didn't want to have. "Boston," I said. "I'm going to Boston."

"Boston?" She scrunched up her nose. "What the hell are you going to do in Boston?"

"Law school."

"Oh, Jesus." She sighed heavily, her breath in the cold air making a little current of steam. "You're just going to walk away from all of this, aren't you?"

"From all of what?"

"Us."

"Us?" I could feel my energy immediately rise. "Are you out of your mind? What 'us' are you talking about? Us doesn't exist, Heidi—except maybe as some eternally neurotic game that——"

"Look, if you're talking about the thing with Shahms——"

"I don't give a fuck about Shahms."

She looked at me, startled. Her cheeks, in the pale light coming from the partially open door, looked suddenly flushed.

"I mean, come on, Heidi. You wanted to hurt me, fine. Shahms too, he's been jealous of me ever since…ever since—but, look, forget it. I only got what I deserved. Besides, it was almost a year ago."

There was a long pause. My energy, which had so quickly risen—just as quickly dropped. I was suddenly freezing, shivering, while Heidi stood strikingly motionless, one hand still on the doorknob. Then, for some reason, at just that moment, I noticed for the first time the big, green, wool sweater she was wearing. She still has this sweater, which was a birthday gift from my father during our senior year in high school, the year my mother died.

"So if you've got it all figured out," she said, flatly, "then what are you doing here?"

I shook my head. The memory of that damn sweater was like a physical ache, something I wished I could just rub away. "I don't know, Heidi," I said quietly. "I don't know what I'm doing here."

"Well…if you don't even——"

"Look, can I just I come in for a minute? I mean, it's freezing out here."

as neighbors huddled in house slippers and pajamas and I argued with that square-jawed pimply-faced fireman…Christ, I've lived through it all a million times. But it's as if I were caught in a tennis rally that just won't end. No matter how I think about it, how well I place my shot—guilt chases it down and comes back with a shot of its own. An unbeatable opponent, to which I surrender. Put simply, Maya is my responsibility. And there's no getting off the hook: a baby girl's innocent soul was dropped into the middle of my messy story, which has unavoidably become a part of her own.

Of course, both Heidi and I have been expecting a letter like this. When I showed it to Heidi, she remained calm and collected, digging up your phone number at once. Her business-like approach was soothing. Over the years, I've had my concerns about Malaika providing for a child on her own. Not that she couldn't handle it. She's tough and strong enough to do whatever it takes. But why should she make her life—and the child's—harder than it needs to be? I've also been rehearsing what I would do when a letter like this arrived, although now that it's finally here this sick, heavy feeling in my chest seems to choke off access to everything I rehearsed.

Bottom line question: what drew me to Malaika in the first place? The mystical East, the stripping off all dual tensions as mere appearance until the soul, in a moment of ecstatic self-revelation, experiences itself as *the* Unity, a la "the way of the Hindu Vedanta." Yin and yang, spirit and matter, form and chaos, being and becoming—Malaika's role was to be my exotic goddess, my "spiritual other," the tough, hard, strong one with whom I'd transcend the world's (rather Jewish) banality. Yes, this was the burden I placed on her and, in this sense, I see now that it was as much for me as for her that she had to have that outrageously ritualized (and dangerous) birth, as if a new life coming into the world would lack glory and splendor without our added theatrics.

Of course, there was also the pure lust. Libido, desire, animal magnetism—call it what you want. The basic truth is that mine and Malaika's isolated moments of ecstasy weren't preserved in the scattered totality of our real life together. And this is where Heidi comes in. Because for her the exploration of "exalted states" is largely irrelevant. Or it's just so different that it requires a different name altogether. She's not interested in some sort of "experience of unity" unless the experience itself preserves all of life's oppositional tensions, each in its proper place. For her, meaning is the unity created out of the realization of these differences, not their dissolution. When the ecstatic shakes it off and climbs down from the world of unity and infinity into the world of multiplicity and boundaries—that's where Heidi makes her entrance, proclaiming, in her own strong, determined way, that *this* is it.

Perhaps I exaggerate the two women's differences. I'm sure Malaika would dismiss everything about Heidi as "head tripping." And a stupid label like that sums up a lot for me, the way Malaika made the impulse toward reflection seem cowardly. Our relationship, that is, was to exist in a region more bold than reflection, as if our love for each other thrived in an area of the imagination more profound than, for example, the tension inherent between what we feel and what we think. Ours was supposed to be a realm outside such distinctions.

But this description, too, Malaika would say, is off. By definition, it's off. Because ecstasy—and, yes, that is what I was after with Malaika—ecstasy stands beyond the communicability of speech itself, which presupposes one person addressing another, which drags us back into the muck of multiplicity.

Yes, rake the muck this way or rake the muck that way—it's still, of course, muck. And so be it. I love Heidi. I do. And though I'll never forget Malaika and Gloria, or even try to, the past is, indeed, the past. Remembrance, in the end, may not be redemption, but to recall the messy (even putrid) truths of the past acknowledges the emotional obligations of the present, however strange they may be. Love as a standing debt of the soul, as Saul Bellow once put it.

But I can just hear Max—dear old Uncle Max, with whom, by the way, my father has begun to spend some Saturday afternoons, it was Uncle Max who once said wryly that "the thing about the past is that with the passage of time, it loses its truth."

A depressing little proverb, which I resist. In fact, this may be the most "Jewish" thing about me, that I wish to insist my past is still somehow presently accessible—not a mere memory, but an experience that continues to legislate its truths, to be felt, and to exert its pressures both on my present and my future.

Which is, alas, marriage. Heidi and me—together, finally, as husband and wife. With everything we've been through up to this point in time—it's something, yes? I mean, we are, if nothing else, not quitters.

About this, I have no doubt.

So I apologize, again, if my candor has been offensive. But I think I'm ready, finally, for your legal advice. Partial custody, visiting rights, or just blind financial support—yes, let's talk about the options. I promised Heidi that I would explore all of the legal options as fully as possible. Then, together, we'll make a decision.